HEROINES

MOCKINGBIRD
STRIKE OUT

MARIA LEWIS

ACONYTE

FOR MARVEL PUBLISHING

VP Production & Special Projects: Jeff Youngquist
Editor, Special Projects: Sarah Singer
Manager, Licensed Publishing: Jeremy West
VP, Licensed Publishing: Sven Larsen
SVP Print, Sales & Marketing: David Gabriel
Editor in Chief: C B Cebulski

First published by Aconyte Books in 2023

ISBN 978 1 83908 217 7

Ebook ISBN 978 1 83908 218 4

Cover art by Anna Astrid

Distributed in North America by Simon & Schuster Inc, New York, USA
Printed in the United States of America
9 8 7 6 5 4 3 2 1

ACONYTE BOOKS

An imprint of Asmodee Entertainment Ltd

Mercury House, Shipstones Business Centre

North Gate, Nottingham NG7 7FN, UK

aconytebooks.com // twitter.com/aconytebooks

For Poppy Rose, a woman of STEM

CHAPTER ONE

There are two hundred and six bones in the human body. I'd only need to break six for permanent damage to a very specific asset. My opponent and I were matched for speed, but I was a better fighter in close quarters. His precision though… maybe seven bones? His hand-eye coordination was superior to anyone I knew, but if I feinted left then I could bring a stave down on–

"Bob? Barbara *Bobbi* Morse?"

"Hmmm?" I snapped back to attention.

"The Palos Verdes property," my lawyer asked, patient. "Are you willing to be bought out?"

My eyes darted to the sharp stare of the man across from me. "You hated that house."

"And now I want it," he replied, petulant as ever.

The fingers of my soon-to-be ex-husband Clint Barton – AKA everyone's least favorite Avenger Hawkeye – were tapping out the beat of a Mötley Crüe song on the table. I hated Mötley Crüe. The quirk of a smile that played across his face told me he knew that I knew what he was doing.

I returned the smirk, thinking about how in that position I could fracture his ulna and radial bones in one swift blow. *Try playing Robin Hood then,* I thought. It was like he could read my mind. Or at least my intent. His own smug expression faltered, and he quickly snatched his arm off the table. We had been many things as a couple, but we were never ones for idle threats.

"All we want is a fair division of assets," Clint's lawyer said. To his credit, he flashed his client a look that expressly communicated "behave". That told me he knew him well.

"And we could have that," my representation countered, "if Mr Barton here would have agreed to the prenuptial agreement my client asked him to sign, which he said that he did."

"Which he *lied* that he did," I mumbled.

Jennifer Walters was extremely overqualified for this situation, and it was out of respect for her doing me this favor that I held my tongue when she kicked me under the table.

"Kick" was a kind word for it, actually, given that She-Hulk wasn't known for her... restraint. I let out a slow exhale of pain, the breath escaping between my teeth so as not to be noticed. Clint noticed, because of course he did. He never missed anything except birthdays.

Straightening in my seat, I tried to look engaged. I tried to look attentive and nonchalant and like I wasn't thinking about how many seconds it would take for me to throw him out that window. Nothing permanent, mind you. I knew he had a trick arrow in that quiver that would have him springing back through the human-shaped hole in the glass and brushing off his shoulder in as many seconds as it took for me to toss him. It was just the catharsis of it all.

It was another full three hours and twenty-two minutes

of back-and-forthing before our lawyers decided to mutually call it a day. At least somebody could agree. I flinched at the thought of what this session had cost me and bitterly wondered if Clint's lawyer had an hourly rate cheaper than mine. *No,* I thought. I wasn't going to do that. I promised myself that no matter how ugly this got, I would not become the bitter divorcée he seemed so determined to make me.

In the bathroom, I splashed water on my face before remembering I wore makeup, but my complexion was unaffected. If this setting spray could hold up under an assault from Skrulls, it could get me through my marriage breakdown. Blinking away the droplets on my eyelashes, I glared at my own reflection. The charcoal pantsuit I had put on to look professional, to look serious, felt more like a costume than anything I wore in the field as the super hero Mockingbird. My usually bright, blue eyes looked dull and even weapons-grade concealer could do little to hide the fatigue on my face.

"Pour myself a cup of ambition," I mumbled to the woman in the mirror, getting myself together. My mother had taught me this. Whenever I needed strength that I didn't have in the moment, borrow it from other women until you believe. In this instance, Dolly. My hands smoothed down the fine lines of the suit's tailoring as I checked for creases and *hell,* my butt looked amazing in this. Head high, "9 to 5" hummed under my breath, I strutted down that office building's hallway like I owned it. Jen and Clint's lawyer waited at the elevators, heads close together in a conversation I only picked up the final sentences of.

"I'm a criminal lawyer, Jennifer," he huffed. "I don't even know what he wants me to do here."

"Besides be criminally annoying?"

He huffed out a laugh and I realized with surprise there was more chemistry between these two than there was in the last few months of my marriage. They separated when the *click clack* of my heels on marble announced my arrival. He offered me a polite nod, his eyes hidden behind red shades as he used a white cane to negotiate his way to the elevator Jen held open for him.

"See you in a few weeks," he told her.

"A pleasure, Matt."

As the doors pinged shut, I tilted my head in a way that said everything without saying anything.

"No," Jen replied, pulling me into the next available elevator. "Not a word."

"I have several, but I'm afraid they'll cost me." I smirked.

"He's a colleague."

"A softly spoken, quite fit and frankly disarmingly handsome colleague."

I was tall at five-foot ten, but I felt tiny as Jen looked down at me over a pair of stylish Gucci frames.

"The only thing messier than negotiating a super hero divorce," she began, "would be doing so while 'negotiating' with the opposition."

"Sustained."

We stepped out into the Los Angeles sunshine right as the influx of food trucks descended for the lunchtime crush. I thought I heard Jen say something like "ooooh, tacos!" but she was gone from my side so quickly I couldn't be sure. It was barely a beat before she reappeared, beaming as she held up two cardboard trays overflowing with food.

"Lead the way," I laughed.

Nestled together on a park bench, our feast spread out between us, we ate in silence as the office buildings emptied out around us.

"Guff pie hove hell aye," she said through a mouthful. I spoke ten languages and conveniently one of them was mouthful, this particular sentence translating to "God, I love LA". I would have agreed with her usually, but I'd lost my appetite. My spicy chicken taco sat half-eaten on my lap as I looked across to a gaggle of fans having flocked to Clint as he'd left the building. He was laughing and smiling with them as he signed autographs, posing for the occasional selfie, his blond hair catching the light.

"I used to love this city," I sighed. "Now it just feels stifling."

"Hey," Jen said, gaze traveling from mine to the scene and back again with sympathy. "Every breakup is varying degrees of bad. One day, with enough time and distance, you'll look back on this and laugh."

"Or fly kick someone out a window."

"I *knew* that's what you were thinking!"

"Not the whole time. I just… I'm sorry. I know you're helping me out with all this, but when we're up there, nitpicking over this car or that bike, I genuinely have no idea how we got here. How did it get to this point?"

"Firstly, you're paying me to be here," Jen began, ticking off points on her green fingers. "Secondly, love is nonsensical. It sands off all the edges of a person, it converts all the red flags to green, it turns every sour note sweet. You can't see it when you're in it and the *only* way to be in it is to blindly jump."

A warm sense of respect and friendship and loyalty spread through my chest as she spoke. I'd been insistent on paying her, knowing the hours it would take and time away from more desperate clients. Even though she'd agreed because I'd annoyed her so much about it, I knew it was a criminally discounted – and still expensive – rate.

"That's a poetic way to say sometimes it works out, sometimes it doesn't." I smiled.

"Eh." She shrugged. "I'm a slam poet."

We cleaned up our rubbish, Jen finishing everything I couldn't eat and I thought grimly about the way my suit didn't fit me like it used to: baggy in spots where it had previously hugged my athletic frame. The stress had caused me to lose weight, my cheekbones sharper and jawline more pronounced. Sunglasses on, chin up, *be your own boss, climb your own ladder* echoing through my skull, we strolled past Clint's growing crowd with only a few passing glances.

"What are your plans tonight?" Jen asked. "I'm on the red-eye back to New York. Early margaritas and karaoke?"

"You know how I feel about karaoke."

"It brings out the worst in people blah blah blippity blah."

"Besides, I've got a mission. My last as a West Coast Avenger, actually."

She cast me a quick sideways glance.

"What?" I prompted.

"Nothing."

"Say it," I whined, rolling my eyes.

"I would *not* want to be whoever is going up against Mockingbird tonight."

The man's broken jaw was the least of his worries as I hurled him into a tower of shipping crates, each one falling on him like novelty Jenga blocks. In my defense, he had tried to shoot me with a spray of bullets from his automatic weapon.

"A machine gun?" I scoffed, somersaulting out of the way and taking cover behind a concrete pillar until he emptied his clip. "I haven't fought an Eighties villain in a while."

The woman next to me grinned, her teeth sharp and her claws even sharper as they retracted with a satisfying *schnick*. Greer Nelson AKA Tigra looked electric as she crouched for cover, our team of just five S.H.I.E.L.D. agents outnumbered three to one. On paper, that is.

"Come on, Bird," Tigra purred. "Give the others an early mark. The two of us can handle these idiots on our own."

The line between flirting and fighting with danger was always blurry with her and the flash in Tigra's eyes made it even blurrier still as the *rat tat tat* of gunfire finally died off. I'd been tracking "these idiots" for months thanks to a tip from one of Tigra's old Confidential Informants from back in her law enforcement days. A "weapons shipment" was all it had been called, but given the lengths these guys had gone to keep it secret – shell companies, shifting dates, even their numbers – it all told me this was something important. Or maybe that's what I wanted to believe, but I was desperate for the distraction: more professional, less personal. That was my new motto.

"They out?" Tigra questioned. "Hey you! Unnamed Agent! Stick your head out and have a look, will ya?"

Such was Tigra's fearsome reputation, the agent almost did it too before I hissed at them to hold their position, unseen. It had cost me to get this far: these guys were the main suppliers for all enhanced weaponry on the West Coast and I'd had to let three shipments of varying import pass through unbothered so they wouldn't know we were on to them. They were clever, having hijacked a nearly perfect pipeline to get their products into the city and undetected under the guise of touring museum exhibits.

Now ancient artifacts have some security, but these fellas were careful enough to make sure their quarry would be of low interest to your everyday thief and therefore your everyday attentive border controls. An exhibition destined for the Academy Museum on the history of the moving image, however, was the perfect Trojan Horse. So effective was their ruse, even Tigra had been uncertain as we'd hidden in place and watched the shipment get wheeled into the empty exhibition space.

"Are you sure?" she whispered. "All the nerds who work here seem to know them."

"Tradecraft 101," I'd replied. "Establish genuine, believable relationships. They've probably been dealing with these guys for close to a year, it seems authentic. But you know what doesn't?"

I pointed out the triceps of the "touring curator" as he signed off on the last crate delivery with his team.

"Museum workers aren't that swole. He looks like a *Die Hard* henchman."

"Yeah, hot and Swedish," had been Tigra's response. I'd been proven right when we'd confirmed that all civilians were out of the museum and made our move. We'd been able to take out a handful before it got to this point, using our lack of numbers and their excess to our advantage. They needed to weave through the Stories Of Cinema permanent exhibition to get to their setup space, so Tigra and I had tracked after them silently.

I'd swept the legs out from under one guy in front of the triangled mirrors of the Bruce Lee section, our reflections distorted with his costume from *Enter The Dragon* behind us. My eyes had fixed on the nunchaku perfectly preserved behind glass as I'd choked that man to unconsciousness, my fingers itching to use them but good girl instincts winning out.

"As little collateral damage as possible," S.H.I.E.L.D. Deputy Director Maria Hill had asked of me. I'd promised. So I cuffed him, marked his position, and left him for the clean-up crew just in time to see Tigra emerge from her camouflage behind the overflowing floral gown from *Midsommar*. She jumped on an unsuspecting assailant's back, taking him out much the same way I did then patting his head like he was having a brief nap.

The two of us had picked them off one by one, the rest of our team holding position until our targets eventually noticed their dwindling numbers. I'd hoped they'd send a few more scouts out to look for them, get a few more on the scoreboard, but they'd gone straight to their generic weapons stash. It had been tucked out of sight so as not to raise suspicion, but I could hear an electric drill now as they desperately tried to crack into their new supply. We needed to take the rest of them out before they got to whatever was in those crates. They were low on bullets and we were low on time.

"I count eight left," Tigra said, sniffing deeply. "Including one who tragically uses Lynx Africa."

I unclipped three surveillance spheres from my utility belt and rolled them out in different directions. I watched on a tiny, handheld monitor as they did their job and mapped out the terrain.

"All right," I began, connecting to the team through our earpieces. "The three of you work to flank the trio with the firepower on the left. Tigra and I will tackle the remaining five who are low on ammo… for now. We move in twenty seconds."

An echo of confirmations came back, Tigra looking at me questioningly.

"I have no cover to get over there," she noted.

"How about a distraction instead?" I connected both ends of my battle staves together until they made a long javelin. Above us, a beloved exhibit close to the size of a Kombi van was affixed to the ceiling.

"Not the shark from *Jaws*," Tigra groaned, realizing what I was about to do.

"His name is Bruce," I said, darting off.

As one half of my team struck theirs, my sudden appearance surprised the others who were late to fire at my footsteps as I sprinted. Leaping onto the handrail of the escalator, I used the speed gained to leverage my javelin and catapult myself upwards and on to the giant shark's back. I had to scramble for a grip over the surprisingly smooth surface, grabbing a dorsal fin at the last minute before I slid right off the other side. Protected from incoming fire by the shark's sheer girth, I had a perfect view of everything below: dispatched bad guys sprawled beneath crates and others cowering behind them. With my free hand, I swung my javelin as hard as I could at two of the three connecting bolts that held the prop in place. Throwing my weight behind it, they burst from the concrete ceiling in a spray and I felt gravity do its work. Planting my feet, I held on for dear life as it started to swing in the other direction toward my intended target.

"Sorry, Hill," I whispered.

I could only imagine what they saw: looking up from their hiding spot as a giant shark descended upon them from the ceiling, mouth first. One of them was actually swallowed whole and I felt him pinball his way through the interior as Bruce made contact. Tigra's yellow, patterned skin was a blur of color as I gained speed and leapt at the crucial moment, spiraling down and on to the shoulders of an attacker. My weight dropped him to the ground – unconscious – before I had to expend much energy on him. The other fella needed work. He was every bit of six-foot-nine and from the way he withstood a crate crashing against him, I knew one blow from him would crack my ribs.

Just because I fought alongside super heroes, that didn't mean I was impenetrable. Half my colleagues had superpowers, the other half were like me: just really freakin' good. My main assailant had height, strength, and weight. I was an All-American gymnast with a catalogue of fighting techniques to pull from and *speed*.

As he swung, I spun and ducked between the blows, using the classic techniques from the Philippines martial art known as Arnis. I made sure not to get close enough for him to grab me *but* close enough that I could hear the crack as I used my battle staves to beat his femur like a drum. Bring him down first. Then immobilize. Hitting the electric charge at the end of one of the rods that had become my signature weapon, I shocked him unconscious as I passed.

Pulling my elbows back, I tossed both staves at the skulls of the last two men standing. They bounced off each with a hollow *clunk* before returning perfectly into my grip with a satisfying weight. Tigra flipped off the shoulders of another, his debilitated form sinking to the floor like his limbs were jelly.

"Hey," she said, only half-annoyed. "I was looking forward to those two."

"Sorry." I shrugged.

"No, you're not."

"No, I'm not."

"AAAAGRH!" The scream came from the guy who'd been Pinocchioed, his body collapsing out of the shark and landing on a bed of broken crates. It softened his fall and he leapt up, spry. He took off at a sprint up the escalator and toward the higher floors. Tigra was practically bouncing on the balls of her feet as she looked at me for permission. She *loved* the chase.

"Can I–"

"Go get 'em, tiger."

She was gone in a flash and I had no doubt that she'd catch that poor guy before he had a second to view the night's sky through the glass dome above us.

"Our targets are managed, Mockingbird," an agent reported, appearing in front of me.

"Great, good job," I said, sheathing my weapons. "Restrain and ready these ones for transport ASAP."

"On it."

Scanning the mess around us, most of this had been brought by the baddies so the damage here wasn't permanent and this scene could be left as spotless as we'd found it minus... well, Bruce. I stepped over his mangled form, patting his tail idly as I made my way toward one of the half-opened crates. I needed to see whether destroying a piece of cinema history had been worth it. They'd mostly got the box open, it taking little more than a heave with a crowbar to unearth the packing materials inside. I was aware of Tigra's return thanks to the whimpering of the man she dragged behind her like dirty laundry, but my focus was on the box.

"What is it?" she asked, having dumped the guy with the junior agents.

"That's a zoetrope," I replied, gently lifting it out and searching for the *true* cargo.

"What kind of damage does it do?"

"Look here," I said, pointing to a small square that she peered through. I used the handle to crank it into gear, the stationary image of a clown beginning to juggle as I wound it up with increased speed. Tigra looked up at me with a grimace.

"Where's the death part?"

I laughed. "No death, just the illusion of animation."

"Huh?"

"This is a real object."

"It's not a weapon?"

"Maybe for the 1870s," I muttered, placing it down gently. The whole point of this ruse was real items among the contraband and I felt around in the crate until I found the false floor. Working together, we lifted the top layer free to reveal–

"Water guns?" an agent asked, looking over our shoulders. He went to reach out for one and I slapped his hand away.

"When has something with a mysterious green goo inside ever been safe to manhandle, Christopher?"

"Never," he mumbled, properly chastised.

"That's right, never," I repeated. "Go get those other crates open, please."

He did as ordered, Tigra shaking her head with a disapproving tut-tut. "I swear they come out of the Academy dumber and dumber each year."

"That's not true," I murmured, only half-listening as I donned a pair of gloves. Christopher had been right about one thing: they did look like water guns. Instead of plastic, the casing was made of fiberglass with an attachable canister at the back that was clear. Inside, however, was the aforementioned mysterious green goo. It had the same texture as mud, sloshing around in there as I tipped the weapon up and down. Tigra took a long, deep sniff.

"It smells organic," she said. This was one of the other reasons I loved having her on my team. She was a vicious fighter, sure, but she'd also worked as a police lab technician and amongst all the brawn, it was great to have another scientific brain to bounce theories off.

"Is that your expert opinion?" I teased.

"Women in STEM!" she responded, too used to my taunts to bite this easily now. Her eyes widened and she pointed excitedly. "Oooh, look at that. I know, I know, no touching."

"Especially no touching," I said, leaning over what looked not dissimilar to a grenade minus the pin.

"How do they go off?" Tigra questioned.

"I do not want to find out," I muttered, eyeing the grooves built into the small, round objects. "I'm going to get an analyst to take these back to the lab at HQ. It's no good disarming a supply of weapons if we don't know what they do and why."

"Sounds like a fun night for someone who's not me," Tigra responded, rolling her neck and looking around with disinterest. "We're done now, right?"

I scanned the second floor of the Academy Museum, debris and disaster around us but victory, too. Arms dealers were being carted off, said arms would soon be safely in the right hands, and S.H.I.E.L.D. operatives were spilling into the space like ants as they sought to clear everything as quickly as possible. I should have felt some kind of satisfaction at a successful mission completed, but my brain was snagging on one detail. I had been a lot of things in my thirty-two years on this planet: athlete, scientist, S.H.I.E.L.D. agent, spy, wife, and founding member of the West Coast Avengers. This was another chapter coming to an end and I wasn't sure how I felt about it.

"Yeah," I finally managed. "We're done for the night."

"Great," Tigra said, clapping her hands together. "Karaoke and margs?"

CHAPTER TWO

In my defense, I'd had three cocktails before coming back to work. Jen and Tigra were, of course, in cahoots when it came to the super-secret mission of "cheer up Bobbi". And they did, for a while at least.

"Happy last mission to the both of you," Jen said, the lime green of our icy beverages spilling with the gesture.

"Cheers!" I responded, taking a small sip before realizing what she'd said. "Wait, the both of you?"

"Surprise?" Tigra winced.

"You're leaving the West Coast Avengers?"

"We're leaving the West Coast Avengers," she corrected. "My West Casa, uh, your West Casa?"

Jen was shaking her head. "That doesn't make any sense."

"Tigs..." I fumbled. "When? Why?"

"Eh, when I heard you and the Pigeon were on the rocks, I figured it was only a matter of time."

For as long as I'd known Tigra, the woman had always had a clear and concise dislike of Clint AKA "Pigeon" AKA "Pigeon Boy" AKA "Errol Flynn" (depending on her mood). She and I, on the flip side, had always gotten along swimmingly but had never been more than work acquaintances at best. As news of the split had spread thanks to paparazzi pics of Clint stepping out with some leggy brunette in Silverlake, Tigra seemed much more willing to take our friendship to the next level: something that had been challenging when you shared a bed with the person she was calling "Katniss Everdeen" in every staff meeting.

"You can't leave because I am," I said. "Clint has a lot of flaws, but he's a great solo team lea–"

I didn't even get to finish the sentence before Tigra blew a raspberry at me while one of the most recognizable super heroes in the world, She-Hulk, cackled next to her. It was a deeply odd yet somehow reassuring sight.

"Please, what are you trying to prove?" Tigra teased. "I'm not wearing a wire, you don't have to gas him up."

"I'm not," I chuckled. "Really. Even if we'd stayed together, that doesn't mean we'd have stayed leading the West Coast Avengers forever."

"Sure," she conceded. "But I need a leader I can respect. And Squawk Eye ain't that."

Jen wiped a tear away from under her eye. "*Squawk Eye,* stop."

Tigra took a dramatic sip. "He just always struck me as one of those white guys who'd wear a 'this is what a feminist looks like' shirt, you know?"

I choke-laughed on a sip of my frozen beverage.

"Selfishly, you leaving was the push I needed, too," she pressed. "Besides, you gotta get out there! This is your time, Bobbi. Take it from someone who had a starter marriage."

Jen clicked her fingers in agreement. "Go have a fling! Take some dumb Polaroids! Make out with a younger guy! Date an older girl! Get a tattoo you'll regret!"

Soon, I was cry-laughing alongside them. Trash talking your ex at a hole-in-the-wall Mexican joint with your girlfriends was a tried-and-true breakup cure. But I had two PhDs and I knew leaving when Jen grabbed the mic for a Mariah Carey ballad was the smart thing to do even if it was still technically early-ish.

I believed in that choice all the way home and through the door of my Burbank bachelorette pad. I had only been renting it for a month, but I loved it, genuinely. I had been able to convert the whole basement into a dojo and that's about as far as I'd gotten on the progress, everything in varying states of boxes. It wasn't as if I was unused to an empty house: Clint and I spent more time on the road together, our lives at risk, than we had at home. If one of us was there, the other wasn't and vice versa. Yet as I paced around the residence, barefoot, looking for something to do and seeing a thousand options but wanting none of them, I gave up.

It was a horrible combination of inaction and agitation. I was quite fine being alone, but I didn't want to be alone with my thoughts. That was how I ended up in the S.H.I.E.L.D. lab at night, looking for purpose where I so often did: through the lens of a microscope.

I'd meant to pop into the West Coast Avengers base when there was little chance of running into anyone, clear out my desk, empty my locker, and bring my stuff over to S.H.I.E.L.D. where I was transferring back fulltime. It had gone smoothly until I'd passed a trainee in the lobby who whispered much too loudly to his colleague, "Is that Hawkeye's wife?"

I gritted my teeth, my fingernails digging into the skin of

my palms as I clenched my fist with frustration. I might have imagined the other looks or whispers, yet I knew for sure there was very little to misinterpret in the laboratory. Science never lied. Science never gossiped. And if I glared just right and looked mean enough, the two other scientists down here at stupid o'clock wouldn't bother me either.

She's just an active child. That's what my mom used to say when she and my dad would fight about it. Gymnastics lessons then karate then taekwondo then Arnis settled my active body, but my active mind… well, I loved languages. I loved history. I loved math and technology and astronomy, but nothing kept me more engaged than science. Biology, specifically.

I always thought Tylin Hii in fourth grade was my first love. The truth was actually closer to the frog I got to dissect in fifth grade; the method behind the madness of how things worked – biologically and organically and chemically – was *true* love at first sight through the microscope. I graduated high school three years ahead of schedule, went to college on a full academic scholarship when I was fifteen and was recruited to S.H.I.E.L.D. two weeks after my eighteenth birthday. It was always a weird juxtaposition, science and espionage, because one was all about facts and the other was all about how you could bend them. That was me in a nutshell, a whirl of contradictions.

"Here's the rest of those samples you asked for."

"Thanks for th–"

My words fell short as I looked up to meet the gaze of S.H.I.E.L.D. Deputy Director Maria Hill.

"Hi." She smiled.

"Hi!" I beamed. She might technically be my boss, but she was also one of my oldest friends going way back to

S.H.I.E.L.D. Academy. Whether it was in combat or in a café, I was always happy to see her.

"Burning the midnight oil?"

"I…" I went to lie, went to come up with an excuse, but didn't have one. "I couldn't sleep."

She nodded with understanding. "I went by the bar to see you off, but–"

"Uh oh, what horrors did you see?"

"Tigra singing Doja Cat, which I will never unsee – you know?"

"I've seen her tackle Alanis so, yes, I do know. Quite intimately."

"How's everything going here?"

"Weird," I said, honestly. "I ran an analysis on the properties in each weapon, which all vaguely have the same chemical markers, but they don't behave like manufactured chemicals."

"Which means…"

"Tigra called it. She said it smelled organic to her."

"A nerve agent?"

"That's what I thought, too. G-agents can smell fruity, but all nerve agents are colorless liquids and this is distinctly… not."

We both looked at the sludge. Her eyes were narrowed in concentration, thinking deeply about what I was telling her.

"So what do they *do*?" she questioned, ever the pragmatist. Hill was direct and she liked direct responses.

"The pseudo grenade is a smoke bomb for all intents and purposes," I replied, pulling up the footage of a lab technician in a hazmat suit letting off one in a controlled environment. "Instead of smoke, though, if you push in here you can see it's actually releasing small spores that would be breathed in and settle in your lungs like an infection."

I handed her a palette with the tiny spores suspended safely in glass and she watched keenly as they floated around, bumping up against the barrier as she shook it slightly.

"Chemical weapons," she murmured.

"That's what I think. If the first weapon is anything to go by, these are designed to attack human biology. I haven't had time to run tests on the goo in the guns yet, but I'd like to use cadavers to confirm."

"It can wait," she said, placing the spores back down.

"Agreed." I nodded. "The bigger concern is where did these come from? And are there more? I can't track the biological source because I don't recognize the make-up right now, but if we start breaking down the design work and where the materials could have been sourced, any design features that–"

"Bobbi," Hill said, this time applying more force to her tone. "I have something more pressing that I'd like to talk to you about in my office. Now."

I was tempted to gulp, but if you didn't smile at a crocodile, you definitely never showed Maria Hill that she made you nervous. An analyst stumbled when he saw the two of us approaching him in the corridor and I swear the faintest smile crept across her expression.

Hill's office was a sharp contrast to S.H.I.E.L.D. Director Nick Fury's, which had columns of books and vital documents towering everywhere. You had to negotiate your way around them carefully in case you knocked one loose and they all came toppling down. Where his was maximalist, hers was minimalist, with clean, clear surfaces and hidden compartments so that even if there was a stack of papers somewhere, it was probably behind some false marble bench.

"Drink?" she offered.

"Sure," I said, taking the tumbler of amber liquid as we stood at a massive window. It took up an entire fourth of her office.

"To your last day as a West Coast Avenger," Hill said, and we gently clinked glasses. "How does it feel?"

"Burns a bit," I replied, earning a smile from her at the multifaceted description. "But it's easier than staying. If we have to go tit-for-tat over who owned *what* appliance when in multi-hour negotiations, I have no idea how we'd run a mission together."

"That bad, huh?"

"I'm pretty sure our lawyers are about to start a support group for each other," I scoffed. "I don't want to leave, but I have to walk away. Clint won't and two leaders bumping heads puts the whole team in danger."

"I agree," Hill murmured. It might have been inching toward the middle of the night now, but S.H.I.E.L.D. was a twenty-four-hour operation. The courtyard below was a reflection of that, with everyone walking somewhere to do something urgent.

"Have you thought about a holiday?" There was a glint in Hill's eye that made me tilt my head with interest.

"If you suggest a singles cruise then I'm gonna have to suggest a bruise."

Hill grinned. "Given your situation, it would be understandable if you wanted to take some personal time between appointments."

Walking back to her desk, she tapped away until a screen behind her displayed a series of images that made my mouth drop.

"Dr Wilma Calvin," she began. "I believe you two are acquainted."

"You know we are," I replied, staring at a picture from over a full decade earlier. My face was fuller, younger, as I offered a bashful half smile while towering over my then mentor, Dr Calvin, and her second in command, Professor Theodore "Ted" Sallis. We looked happy. Hopeful. High on the lack of a clue about what was to come. Hill swiped across the screen, showing a more recent series of updates on Dr Calvin.

"As you know, since Project Gladiator she has struggled to find work in the US," she began. "When was the last time you two spoke?"

"Probably around then as well," I noted, Hill nodding like she already knew this fact. She probably did.

"For the past three years, your old boss has been working out of the Department of Biochemistry at Oxford University as a visiting professor."

"Good for Wilma," I said, knowing how hard it was to secure tenure anywhere, let alone an ongoing placement at one of the world's oldest universities. Not to mention as a semi-disgraced American *female* scientist.

"Sure." Hill shrugged. "Not so good for Wilma is the fact she has gone missing."

"Missing as in *missing* or missing as in likely murdered and the body just hasn't been found yet?"

"I don't know, but to be brutally honest the latter would be preferable," she replied. "The specifics of Project Gladiator remain confidential, but her area of expertise puts her on a list."

"Let me guess," I murmured, thoughts dark. "It's a very small list with a very specific area of expertise that could be invaluable to S.H.I.E.L.D.'s enemies."

"Obviously we continued to monitor Dr Calvin once the project was shut down. Per her plea agreement, she was unable to use or publish any of her findings from her time working with S.H.I.E.L.D. Our surveillance suggests she has not continued her research–"

"And she wouldn't," I interrupted. "She would never. Not after what happened. It devastated her. She pivoted away from that field altogether."

"Exactly," Hill agreed. "But if she is missing, not murdered, that begs the question of who took her and why?"

"You think Hydra."

"I fear Hydra. They're not above abducting an old woman and forcing her to finish the research she started if it means being able to recreate something as close to Cap for their own means as possible. In fact, I'd say that's right within their purview."

My silence was a firm agreement. Hydra had and would do much worse.

"What do you want me to do?"

"Go on vacation, Bobbi." She smiled sweetly.

"To England."

"Why not? I hear Oxfordshire is lovely this time of year. A change of scenery can be very helpful when going through a significant life upheaval."

I grinned, unable to help the excitement creeping through my veins as I was filled with purpose. I *did* need a change of scenery, somewhere that wasn't filled with the echoes of dates had and memories now soured by how things had ended. Hill had done me a favor by finding the weapons trafficking assignment that could divert me from dealing with Clint on a day-to-day. This was that times one thousand.

"The West Coast Avengers shouldn't have had to lose you," Hill said. "I don't want S.H.I.E.L.D. to either, and frankly, there's no one better placed for this mission given your personal history with Dr Calvin and your competence in the field."

"What do you want me to do?" I asked, calm, confident, ready.

"Go there. Dig around. See what you can find out, but do it discreetly. It's only because we kept track of her that we were alerted to anything at all. A generic email was sent to her supervisors advising of a family emergency stateside, of which she was granted two months' leave to attend."

"She has no living family." I frowned, spotting the first red flag. Whoever sent that email, it definitely wasn't Wilma.

"Correct. And she never returned stateside. Who sent the email and why? Where is Dr Calvin?"

"And why are they trying to hide the fact that she's AWOL?"

"Correct again. There's a professor from St Andrews filling in temporarily and you're used to navigating that world of stuffy academia better than anyone else I could deploy. Not to mention you're handy in a fight."

"Handy?" I smirked.

"Very handy." Hill looked at the time and gathered her things. "Come on, I'll walk you out."

It was a cool, February evening for Californian standards. I knew that where I was going it would be a whole lot colder and barely at the tail end of their winter. Jeans and a loose jacket wouldn't do, and I reveled at the opportunity to plan for this mission in every minute detail. Our footsteps were in sync as we strolled towards the parking lot, Hill handing over a laptop as we walked.

"Everything you need is on there," she began. "All our surveillance up to date, current case files on Dr Calvin and the archives from Project Gladiator."

"How long has she been missing?"

"The email was sent a week ago. We don't know who's in play."

"Go in undercover," I cut in, thinking out loud. "Get a lay of the land and identify the players. Old school spy shenanigans."

"I believe that's the technical term, yes."

I huffed a laugh. "When do I leave?"

"Tonight. We've got a plane ready to take off in an hour."

"Oh! Do I get to–"

"We have a pilot. I figured you'd need that time to get up to speed."

"Sure," I sighed, her logic making sense but the disappointment of not getting the metaphorical keys to a S.H.I.E.L.D. jet still being very real.

"Identity documents," Hill continued, handing me an envelope. "Your personal leave is obviously the cover for the story here and that's what we'll maintain. You've got a burner device in there to contact me with updates as you find them."

We came to a stop at my car, my pride and joy: a pink 1973 Torana. I'd purchased it outright, long before I'd met Clint, so thankfully it wasn't part of the divorce negotiations. But all of that was a later problem. That was something for future Bobbi to deal with. Right now, I had a go bag to get, a plane to catch, mission specs to lay out and a case to brief myself on. I had the best kind of distraction a girl could want: an international mystery.

"You should get Tigra in the lab to keep working on the weapons," I said to Hill. "She quit the West Coast Avengers too, but if you asked her, I'm pretty sure she'd do S.H.I.E.L.D. work on a freelance basis."

Her eyes twinkled with amusement. "Already hired her."

I laughed, classic Hill – always one step ahead. "Well, speak to you soon."

She nodded, watching as I got in the car and revved the engine to life. I was about to pull out when she approached. I rolled down the window, letting her lean on the frame.

"You were always great on your own, Bobbi," she said. "It's time you remember that."

CHAPTER THREE

Hill's words still echoed in my head when I pulled up on the tarmac with ten minutes to spare. A Cessna Citation Longitude was waiting, your standard super midsize jet, and I wished it was something more tactical, something I was more familiar with, but the whole aim was to blend in. I recognized the pilot immediately as the very same one I had done my most recent flight training with. He'd told me his surname was Serbian for "clan of wolves" and it made sense on the day as he flew like a wild animal behind the controls. At S.H.I.E.L.D., a flight instructor with edge was desirable.

"Good evening, Mr Vukojevic," I said, offering a friendly wave. "It's nice to see you again."

"You too, Mrs Morse, the best student I ever had."

If he noticed the way I flinched at the "Mrs" he didn't say anything and I followed him on board, eyes scanning the aircraft's interior where six passengers could sit very comfortably.

"This all looks very pedestrian for you," I teased.

"Funny, I was about to say the same."

His hand pressed against a digital panel built into the wall and suddenly the generic cream seats and wood paneling disappeared. Like a tiny house in transition, I watched chairs sink into the floor and tables rotate back into the walls, clicking into place seamlessly. My mouth popped open as the layout transformed into a mobile control room with everything a spy in transit could need. I all but rubbed my hands together with glee, itching to dive in and get started on what would be every bit of a ten-hour flight.

"There's the pilot I saw do a barrel roll at seven hundred feet," he said, eyes twinkling as he watched my obvious delight. "In a helicopter."

"Hey, you taught me that maneuver!"

"It was a refresher course, not an air show." He smiled. "Wheels up in five."

"Is it just us?" I asked, whirling around. "No co-pilot?"

"You're my co-pilot," he noted. "If anything goes wrong, that is. Deputy Director Hill said she wanted to keep everything as tight as possible."

Ah, that I understood. The more people who knew, the more people who could tell. He excused himself and made for the cockpit. Keeping my backpack handy, I tucked away a small suitcase and felt my phone buzz in my pocket. I checked it as I settled into my seat and buckled up. It was from Jen, who I'd quickly fired off a message to in my mad dash to the airport, fully expecting a response in the morning. She had her own plane to catch, but she was as efficient as ever.

"Just spoke with Barton's lawyer," the first message read, dots as she continued to type the rest. I quickly shot off a reply.

"The hot one?"

"The completely regular looking one," she pinged in

response, her words almost audible in my head. "Took some work, but the next mediation is officially moved to the start of March, and we can push it further if you're not back by then."

"Took some work?"

Jen was careful about what she said with regards to my ex, her reception to Tigra's digs earlier the first real clue I'd had about how she felt. The super hero business had a lot of big fish in a small pond. She kept it civil, knowing odds were she'd have to work with Clint at some point out of the context of divorce proceedings. She maintained that standard now, replying with just three emojis that told the story for me: red-faced smiley with steam exploding from its head, skull emoji, followed by a baby. He would've been annoyed by the delay and seen right through the "personal leave" excuse, but work came first for the both of us.

If I had to guess, the thing Clint would have been most annoyed about was not knowing where I was going, what I was doing, or what mission I was on. He'd lost the right to that and now, he could get used to being the one in the dark for once.

The rumble of the plane whirring to life vibrated through my seat. I switched my phone off, removed the SIM, and slipped both into an airtight security satchel with magnetic foil lining. My digital footprint needed to be nonexistent when I hit the ground and I switched to the clean phone, having transferred over anything essential I needed. The plane's acceleration forced me back into my seat, but I barely noticed, already flipping the laptop open and setting it on the magnetized bench in front of me so I could dive into everything I needed to know.

American academia had no place for Dr Calvin following

the *incident*, so she'd left. Her field of expertise was broad enough and her mind brilliant enough that she could pivot to other areas of interest, working intermittently on research projects across Europe for several years until she landed the posting at Oxford. The university was historic, prestigious, significant and for someone of Dr Calvin's caliber trying to rebuild their reputation after a disgrace under vague circumstances, joining their Department of Biochemistry was a tangible step to clawing her way back.

"Atta girl," I whispered. Yes, I had a huge part to do with her being in that situation in the first place, but I couldn't help but root for her. She'd always had guts. It was right there in her psychological profile when she had been contracted by S.H.I.E.L.D. over a decade earlier: resilient. That's why I knew – and Hill had, too – that something had gone seriously wrong. The impulse might have been to suspect she'd done a runner, knowing that she was being monitored and finally cracking under the pressure, wanting to go off the grid and have her freedom like before. Yet her work had been everything to her when I had known her. Given the frequency of papers she'd published in the last few years alone, that hadn't changed.

Using a fake portal login, I scanned the titles: her findings covered everything from discovering a new bacteria-expanding mechanism to radiation damage in proteins. Dr Calvin was the supervisor for my first PhD on molecular DNA modifications, which tied in perfectly to my time working under her on Project Gladiator. I'd gained one more since then, straying away to examine natural alternatives to extending cell lifespans, but even so this was... dense.

I was smart, but everything from her terminology to her

case studies strained parts of my brain that often felt dormant amongst all the physicality of being a West Coast Avenger. *Former*, I corrected myself. From the surveillance documents, it was clear Dr Calvin had to split her time between teaching and research hours – standard practice – which was not the first, but certainly one of the loudest alarm bells. She had loved to teach, but she had *lived* to research.

The "family matter" was either an outright lie or a forgery. Fact. The result was the same. Fact. So, there were two possibilities: either she fled voluntarily or she was taken involuntarily. The former seemed so unlikely that I wanted to rule it out altogether, but until I could get into the cottage she'd occupied on the outside of town to see if anything was missing, I couldn't be one hundred per cent certain. My instincts and logic told me that she was taken and the voluntary aspect of it all was staged. The question was then, by whom?

Any myriad of power-hungry global organizations could view Dr Calvin as valuable. They'd view her as invaluable *if* they knew the specifics of her previous work, but Project Gladiator was supposed to be confidential. In this business, "confidential" was more of a guideline than a rule and I knew I wasn't the only operative who shared that belief.

Hydra was suspect number one, yet hyper-focusing on them could lead to confirmation bias and leave us blind to any other possibilities. Oxford was in S.T.R.I.K.E.'s backyard, S.H.I.E.L.D.'s British equivalent, even if this wasn't their usual – how would the English say it, cup of tea? Any megalomaniac mad scientist a stone's throw away was also on the roster and I'd had Hill send me over a shortlist of possibilities to consider: Doctor Doom, A.I.M., Beyond Corporation and Hellfire, just to get started. So. A needle in a haystack. The seatbelt sign pinged off and I got to my feet, stretching out my body as I ran through a series of fairly basic moves that kept me limber but also helped ease the lingering muscle tension from the fight at the museum.

Movement helped me think. Using my body weight to stretch my arms out above my head, I stared at the mounds of blackish purple clouds out the window. *You were always great on your own, Bobbi.* I'd gotten used to being part of a team, being part of a pair, being part of a whole. I knew I'd definitely gotten lost in there somewhere. Trying to navigate all of those interpersonal relationships alongside the professional ones had felt like running blindfolded through a hedge maze at times. Now it was just me, striking out on my own, with the added assistance of S.H.I.E.L.D.'s resources in my back pocket. Rolling my shoulders and blocking out the gorgeous view, I recentered myself. This is what I was good at.

Start micro, move macro had been one of my first and most useful lessons so that's what I did. I knew what was in my suitcase intimately, every item having been packed with intent and specifically for situations just like this when I needed to depart ASAP. I didn't know exactly what I would need, when or why, so I went with the basics.

Battle staves, lockpicking kit, portable lab basics, handgun, dismantled shotgun, covert ops suit, and Mockingbird tactical suit – one should never travel without it. Then there were the hasty additions: everything I would need to match my cover as Millicent Porter, a Brown transfer doing a semester abroad and working her way through a Masters in gender studies. Languages I had no trouble with, but accents were not my strong suit, so the most fitting ruse was adjacent to the truth. I had studied at Brown, actually, but only for two semesters while on temporary assignment. I would seem just like any other American there to annoy the English.

By the time Mr Vukojevic touched down at a private airfield not far from Gatwick Airport, I'd forgone a nap to make sure the ensemble cast of my one-woman play was ready to take the stage. I completed the finishing touches in the short cab ride to the main airport. In a brown, bobbed wig, all-white cashmere fit and delicate gold chains, the aim was to look like a svelte soccer mom as I joined the throng of people catching the train from the airport to the city. If there was anyone on me, that would be the easiest and quickest way to spot a tail. Sure enough, it didn't take long to pick up a shadow as I rode the train towards London. They weren't Hydra, that's for sure: those guys tended to have a kill first, ask questions later policy. And – much as I hated to admit it – they were usually semi-competent. These two looked like they had watched too many Bourne movies, their tight clothing and twitchy jawlines a dead giveaway.

I rode the train past my intended stop, eyeballing it until I found the station that looked busiest and most chaotic: St Pancras International, the interchange for King's Cross, from where I could pick up an Underground train to my final destination. It would have been easy to lose them on the walk over to King's Cross, among the crush of people rushing to get home as it ticked over into peak hour. That would have been a waste though. Knowing who they worked for would tell me information I couldn't find elsewhere.

Annoyingly, I had to slow down and pretend to adjust the strap of my ankle boots when they lost me and once on the concourse, I diverted into a newsstand after they'd clocked my frame. I browsed the rows of magazines, fingers dancing over the glossy volumes as I wandered past the taller of the two men following me. He was focusing so hard on pretending to read a magazine – upside down – that he didn't notice as I slipped a hand into his jacket. *Bless his heart,* I thought. This would be a lesson he'd learn the hard way.

The other guy was an eager beaver, following way too closely to remain unnoticed and even bumping into an older lady as he went to blindly follow me into the bathroom. He lost precious seconds profusely apologizing to her and by the time he was done, I was locked in a cubicle and reading all about my new friends via the tablet I'd pinched from Junior Jason Bourne.

Swiss Army Knives were overrated in a world where multifunction hair clips existed and I pressed down on one now, releasing it from where it was pinned. It was basically a tiny toolbox resting on your scalp, looking exactly like a regular hair clip until you peered closer. There were tiny, serrated teeth on one side that could cut through almost anything with enough pressure applied, along with nodes for a variety of screwdriver sizes, ruler marks and wrench. I was ready to unscrew his device and override the security mechanisms from the back end. Turns out, I didn't need to as he hadn't bothered to lock his tablet.

"Ugh," I moaned, clipping my tool back in. So annoying. This was much less interesting: teams of two had been deployed to follow and monitor *all* passengers incoming via private airfield due to an increased terror threat level. Disappointment again. I hadn't even been made, just assigned these two idiots because of procedure. I poked around a little, noting that the alert had gone out five days ago – before I'd even been assigned this mission – and this duo worked for S.T.R.I.K.E. *Curiouser and curiouser.* What took their terror threat level from the official designation of low to substantial? When I tried to follow the file path back to that crucial piece of information, I couldn't get any further without facial recognition.

I could drag them in here, knock them out, and get my answers. The downside of that whole equation was eventually they'd wake up, realize what had happened, and raise the alert. The woman they had been following with disinterest due to standard operations would become someone of great interest to them. I'd probably have twenty-four hours at best before my cover was blown, and the entire backlot of S.T.R.I.K.E. knew there was a S.H.I.E.L.D. agent among them. Then the question of why would become much more of an issue.

I followed all these thoughts down the rabbit hole in a matter of seconds, making my decision as I washed my hands at the sink. Eager Beaver was – again – lurking too close to the entrance to the bathroom, basically vibrating on the spot as I exited and then panicking when he realized what he was doing. He followed too far behind now and it wasn't long before I spotted Junior Jason Bourne, locked his tablet, and slipped it back into his jacket while I passed him in a line. These two were – respectfully – fools. Or at the very least, *super* green. If they lost me, it would be a reflection of their incompetence and not my superiority and that's exactly what I was counting on as I pivoted out of their line of sight, away from a camera, and into an electrical closet. I disrobed quickly, switching outfits into a boring black and white business suit, and ditched the wig.

I looked just like any other corporate darling as I pretended to be on the phone to my spouse, bemoaning the guy in accounts who just "couldn't get anything right!" The woman who had traveled to London was more of a Cassandra – Cassie to her friends – but I saw this identity with a name that was more classic and unexpected: Blythe, boss of the boardroom.

My third and final switch was a deviation from both of those, because the reality was the more I could work a disguise into what was naturally there physically – just like the fiction crafted around her – the more it could stand up to scrutiny. It had been easy enough to find a discreet and private rest room to take over in this massive station, sincerest apologies to the mothers whose changing table I was occupying for fifteen minutes. With a triumphant flip, I snapped my head back and scrunched the wet hair with a paper towel, getting rid of the last few droplets.

"There you are," I beamed.

By the time I strolled back out onto the concourse, Millicent Porter had gone from an idea to a living, breathing reality. Wigs were great in theory and lace fronts had saved my butt more than once, but to a trained eye they could be spotted easily enough. My usually blonde hair looked pink because it *was* pink. A cheap box dye, but precisely the kind of thing a student abroad could afford. I'd slapped some stickers on my suitcase, torn at them a bit so they appeared aged enough, then leaned hard into the aesthetic with a pastel pink trench coat, knitted houndstooth sweater in a complementary shade and pair of cat-eye fuchsia frames with glass in the lens to subtly change the shape of my face. The best way to blend in sometimes, was to stand out.

My point was proven by how easily I merged into the crowd, thousands of bodies pressing against each other as they chased an invisible timetable only they knew. Descending the escalator and making my way toward the transfer I needed to get to Paddington Station, I smiled as I looked up at the huge, steel structure that was built into the archway of the roof like a cascade of conflicting metal lines. Colored lights were projected against it, changing the shade every few seconds, and it transitioned from purple to pink just as the echo of my boots hit the pavement.

Millicent would have stopped for a selfie, so I did too, immediately setting the shot as my new lock screen. One more tube and then I was shivering involuntarily while looking for my platform at a station that was better known for the famous fictional teddy bear named after it. My ride was running five minutes late and by the time it pulled up, I all but jumped into the cozy interior.

"Someone's keen," an old man chuckled as he boarded the train behind me. I grinned, chattering my teeth dramatically. "Not from around here, love?"

"America," I replied. "First time in England."

"Ah." He smiled, nodding. He turned to his wife with a curled lip and whispered "*Yanks*" with disgust. I had to suppress the urge to laugh, because although the chill of February back home and February here had given me whiplash, this was maybe my thirtieth time in the UK if I had to guess. The first five times are always special, then it's just a matter of "what's the time difference?" My unintended but not entirely unanticipated detours had thrown off my arrival time by an hour, but on the plus side meant the train to Oxford was quieter than I had expected and it wasn't hard to find a comfy seat on my own. As we chugged out of the station, the lights of a gray London city whirring by, I settled in for a cruisy fifty-minute ride until I'd be on the ground.

There wasn't a whole lot to look at thanks to the night sky's impenetrable blackness, so I watched the passengers around me instead. A snoring woman rested her head on a friend's shoulder, both of them looking like fellow university students. A mother was breastfeeding her young son, her other child watching *Bluey* with rapt attention on her phone. The old man who was distinctly anti-Yank handed the newspaper to his wife, tapping at an article he wanted her to read. It was such a casual gesture, so unremarkable, but it struck me immediately. I pulled my laptop out of my bag, firing it up as I connected to the academic portal and false permissions S.H.I.E.L.D. had set up on my behalf. Whoever was interested in Dr Wilma Calvin had likely gone through the exact same process I did: scanning her articles, downloading them, reading them. And that was trackable. All I had to do was come up with some parameters.

Years ago, I had made a custom piece of software to track DNA markers across super-powered humans, looking for and identifying patterns. I'd called it Library Card, because it was essentially a pass to access all kinds of information you didn't know you needed. It was rarely used at S.H.I.E.L.D. now – there being a thousand better ways to do the same thing – but the plug-in came as part of all your standard operating software on a mission laptop, so it was easy enough to access.

Jumping into the backdoor of the code, I made some tweaks to what Library Card should be looking for. I'd start with her past three years at Oxford, expanding the search wider if I needed to, but flagging any recurring names that frequently accessed her papers online. That would give me a lot of filler, students and fellow lecturers and professors who were consuming her work quite innocently as part of their day-to-day roles. So I added additional search fields, slotting in attendees at conferences she had spoken at, names that had been in her classes, folks who had emailed her. I hit enter and watched the percentage bar inch along until a satisfying ping told me the results were ready.

"Sheesh," I mumbled. Even with those parameters, it was a lot of names – some fifty or so – but it was a starting point and I had nothing but time to kill on this train ride. There's this stereotype that spy work is sexy and sometimes, under key circumstances, it can be. Mostly, it's just going through a spreadsheet and looking for the digital footprint of every name on the list while alternating with painting your nails a matte pink.

Library Card's results hadn't proved super fruitful at first – students, lecturers, scientists, as you'd expect – but then I got an interesting result on the name "Lynval Golding". He was a real person all right, just like the others, yet he didn't fall into any of the other categories. A Jamaican-born British musician and founding member of a ska band I'd never heard of – The Specials – he was well known enough that trying to find anyone else under that name was impossible. All online searches, social media profiles, and image results came right back to the musician. It was a specific enough name that there couldn't be that many Lynval Goldings out there and I set it to the side, marking it for further examination later.

Later came quick as just a few entries down, I had the same problem with "Steven Severin" – a name that was satisfying to say out loud but borderline impossible to search as he was a founding member of *another* British rock band, Siouxsie and the Banshees. I didn't even bother searching for "Robert Smith" when I got to it as I was enough of a Cure fan to know that was hopeless and "Kate Bush" was really just having a laugh by that point. By the time a voice crackled over the intercom telling passengers Oxford Station was the next stop, I had the pattern I had been looking for.

Either a who's who of specific British musicians were interested in how severe cooling compacts chromatin and changes subcellular transcriptomes – and had attended lectures on that very subject – *or* someone had used those names as cover when digging into the specifics of Dr Calvin's work. There was a cleverness to it that I appreciated, as annoying as it was. None of the names were, say, as obvious as "Lady Gaga" and would leap out immediately. They were *just* popular enough that they were unsearchable if you had the sense to do the kind of digging that I was trying to do. Someone had been curious about her work and that someone had a sense of humor, which was something at least.

As I stepped off the train, cold air blasting my face and The Specials now singing about a "Ghost Town" through my headphones, I couldn't help but smirk. If I had to take down a Hydra operative, at least let them be funny.

CHAPTER FOUR

God bless college dropouts. That was my first thought as I finally came to a stop after a solid sixteen hours of traveling and collapsed on the single bed of a room at Magdalen College. There were more than thirty different colleges under the Oxford banner, and I'd gotten lucky with someone forfeiting their room midway through the second term of the academic year, Hilary. Not to be confused with Michaelmas – which came before – and Trinity – which came after. This country was confusing. *And cold,* I thought bitterly as I watched my breath form a small steam cloud inside the room. It took me a solid five minutes before I was able to establish that the fireplace was ornamental and to find the functioning heater.

Could the person here before me have frozen to death? I was whining, I knew it, and once I had a searing hot shower in the *communal* bathroom – kill me – I was starting to feel more like myself. This room being vacated in a hurry meant that half of it was still furnished and if anyone bothered to check, it would look like a student lived here. A slightly more mature student compared to some of the others I'd passed in the hall, but the dead succulent in a sad little pot plant was an authentic detail.

I was bone tired but strangely wired and as I unpacked, I listened to the playlist I'd haphazardly put together with all of the pseudonyms from the operative I feared had taken Dr Calvin. This space wasn't secure, and I had things to do that would allow me to sleep at night, so with my portable toolkit I got to work. First, refit the existing lock and add three more: two to the main door and one to the window. Second, connect all of them to motion sensors so I'd be alerted the second someone was trying to break through. Three, layer the existing window with a bulletproof film that peeled off one surface and on to another in any shape that I cut it to. Four, make sure the fireplace was actually blocked off and a surveillance drone couldn't be fed down it. The fifth and final step was a tiny security camera that I fitted rather seamlessly into a black, ceramic ornament that had been left behind. If I tilted my head just right, it kind of looked like a horse. Kind of.

I taped a handgun under the bed and positioned my battle staves within reaching distance of my pillow before inspecting the contents of the mini fridge. Depressingly empty but clean. My last meal had been on the plane, chatting with Mr Vukojevic while eating an overstuffed salad sandwich in the co-pilot's seat. He'd chastised me for leaving shredded beetroot behind. My stomach rumbled at the thought and I grabbed a protein bar from one of my stashes. Wrapping a throw blanket around me, I stared out the window at Oxford by night. It was quiet right now, a Tuesday evening on the other side of midnight not cause for much ruckus, but it was still satisfying nonetheless. I was up on the third floor in a room that faced away from the college's famous grounds and instead gave me a view of a chapel that looked much more like a cathedral. That was apparently something British colleges had: *cathedrals*. This place didn't quite seem real and all I'd seen of it so far was the walk from the train station to Magdalen College.

And yet… I was excited to be here. I had leads. I had a plan. I had an advantage in that I knew Dr Calvin, probably more than I would have liked if I was honest. Although I'd be playing catch up in terms of trying to backtrack through the movements leading to her disappearance, I was on the ground in a place I'd never been before and getting to do one of my favorite things in the world: problem solve. It was such a comforting thought, I barely spent any time thinking about how weird it was that a sink was fitted into the center of the bookshelves. College dorms, a unique puzzle box of their very own.

The best way to know a city was to run it. Literally. The fact jogging was scientifically proven to help combat the effects of travel fatigue was an added bonus. Thermals on, beanie pulled tight, body stretched, music up *loud* and soon I was pounding the pavement of one of England's oldest establishments as sunlight broke over the horizon. It didn't take me long to run to the edge of Oxford, which was too small to be a city, but didn't feel quaint enough to be a town either. So I turned around, getting my bearings as I negotiated every alley, every side street, and every lane as they twisted around and doubled back and looped in on each other. There were beautiful rivers that cut through the township, and I joined the throng of people biking alongside them, maintaining a steady pace as I used the intermittent bridges to dart from one bank to the other.

As the morning crept on and the sun rose higher, the waterways got just as busy. It was like an aquatic version of a Los Angeles freeway, rowers bumper to bumper as they paddled on despite what seemed like freezing temperatures to me. Most were in multi-person crafts, everything from a K2 to a K4, but when I saw a lone figure bundled up in layers of protective clothing slicing through the water with their paddles, I couldn't help myself. I'd been aiming for distance, not speed, but I was a naturally competitive monster. My tread increased as if of its own accord and I pumped my arms, darting around the human obstacles on the riverside path as I chased the kayaker. They must have noticed after about half a mile and their own pace picked up too, while I matched it. I had better endurance and soon, my long legs were doing what it felt like they were born to do as I strode faster and faster until I had ironically run out of runway.

Exhilarated, I laughed as I slowed to my regular jogging pace and mounted the steps of the small bridge that arched over the waterway. Looking down at my competitor, I was surprised to see that he was… cute. Handsome, even, the little of his face I could see. His eyes were hidden behind a pair of polarized sunglasses and a beanie was pulled as far down on his head as he could manage. His jawline was clean shaven and sharp as he smiled up at me, dimples pronounced. He didn't stop paddling and I respected that, returning the small wave of acknowledgment he offered as he passed underneath me.

Checking my position, I started a wide loop around the green lawns of University Parks just like any other annoying exerciser that morning. Conveniently, it gave me a great view of the New Biochemistry Building, which Dr Calvin had worked out of. It was an example of a rare structure in the town that was new, modern, with the sunlight catching on autumn-toned glass panes that were fixed into the exterior of the building. I paused in front of a student noticeboard, scanning the leaflets there asking for test subjects on various research projects and advertising for everything from housemates to personal tutors. My eyes caught on a flyer for a function happening that evening and after a quick glance to make sure no one was watching, I unpinned it from the board and slipped it into my pocket. Dr Calvin's residence was a walking distance of twenty minutes or a hop, skip and a jog in my case, my eyes running over the names of the cafes and restaurants and shops nearby that over the past few years she would have become a regular fixture at.

By the time I was walking off a tidy twenty miles at a not too shabby pace, if I do say so myself, I felt confident in my basic geographical understanding of Oxford as a whole. Specifically, the places I would need to start picking apart Dr Calvin's life and whoever might have wanted to disrupt it. Wiping sweat from my brow and relishing in the exertion that had clothes sticking to my skin, I was thankful that my next step required slightly less physical effort and considerably more mental patience.

"You there! Pinky!"

A man whose jowls had jowls was clicking his fingers at me aggressively. A strained smile on my face, I made my way over to him with the tray of canapes that was the object of his affections.

"What are these?" he barked, fingers dancing over the appetizers, each one under threat.

"This is sweet pea pesto crostini," I replied, moving on to

the next dish before he got a chance. "And spinach-artichoke stuffed mushrooms."

"Where's the *meat*?" he snarled, all teeth.

"These are the vegetarian options, sir, but I can send one of the meat servers this way if you like."

"Promptly."

I nodded politely, about to dart away when one of the men stopped me. I hadn't had the time to notice much about him except that he was the youngest of the professors and instead of wearing pants, had on a red tartan kilt with his suit jacket.

"May I?" he asked.

"Of course," I responded, pivoting back politely and meeting his gaze.

"I love mushrooms," he said, Scottish accent thick. There was just the faintest hint of humor dancing in his eyes and as he raised them to the roof and back again, indicating his thoughts on the present company, I bit my lip to hide a smile.

"Take a few then," I whispered. "No one else likes them."

There were streaks of silver in his fiery red hair that glinted in the low light, and he went to reply, but one of his colleagues called his attention.

"Did you read Nijin's latest findings?"

"Aye." He nodded. "I thought they were quite rudimentary."

I took that as my cue to leave, navigating my way around the sea of Oxford's scientific elite as they all congregated in the one spot to honor… someone, for something. The specifics weren't that interesting to me, but the opportunity to work at a function being held two floors above Dr Calvin's office and primary laboratory was *very* interesting. So, too, was the added bonus of getting to scope out her peers, the people she had worked alongside since arriving in England and even those she had just given a passing head nod to in the hallway. Using trays of food to circulate through the space, it looked like any other function at a university as the different departments under the broad "science" banner converged. Mostly white, mostly older men made up the bulk of the room, with clusters of outsiders trying to cross enemy lines and infiltrate the different departments with idle chatter on a variety of dry subjects. Of course, the chatter was never *really* idle. It was always loaded with intent and strategy as each person here tried to secure their forward mobility in the cutthroat world of academia. I didn't miss this.

Returning through the swinging doors of the kitchen, I was able to keep my eyes on the players as I reloaded and reshuffled the array of snacks that needed to head back out in a matter of moments. It had been easy enough to get on this catering staff list. I slipped in my name for someone else's on their online roster once I saw the event flyer earlier that day. It was too good a chance to miss and the most seamless, easy way to get access to the building and access to Dr Calvin's colleagues simultaneously, while using my temporary undercover identity. Sure, I was dressed in a black and white uniform that had an annoying satin waistcoat and even more annoying bowtie, but comparatively this was nothing. I shuddered at the memory of having to go undercover at a Juggalo convention to infiltrate a ring smuggling underage mutants. A gentle elbow to my side thankfully shook me out of the traumatic recollection.

"I saw you chatting to Kilty McKilt over there," said a woman whose name I had to strain to recall. Thank heavens for the name badges. "He's the only fit one among the lot of 'em."

"Do you know him, Elle?"

During setup, I listened as all the other waiters chatted and I identified her as the most useful among them. She worked this circuit *a lot* while studying for her Master's in environmental science, so she knew pretty much everyone.

"He's the new professor from St Andrews."

"Ah." I nodded. "The kilt is the giveaway."

"Right?"

"Shame about the Tom Selleck moustache."

She laughed, braids clinking with the gesture. "I dunno, I'm ticklish so… quite the fan. Plus, I love redheads."

"He's the one filling in for Dr Calvin?"

"Yeah. I have a friend who's in his classes, says his whole presentation is a bit robotic, you know?"

"What's his name?"

"Professor Halkner, Falkner, something like that."

We swapped trays and I headed back out, the smoky wrapped bacon parcels and quiches proving much more popular than my previous vegetable dishes. The second the last morsel was gone, so was I. I took a hard right as the speeches began and everyone's attention turned to the front of the room. It's amazing how many places you could get access to if you moved like you had purpose and I jogged down the maintenance stairwell quickly, busting out on to the third floor and a corridor that put me closest to Dr Calvin's office. I still had to negotiate a very visible and public walkway to cross from one side of the building to the other. The whole center of the space was light and airy in a way that looked beautiful from the ground floor as you arched your neck skyward to the exposed stars protected under glass, but it was annoying for sneaky purposes. Thankfully, everyone who was anyone was upstairs and I could hear the noise from the party as I walked swiftly, tray laid flat as I smiled politely at a passing student.

C Wing was empty, and I'd swiped a key card from Kilty McKilt that allowed me access with a satisfying *ping* as I ran it under the security reader. I had what looked like a novelty pen in my pocket and the second I was somewhere that I shouldn't have been, I pressed the button at the end of it that *should* have ejected ink into the nib's tip. Instead, it made every security camera in a fifty-meter radius capture nothing but white snow until I was out of range. There was only a standard lock on Dr Calvin's door and I hesitated for a moment, wondering if I should tackle this first or her lab just down the way. The office was closer, so I dropped to a crouch as I unclicked my fake pen to reveal the tools encased in the plastic within. I wedged a hook feeler pick into the lock, adding a tension wrench as I got to work. It was only a matter of seconds before I heard the satisfying clicks of the pins and the door popped open.

Gently shutting it behind me, my eyes ran over the organized chaos of her space, which looked pretty much the way it did a decade ago except with better furniture. Most of it – I knew – would be largely unused as Dr Calvin was someone who believed her best work was done in a lab coat. My fingers ran over the white fabric of hers where it hung on a hook at the back of the door, smiling at the detail of her name sewn into the pocket with blue thread. Sentimentality could wait. I had about fifteen minutes before someone would notice I wasn't working the floor, twenty if Elle took the initiative to cover for me. I moved through the space methodically, slipping on a pair of gloves and clicking at the side of my glasses until the view switched to UV light. There was no blood, no fluids, no sign of anyone attempting to clean up a crime scene. I could faintly see where she had been, however, tracking her movements with the neon blue smears left from the everyday human bacteria on her skin when she had been here, alive, well, and shuffling through this space in the harried manner that was distinctly hers. There were four volumes on the bookshelf that she had returned to repeatedly and I pulled them down, shaking them one by one to see if anything fell loose. Nada.

Her desk was just as fruitless, each drawer full of half-chewed pens and knick-knacks designed to keep the impulses of fidgeters at bay. A drawer of graded papers and another of university documentation hid nothing, but I checked under her desk just to be sure, my fingers running along the smooth lines of the craftsmanship, searching for imperfections. Nothing. I followed the route of several cords to what should have been a laptop, but her computer was gone. The impression of where it had sat over countless hours was still there, the rectangle shape set into the paper of her day planner. I quickly snapped a shot of it, the current month laid out ahead of her with meetings and dates and details filled in. Flipping through the next several months was just as vital, with each hastily scrawled square telling me that she had intended to be here in March, in April, in May, in fact right up until the end of the Trinity term.

Laying a square of paper from the printing tray flat, I used a pencil to hastily etch out the markings of whatever the last thing she'd written there would be. I didn't have time to look at it now, but it may prove useful later. I checked the room for bugs, cameras, any kind of monitoring device that would indicate Dr Calvin was being watched by someone besides S.H.I.E.L.D. The space was clear. Turning back to the printer, I punched through the settings until I was able to find the "print last job" mechanism and hit the key. A series of papers chugged out of the machine, with only two pages to go when I heard an enormous crash down the hall. It sounded like someone had smashed an entire cupboard of fine china and – most importantly – it sounded like it had come from the direction of Dr Calvin's lab. I bounced on my toes with impatience, waiting for the final documents to be spat out. Grabbing them, I ran for the door and folded everything I had into a neat square.

I was conscious of the fact I wasn't meant to be here and quickly snatched Dr Calvin's lab coat on the way out. Buttoning it up around my catering uniform and tugging off my bowtie, I hoped it would help me pass as a student as I jogged down the hall and skidded to a stop in front of... well, chaos. There was no other way to describe it.

The door to the lab had been blown from its hinges, the glass viewing window laying smashed in tiny pieces on the floor. That was only a layer to the cacophony of sound that had drawn my attention, however, and my eyes were drawn to the rest of the lab. It looked like every single piece of equipment – every microscope, every beaker, every test tube – had been obliterated. Slippery glass crunched underfoot as I inched deeper into the space, and I reached out to steady myself on one of the tables.

"Ugh." I grimaced, yanking my hand away as I made contact with a wet, slimy substance. It was clear, almost translucent. You couldn't tell it was there until light reflected against it or you had the misfortune to touch it.

"Absolutely not," I groaned, wiping my hand hastily against the lab coat. It was only then that I realized I wasn't alone, the other occupant of the room having remained perfectly still in the hope I wouldn't notice them. Spinning on the spot, I drew my staves and turned to face the corner behind me in a flash of motion. Dr Calvin's replacement was frozen behind the desk, his hands flying up and his back pressing against the wall in surrender.

"I swear, this isn't what it looks like," he said, Scottish brogue absent.

Unfortunately for him, the motion of his lips as he spoke caused his thick and apparently synthetic moustache to slowly peel away from his face. It dangled there for a moment, lopsided, before dropping to the ground and into a ball of slime with a wet *thunk*. He closed his eyes with annoyance, letting out a long exhale of frustration.

"Okaaaaay."

"Kilty McKilt." I smirked. "Your Scottish accent sucks."

His eyes flashed with a hint of amusement. "Your hair sucks."

He never had a chance to hear the biting reply on the tip of my tongue as a voice cried out behind us.

"All right, hands up! Nobody move!"

CHAPTER FIVE

A curse escaped his lips, but I remained silent as I did exactly what they said and raised my hands. The motion allowed me to slip my staves into the sleeves of the lab coat, my thumbs pressing against their weight to hold them in place.

"I'm not sure w-what's going on," I stammered. "I was just working in the lab down the hall when I came to investigate the nois–"

"Quiet!" the guy yelled, asking me to turn around. I was surprised to find four men dressed in the security uniforms of the university. They were so aggressive, I assumed they were cops.

"I'm Professor Falkner," the man who was definitely not Professor Falkner said, Scottish accent back in full swing. "This is my laboratory, I have every right to be here – look! I'll show you my access pass."

He fumbled in his pocket for it, hands patting around as he searched for it to no avail. He looked guilty as heck.

"It's here, I swear…" His gaze cut to mine sharply, as if

knowing I was the one who took it. He was right, of course, but I blinked back innocently.

"We've never heard of any Professor Falkner," the leader snapped. "This is Dr Calvin's lab."

I frowned, Kilty McKilt doing the same. Our eyes met for a brief moment.

"Really?" he asked. "Because that's my name on the door."

He nodded his head in the direction of said plaque, which they were standing right on top of given the door was beneath their feet. The name "Professor Falkner" glinted ever-so-slightly under the sticky film of slime that seemed to coat everything. They didn't bother to look down.

"That's a pretty remarkable response time for campus security," I murmured. "Something explodes here, and you guys happen to be not only on the right floor, but eight seconds away?"

"Ten," Kilty McKilt corrected.

"Very remarkable," I agreed. They seemed to realize we were on the same page at precisely the same time. What should have been electric currents firing from their tasers were bullets instead, but I had already anticipated this and thrown myself through the air by the time they started firing. I landed behind the thick, almost impenetrable laboratory bench at the exact same moment as Kilty McKilt, our shoulders colliding together with an *oomph*.

"Pretty spry for a professor," I shouted over the sound of weaponry firing.

"Oh, shut it," he scoffed, a South London accent now seeming much more comfortable in his mouth than the Scottish one. "Going to offer me a canape?"

"I would," I replied, quickly grabbing one of the only

unbroken petri dishes laying at my feet. "Think they'd stop firing at us for a few seconds so I can ask their dietary requirements?"

He barked a laugh, head swiveling as he looked around for the best exit. While his attention was elsewhere, I quickly scooped as much of the mysterious goo as I could into the plastic container and twisted the lid shut. By the time he looked back, it was tucked into Dr Calvin's lab coat.

"They have us pinned down," he said. "That window is our only hope."

"Where does it lead to?"

He shrugged. "Find out?"

I muttered a string of curses under my breath. There were two things I knew for certain: these guys were *not* campus security, and the man next to me could *not* be trusted. Yet sometimes knowing where the trap was made it easier to divert around it. At least that's what I had to tell myself because the truth was, I needed out of there and out of there *fast*. If through a window with a stranger was my only option, then so be it. My grip tightened around the staves, blue sparks shooting from the ends as I tested their charge. Face grim, body crouched into a fighting position, I made my choice.

"Fine," I murmured. He nodded back at me, unwrapping a belt from around his waist that I didn't even know was there. Did kilts need belts? *Stay focused,* I snapped at myself. Both of us knew the signal without needing to communicate it and as soon as there was a pause in firing, we sprang into action. I slid across the bench, trying not to think about the fluid underneath me that was giving me extra speed as I slicked through it, and kicked the first man square in the face. He hit the ground cold, and I only had to throw one stave to take out my other target, tossing it against the wall so that it ricocheted off a cabinet and into the skull of the man just as he raised his weapon at me. He dropped like a sack of bricks, collapsing at precisely the same time my stave bounced back into the palm of my hand.

"Good girl," I whispered, forgetting that I wasn't alone.

"Are you talking to a baton?" my comrade asked.

"It's clearly a stave!"

"Are you talking to a stave?" he grunted, belt around the neck of a security guard as he choked him to unconsciousness. The other assailant was hunched over in the fetal position, clutching his leg like it was about to drop off. My ersatz Scotsman had managed to do all that in a kilt. I'd fought in skirts before and I couldn't say that I wasn't impressed. Very impressed.

"Are you asking him out on a date or can we go now?" I responded, showing it not one bit. He flashed a grin at me, the white teeth and dimples immediately recreating the image from that morning. "Kayaker."

The grin grew even wider if possible. "I was wondering if you'd notice me. Here I was thinking it was just coincidence, the beautiful woman from this mo-"

"Ick," I gagged. "Give it a rest."

A door banging open sounded behind us, footsteps echoing down the hall and shouted voices as more bodies rushed to greet us. There was no time to waste. A chair was hurled at the window, it shattered into miniscule pieces as we both ran towards the newly opened exit point. As I leapt, I heard a yell as someone caught sight of our figures disappearing through the gap. We were suspended in the air for only a few brief seconds, cold rain splattering against my face as the sky opened up.

"Ooooft!"

I landed with a grunt against a hard bed of concrete roof tiles, several sounding like they cracked under the impact. My companion landed just as ungracefully but with more momentum, his hands scrambling for a hold as he started to slide downward. I'd managed to grab on to a ledge with one hand and connected the staves in a flash, extending their length toward him as he fell.

"No way I'm grabbing that!" he panted. "I've seen what you can do with those things!"

"Trust me or die!"

The words must have gotten to him as he clutched the long security of the rod at the last minute. His trajectory now stopped, I strained to hang on with the additional weight but was eventually able to pull him back up. He collapsed next to me, puffing and soaked as we lay there for a moment.

"Thanks," he sighed.

My glasses had skittered off the side of the building, giving me a clear view of his face as I turned my head to analyze whether he was really meant it or if this was just another lie I had to contend with.

"Oi! There on the roof!"

We sprang up in an instant. Thankfully it was actual campus security yelling at us this time. I could tell given this guy was at least twenty years past his physical prime and hesitant to climb out on to the roof after us. The first group would have been in hot pursuit. Sirens moved from the distance to near proximity, red and blue lights flashing against the reflective glass of the building as we scrambled across the wet tiles. It was like for every five steps of traction I gained, I lost another two and let out a pained yell as I slipped and hit my knee.

He grabbed me before I could fall much farther, both of us unsteady as we regained our footing.

"Follow me," he said. With my staves sheathed and my hand gripping his for support, we maintained the best pace we could along the length of the building. The yells of "whoa!" and "watch out!" told me we were being followed, but this was a treacherous path and our pursuers would soon fall behind. Or we'd break our necks, whatever came first.

"We need to get down from here," I said.

"One more block," he grunted in agreement, pointing out the spire of what I had to assume was a nearby church. That was our line of sight and challenging as it was, we were able to get there as the rain increased and flashes of white lightning struck across the skyline. Getting down was just as hazardous, a windowsill properly giving way and falling some four stories when I put my weight on it. We both watched its descent in silence, knowing it could have just as easily been us as it clattered against the concrete.

"This building is six hundred and fifty years old," he said, so quietly I had to strain to listen.

"RIP?" I offered.

He cackled, a slash of lightning drawing our gaze to the silhouettes of cops and security delicately trawling the rooftops.

"We need to lose them. And I know the perfect place."

I can't say watching a sopping wet man in a kilt swing his way through a window was on my bucket list. Yet when it happened in the moment, it was truly a shame that it hadn't been. A second later, a hand shot out in the darkness.

"Coming?"

I took it, letting him pull me inside. We both examined

the disgusting disarray of someone's dorm room for a beat. A straight man's, clearly, given the interesting curation of posters on the wall that featured various stages of undress. He moved first, grabbing the blankets off the bed and tossing me one.

"I don't know if I want to touch that," I grimaced, holding it at arm's length. "Have you got a towel?"

"Like a towel's gonna be any better," he snorted. "And it's not to dry off – wrap it around you."

He demonstrated by showing me, the result looking very close to a bargain basement Julius Caesar. If it wasn't for the sirens and footsteps I could hear thudding overhead, I wouldn't have done it. Yet the second I had a semi-stylish loop knotted around my shoulder he was urging me on. Soon it became clear to me, us passing clusters of students in the halls all with bedsheets haphazardly fastened and drinks in hand. There was a woman up ahead with a brightly colored flower crown that didn't fit the Roman aesthetic at all and he winked at her, using her flushed response as a distraction to deftly pluck the crown from her head. He threw it at me like a frisbee and as reluctant as I was to attend Coachella, I knew the reasoning: it would cover my hair. He tugged at his own, his red mass lifting off to reveal slick, black hair in its place and he immediately looked ten years younger. The wig was positioned on the head of a bust as we passed it, seamlessly fitting with the décor. We hit the ground floor of what looked like a nightclub at the same time as the police, but he had an answer for that, too. "Toga, toga, toga," he said, fists clenched and pumping as we were pulled into a larger group. It was like a contagion, his three cries catching immediately as everyone joined in.

"Toga! Toga! Toga! Toga! Toga!"

It was deafening and had the required effect. The police couldn't see anything, couldn't hear anything, as we were lost amongst the rabble. We were invisible and eventually they were gone. It was easy to slip through after that, both of us staying crouched so our mutual heights wouldn't give us away if anyone remained. Yet the word "toga" was echoing through my skull so profoundly, I doubted anyone over twenty-five could stand it. We collapsed into a dining booth near the door, both our backs pressed to the wall so we had a view of any incoming danger.

"Best to wait it out for a while," he said, using a serviette to wipe the water from his face. I could only nod in agreement, my heartbeat still pounding from the pursuit. A woman passed us with a tray of jelly shots and he waved her down, taking a handful of six and splitting them between us.

"No," I said, shaking my head and pushing them back. "I need to stay sharp."

"Loosen up." He beamed. "Live a little while running for your life!"

I smirked, watching as he slammed them back one by one. When he was done, eyes closed with satisfaction for a beat, I made my move. His eyes flew open as I cuffed one of his wrists to the stabilizing bar beneath the table. He didn't look surprised, just disappointed.

"C'mon now, love, was that necessary?"

"What's your name?" I asked, ignoring his question for my own.

"Lancelot," he scoffed. "What's yours?"

"Guinevere. Who do you work for?"

"Ya mom."

"My mom's non-responsive."

He winced. "Jinx. Me, too. Welcome to the Dead Moms Club. Hey, did they tell you that's why you became a spy? The mission therapist goes on *and on* about it with me."

"What did you do to Dr Calvin?" I asked, ignoring his earlier assumption.

He perked up at that. "What did *you* do to Dr Calvin?"

Ruined her life. Destroyed her professional reputation. Set her on this path to disaster.

"Gah, don't give me the silent treatment," he whined. "You're too good. I can't read your face, so I need you to actually verbalize things if I'm going to pick them apart."

"Do you just… say the first thing that comes to your mind?" I asked, genuinely baffled.

"Well, no. Hazard of the job, obviously. But that's what makes this so great! You've got me literally chained to the spot. No games! Let's make this our *Out of Sight* moment."

I frowned deeply.

"You know, the George Cl–"

"The Jennifer Lopez movie," I interjected.

His dark eyes twinkled with delight, and I was amazed that even with the disguise, I hadn't recognized him as the racer from the river this morning. He'd been sans moustache then and practically wearing a balaclava, but it was the energy of that *look*.

"It's a great film," he said, voice dropping low. "You know I–"

"Toga! Toga! Toga!"

"Yeah, yeah, toga etcetera," he huffed, annoyed at the interruption that had saved our skin not twenty minutes earlier. The guy moved on, looking deflated until he hit the next group and the cycle repeated.

"Name," I pressed. "The police could burst in here any minute. Campus security. Or worse, whoever tried to pass themselves off as them. You'd be stuck here in a toga and a kilt. I'd be gone."

"Quite a confliction of cultures, innit?"

"Quite. Tell me what I want to know and I'll let you go."

He narrowed his eyes. "Would you though?"

"Yes," I replied, trying to let the veil drop and allow him to see the truth on my face. He was quiet, gaze darting over mine like a lie detector until he was happy with what he saw.

"OK," he huffed, like he'd regret this later. "Quid pro quo, Clarice. My name is Lancelot."

"Oh, com–"

"Seriously," he snapped. "Everyone calls me Lance. You can too if you're not comfortable with, what was it? Kilty McKilt?"

I laughed despite myself. "Lance what?"

"Lance Hunter," he said, extending his free hand across the table to shake mine. "S.T.R.I.K.E. agent."

Rolling my eyes, I shook his hand with reluctance. "Not another S.T.R.I.K.E. agent."

"Another?"

"I had two follow me from the airport. Very annoying. Very incompetent."

He was laughing, chest full on rumbling with the motion as he threw his head back. "I bet you ate them alive."

I didn't respond.

"And for the record," the man whose third name for the night was now Lance Hunter began, "I didn't do *anything* to Dr Calvin. It's my fault she's missing in the first place."

"Your fault? How?"

"I was supposed to be remotely monitoring the old bird,

wasn't I? Make sure she wasn't selling formulas under the table."

"She wouldn't do that."

"You seem very sure."

It was a stare-off. I crossed my hands over my chest, tilting my head and indicating that he should continue.

"She fled right under my nose," he said. "Now my arse is grass unless I find her, which is what you caught me trying to do tonight."

"What was with the goo?"

"That wasn't me!" he pleaded, throwing up one hand as if to pledge Scout's honor. "I swear! Searching her lab seemed smart and logical. Someone else clearly thought so too, as they got there before me. It really wasn't what it looked like."

"Then I showed up," I said, adjusting the condiments on the table into a logical order. "Then not-quite-campus-security. Then actual campus security. Then the police."

His eyes tracked my fingers, bouncing from the salt to the pepper, to the mustard, to the ketchup and then the grime of the table.

"That's a lot of chess pieces on the board," Lance agreed. "Even for S.H.I.E.L.D."

My eyes flashed up. "I never said I was S.H.I.E.L.D."

"I *mean*, you're American and obnoxious, so it makes perfect sense. Besides…"

He pulled the handcuffs up from under the table, dangling them in front of me. They were specific, a matte gray rather than metallic and said to be unbreakable. Said to be.

"These are S.H.I.E.L.D. standard issue," he continued. "Look, that's the li'l bird logo there, innit?"

I snatched them from his hands, pulling them out of sight

before anyone wondered why two toga wearers were playing with enforcement equipment at a party.

"Why would you just sit there pretending?" I snapped.

There was only a faint smile on his face now as he answered, sincere and serious, "So we'd have this moment: one where I answered your questions and told you the truth when I didn't have to. And you would know that I had a choice in the matter, that I could have left, but I didn't."

The toga chant had started again somewhere in the party, but it sounded far off in the distance as we sat across from each other, staring and engaged in an entirely different conversation.

"Why?" I asked.

"Simple," Lance replied, laying both hands palm up on the table. "Trust."

"Not the *t* word."

"I need you to trust me, so you'll work with me," he continued. "Rumor has it Dr Calvin was one of yours and you being here means that you suspect her disappearance has something to do with her S.H.I.E.L.D. work. I need your insight, I need your information, and I need your resources if we're going to find out what happened."

Chewing the inside of my cheek, I thought it over. Our agencies were closely aligned on this according to him, but that still didn't mean there wasn't danger. This could be an elaborate S.T.R.I.K.E. scheme to find out the specifics of Dr Calvin's work in the hopes of recreating it for themselves. They could have even taken her, using her disappearance as bait to force our hand. She could be in one of their cells as we speak. These and about a hundred other theories whirred through my head in a flash as I tried to run the risk calculus required. At the end of the day, this wasn't a call I could make fortunately. It was *way* above my pay grade.

"It's not up to me," I said. "But let me ask the boss."

He brightened. "I'll ask mine if you ask yours?"

Lance Hunter held out his curled fist, flesh-to-flesh contact seemingly very important to him. I watched the handsome devil practically bat his eyelashes at me. In a split-second decision, I had to trust my gut.

"Deal," I replied. We bumped on it.

CHAPTER SIX

We stayed at the toga party an additional long, painful hour. Just to be safe. Although he'd made the peace offering, I wasn't fully sure if I trusted this Lance Hunter. I was certain he didn't trust me either and, frankly, I respected him more for it. So we left the booth, standing shoulder to shoulder, neither quite willing to let the other out of their sight as we leaned against a wall with our arms crossed and our clothes soggy. It was the stereotype of two old fogies watching on as "the kids" danced to a very poor excuse for music that I just couldn't get behind, no matter how hard I tried desperately to find the rhythm to pass time. When the crowd started to thin, I practically sagged with relief as that was our cue.

The second we were outside, I was immediately shivering. The rain had stopped but somehow it was even colder. I always associated rain as the entrée to sweeping humidity, much as I tried to leave the Californian mentality behind. Lance took one look, ducked back inside the party, and returned with a thick puffer jacket that made me look like a very tall marshmallow woman.

"Here," he said, shoving it over my shoulders and (wisely) not waiting for a response.

"Whose is it?"

"Does it matter?"

He had a point. We started making our way through the town, slowly, to scan for threats. We added some intentional stumbles here and there so that we looked just like any of the other students around us, annoying the locals and blending in with the frivolity.

"Where are you?" he asked.

"Magdalen."

He nodded, as if that made perfect sense, and we readjusted our course. It wasn't long before Magdalen College tower came into view as we walked over a bridge, a blueish purple light projected against the ancient structure. The River Cherwell was hushed beneath us, quiet, as if it knew these were the hours all good rivers should slosh and splash discreetly. I leaned against the railing, looking down at the glistening black waters below.

"You know I haven't asked for your name," Lance said, mimicking my pose.

"I know."

"Would you even tell me?"

"Sure. It's Pinky."

"Ha," he barked. "OK, *Pinky*. We have the same goal."

"So you say."

"So I say. Here's what I'm thinking: we call an hour truce. You speak to your people, I speak to my people. You've got *my* name, so run the checks that you were going to anyway. Get the permissions. Vet me. If green is go, meet me across the cloister in sixty minutes. If red is no, then an hour is plenty of time to vanish, abort the mission, and never be seen again."

It was my turn to laugh then. "And leave Dr Calvin to you? I saw what you did to the lab with your... *goo grenade*. No way."

My amusement wasn't returned, and he grabbed my arm, face serious as he spoke low and fast.

"Listen," he urged. "I told you that wasn't me. That's how I found the place. And the S.T.R.I.K.E. agent who had this job before me? Disappeared. *Whoosh*. Just vanished off the face of the earth. I always suspected Dr Calvin was involved, but I could never prove it. Now I think I was wrong. Something much worse is at play and I think you know that, too."

He released me, stepping back as he tried to tone down the desperation just a tad. I didn't like that he was right.

"An hour," I said, holding out my fist. He looked at it about as uncertainly as I had his. He bumped it, the motion slow as if I had a gag hidden beneath my sleeve and was going to zap him. I did consider it. "And my name is Bobbi Morse."

I left Lance Hunter on that bridge, my mind racing through all the possibilities and plotting a potential path forward in my head. Pebbles crunched underfoot as I jogged, weaving between the ancient pillars of the college and I rushed to make the most use of the time I had.

"Ooooh, cute flower crown!" a girl cooed as I passed her.

"Thanks, babe," I replied, not slowing as I took the stairs to the student accommodations two at a time. I checked my security mechanisms, the room untouched and unentered since I'd left it, then darted inside. Part of the job was being ready to go at a moment's notice, so I was repacked and retooled in five minutes flat. The next most important issue was regaining feeling in my extremities. There were few things a hot shower couldn't fix and I stripped off quickly, washing myself clean with searing water and using a high pH shampoo to rinse the pink from my hair. Towel wrapped tight around my body, a quick treatment scrunched through my ends, I felt somewhat like a human being again as I grabbed my bundle of discarded clothes and headed back to my room.

It was only when I threw them down on the ground that I noticed the metallic jangle that came with them. My keys were on the bedside table, next to the slime sample and the papers I had taken from Calvin's office and was optimistically trying to dry out. I'd removed everything I needed from my pockets, my staves were cleaned and stored, I–

"Wilma," I whispered, digging through the soppy bundle until I was able to retract her lab coat. I hadn't examined this properly, just grabbed it and ran, but I studied it closely now. Nothing looked unusual about it to the untrained eye, but now I could feel the additional weight on the left side. It was incremental, but it was enough. Using one of my tactical hair clips, I picked the stitching on the front pocket free until I was able to reveal a hidden layer of fabric. I unwrapped it like a present until inside the bundle was a set of keys. Just three, each looking old and rickety like they were intended to open the door of a haunted house or something ridiculous.

How did I miss this before?

Doesn't matter, I told myself mentally. I had it now. Glancing at the time, I quickly began activating the cloaking bubble I'd set up, with four flat interceptors placed around the space so anything I said couldn't be heard even if your ear was pressed flush against the door. Then I did what I had been dreading: I called Hill.

•••

Lance Hunter was waiting for me exactly where he said he'd be, at exactly the precise time, and on exactly the kind of motorbike I loved to ride: a Ducati. Kicking him off and racing into the distance wasn't an option, sadly. I had my orders and they were to – and I quote – "play nice". Even so, I may have been walking into a hastily negotiated inter-agency truce, but that didn't mean I shouldn't be mission ready. In all-terrain boots that came up to my knees and a bodysuit that had more secret compartments than the Quinjet, I'd thrown a thick, warm trench coat over the top to soften the look. It was black on black on *black* and with Lance's all black leather riding suit, it wouldn't have been hard to believe we could just fade away into the night. A cool breeze – was there any other kind here? – whipped my still drying hair behind me as I paced toward him with purpose.

"Blonde?" he said.

"Stop gawking."

"I thought that was your real hair."

"It was."

"But… an hour… now blonde," he stammered.

I took the spare helmet he had in his hands while he continued to stare. "The base of the pigment is only semi-permanent. If you already have a lightened follicle underneath, introduce a high pH shampoo and the coloring slips away."

"Huh?"

"Science," I simplified, swinging my leg over the back of the motorbike. "Semi-permanent science."

I watched him turn the key and hit the start/stop switch once, waiting for the sound of the engine turning on. It told me a lot very quickly, with the Ducati 1098 having a feature ninety per cent of bikes didn't have. The computer took over the start sequence as soon as you hit that button and I'd watched many a dude fool around, finger held down like it was faulty as they waited for the ignition. Heel flicking away the kickstand with ease and two quick revs of the throttle later, we were off. Leaning into the turns, we sped through the few streets of Oxford and into the country. There were no other cars at this hour, the lanes and roads empty. Switching the headlights to full beam, that's when Lance really opened up. We were well beyond any legal speed now and I relished it. I was never that person who clenched their eyes shut and buried their head in fear. I loved to go fast, faster than was safe, and I felt exhilarated as we bulleted through the English countryside in a flash of motion.

It was disappointing when we hit the highway, the dotted lights of London dancing up ahead and growing bigger and bigger as we neared. Just over an hour didn't feel long enough. *Keep going,* I wanted to say. *Just keep driving to Scotland, I don't care.* The faster you went, the harder it was for your problems to catch you. That never really worked though, not in the long run. And with a jolt, the smell of fuel and the feel of leather took me back to an involuntary memory with Clint. It wasn't anything special, just a rare afternoon we'd had together and an impulse decision to drive down the coast, find a hotel, lose a few days. The mind could be so nasty like that, something tiny in the present throwing you so quickly and efficiently back into the past. It wasn't a simpler time, it was never simple, but for a stupid few seconds I remembered what it was like to be happy. With him.

"You all right?"

Lance's question shook me out of it. He must have felt me stiffen against him, my hands now gripping the rail underneath the seat rather than his waist. We were waiting at a traffic light I didn't even remember stopping at. I tapped him on the shoulder as the light went green, ignoring the question and refocusing as we drew closer to the city center. He slowed as we entered a roundabout, and I eyed the train station to my left suspiciously.

"We're not going to have to charge a wall between platforms, are we?" I asked.

His shoulders rumbled beneath my grip with a chuckle. He pulled on to an offramp for an underground parking garage, his laminated pass beeping at the security station as a boom gate pulled back to allow him entry. The concrete decline into the bowels of the structure felt foreboding, but as we kept going deeper and deeper and deeper, I gave up trying to count how many levels we'd navigated. It seemed like we must be close to the earth's core by the time he pulled to a stop, docking the bike near a guard station manned by a cheery looking fellow who offered him a wave.

"'Ello, Lance!" he called. "Want a cuppa?"

"No thanks, Daf! Gotta sign in a visitor."

"Oh, righto then," the portly gent called, ducking back into his security hut to gather the materials.

"Don't be frightened of Dafydd," Lance said, his hair wild as he pulled off his helmet. "I know the persistent offer of quality tea scares you people."

"You people?" I scoffed, hopping off the bike. He took my helmet, clipping them both away into a compartment.

"*Americans,*" he offered, giving his body an all over shiver for emphasis. "With your terrible coffee and brash manners. Wouldn't know a good Earl Grey if it slapped you in the face."

"Wouldn't mind slapping a face right now," I replied.

He winked. Winked! Our steps echoed through the concrete prism of the seemingly endless parking garage, Dafydd meeting me with a scanner at the ready.

"The request for a visitor pass came through just before you arrived, Mrs Morse." He beamed. "Just sign here and hold still for the retinal scan."

I did as he asked, jaw clenched as I waited for an aside from Lance. Nothing came. I clenched my jaw harder. A small, glossy card popped out the bottom of his tablet and he affixed a clip to it, handing it over.

"There ya go, love," he smiled. "Just attach it to your person and keep it visible at all times."

I frowned down at the picture of me, which frowned right back.

"Have a great night! Oops, I mean morning now."

"Thanks, Daf," Lance said, slapping him on the shoulder in that way men do. We strolled toward a nondescript steel door that had been weathered to look like it was as old as everything around us. Lance scanned his pass, I scanned mine, and a long, chrome hallway stretched before us.

"Usually I'd drive us right through, but there's one more security che–"

"Just say it," I snapped, cutting him off.

"Say what?"

"What you're dying to say. What everyone is always dying to say."

He puffed out his cheeks, looking tense. "All right. Born Barbara 'Bobbi' Morse AKA Mockingbird AKA Agent 19. You're an Olympic medalist – bronze in parallel bars, although you were robbed for the silver – and competed at two World Titles across disciplines. Although I heard from a sneaky source of mine that you would have fared better competing in taekwondo. Overachiever."

I looked sideways at him in disbelief, but he kept his eyes fixed right ahead.

"In fact, 'overachiever' should be the title of your memoir. It comes up a lot. You're a proficient pilot across almost every form of aircraft and prefer vehicles pre-1980 when forced to be on the ground – faster the better – or any kind of motorcycle with modifications that are not strictly legal."

"It's only illegal if you're caught," I murmured.

"Eldest child of Susan Morse, parents divorced when you graduated high school at a freakishly young age, mother in a persistent vegetative state, dad AWOL. A master martial artist, holder of *two* PhDs – which would technically make you Dr *Dr* Morse – and prodigy of one Dr Wilma Calvin on a project that is presently classified to my organization. Former West Coast Avenger, signature weapon two scarily designed battle staves, pain in my butt so far, and one of the best operatives S.H.I.E.L.D. currently has on their roster."

We'd reached the end of the hallway, but I barely noticed as I stared at him. He met my gaze.

"Anything I missed?"

"No," I replied softly. "That about covers it."

He nodded, swiping us through two more doors and into a security checkpoint where I was examined, questioned, searched and picked apart. I didn't really notice. Instead, I was stuck on the small kindness of being defined by my achievements and not by my association with a certain bow-wielding crime fighter. Given it was on the stupid badge clipped to my coat, it was clearly in their records. Yet he didn't mention it even when Dafydd seemed so keen to.

"You're cleared, ma'am."

"Uh, thank you," I responded, slightly unsettled by the "ma'am" of it all. Lance was waiting for me on the other side, a huge, cavernous space stretching out behind him. It looked like an aircraft hangar, but with better lighting and what was clearly excellent central heating. I was the warmest I'd been since arriving in this country. There were screens positioned throughout the space, displaying various news broadcasts from around the world along with key data points visible along a side bar. Offices stretched upwards toward the arched ceiling, all of them transparent and looking like little glass Lego cubes stacked on top of each other. Even the elevator was see-through, which was admittedly very Willy Wonka of them.

"Are you gonna do me?"

His question jerked me out of gawking. "What?"

"My turn," he continued, gesturing at me like he was ready for a fight. "Lemme have it."

"All right," I smirked, looking him up and down. "Lancelot Hunter, which is somehow a real name, known as Lance to people who have no sense of humor. Age twenty-nine, orphaned at a young age, raised by an absentee aunt in a South London housing project, street hustled to survive, hence the adept skills with previously thought to be unbreakable handcuffs."

"I'm good with my hands." He grinned.

"Arrogant," I continued, watching that grin falter. "Following a string of offenses, was given a choice between jail time or serving in the Royal Navy. Picked the latter, excelled with a structure and outlet to deploy many talents, earned a Master's in engineering, and quickly elevated through the ranks before being recruited to MI6 and eventually S.T.R.I.K.E."

He raised a single eyebrow, encouraging me to go on.

"A Leo on the cusp of Virgo," I finished.

"There ya go." Lance beamed. "Feel better?"

"Li'l bit."

"C'mon then, let's watch our bosses bicker with each other."

It was like he brought his will to life with the comment, a very small man suddenly standing right behind him. Lance jumped, placing a hand on his heart for emphasis.

"Every time," he whispered. "Good morning, director."

"Hunter," the director replied, barely giving Lance a passing look before extending a hand to me. "Mrs Morse-Barton, it's an honor to meet you. I'm S.T.R.I.K.E. Director Tod Radcliffe."

I shook his hand, surprised by the firm grip and quietly seething at him addressing me by a hyphened surname I'd never taken. If S.T.R.I.K.E. couldn't even get that right...

"Thank you for having me," I said through a fake smile.

"An advanced warning that a S.H.I.E.L.D. agent was operating within our borders would have been preferred to a thank you," he replied.

"S.H.I.E.L.D. has international jurisdiction," I countered. "Just like S.T.R.I.K.E."

"And S.T.R.I.K.E. has manners, unlike S.H.I.E.L.D. it seems."

Touché. "Better to ask for forgiveness than permission, in this case."

"Hmmm. I can see why you and Hunter get along."

I opened my mouth to rebut him, but over Radcliffe's shoulder Lance was pulling a finger across his throat, begging me to stop.

"I've been having some very fruitful conversations with Deputy Director Hill over the past hour," he continued. "If you'd be so kind as to join us in the briefing room, I believe we can get started."

He spun around sharply, the ugliest pair of brogues I'd ever seen making almost no sound as he marched in the direction of where we were supposed to go. This was clearly a man used to being followed, from orders to general geography. Lance elbowed me as we dropped behind, navigating our way through passage after glass passage.

"Stop making this worse for me," he hissed.

"Me?"

"He's a nasty wee man and he already hates my guts."

I cast a glance toward the assistant that had appeared out of a doorway to join us, their posture stiff and their face strained as he barked an order at them.

"Are you sure it's not broadly humanity that he hates?" I asked.

"Omigod," he groaned, running his hands over his face. "A death wish. I'm stuck with a lanky broad who has a death wish."

Lance's wasn't the only file Hill had sent over in the brief time I'd had before leaving Oxford: she'd been sure to include S.T.R.I.K.E. Director Tod Radcliffe as well.

"When he pushes you – and he'll push you – you have to push back," Hill had said. "He considers anyone who bends to his will weak. It's in the psych profile."

There had been juice about Lance in his, too – adaptive and adventurous, someone willing to bend the rules in order to get the job done, a charming bad boy with a danger streak – which I'd found more interesting reading. A big softie with a strong sense of morality was the psychological evaluation I'd left out of my recap to him. Stepping into the briefing room, a button was hit and the glass shifted tone so that the outside view of what was happening in here would be completely blocked. There were six other people in this room, the ranks swelling to ten once we joined them, and I was immediately annoyed. If I didn't know these people, I couldn't trust them, and it felt like a flex on S.T.R.I.K.E.'s behalf. When the door clicked shut behind us and Hill appeared on the screen from Los Angeles, I had to fight to hide a smile. There was exactly double the number of people gathered around her and she'd assembled her team in a much larger, flashier space. I knew it was actually across the other side of the building from her office. Hill could flex just as hard as anyone when she needed to.

Her decision had been simple. She didn't fully trust S.T.R.I.K.E., but if they were investigating Dr Calvin's disappearance as hard as we were, then the most logical conclusion was they weren't responsible. She didn't want to share information. Yet as she and I had talked it through, Hill had begrudgingly come to the conclusion that we had to: even just to find out what it was that they knew. Once that was established, we could reassess with all of the relevant information.

There were only two seats left available, both at opposite sides of the room, and I took the one closest to the screen. Hill's eyes tracked my movement, as if reading my body language for any signs that something was awry. I gave her a small nod, indicating that everything was fine on my end.

"Good morning, Director Radcliffe and your team," Hill began, taking charge of the meeting at the first possible moment. "Thank you for assembling at what I know is an extremely inconvenient hour. Although our agencies haven't always worked harmoniously together, our desire to locate Dr

Wilma Calvin alive and well is a shared goal. So, in the interest of achieving that, we will put everything that we have on the table and in exchange, S.T.R.I.K.E. will do the same. Agreed?"

"Agreed," Radcliffe replied, mouth tight. Hill's gaze flicked to mine.

"Bobbi, why don't you explain how yourself and Dr Calvin first became acquainted?"

"I worked under her as a PhD candidate during Project Gladiator, which was a S.H.I.E.L.D.-funded attempt to recreate Super Soldier Serum."

"Attempt?" someone asked.

"It failed. Concerns had been raised about her methods and when the project was terminated, Dr Calvin rushed to human trials – namely her right-hand, Professor Ted Sallis – who died as a result. She avoided prosecution largely because the work was confidential, but she was unable to find employment within US academia again. This was just over a decade ago, but her research for us and unique area of expertise was significant enough that when she relocated to Europe and eventually here, there were tabs kept on her activities – mainly her work – to make sure that she never strayed too close to Project Gladiator again or ended up in the hands of the enemy."

"Hydra," Lance said, his gaze penetrating mine.

"Anyone," Hill corrected. "But yes, Hydra would be worst case scenario."

Radcliffe cleared his throat dramatically, making sure the attention was back on him. "Fortunately for all of us, no Hydra operatives or affiliates have been identified," he said.

"So far," I said. "But someone was on us tonight posing as campus security."

"We'll look into that," Radcliffe added.

"And what about who was there before?" Lance asked, earning blank looks from everyone except me. "Before I got there. Who destroyed the lab?"

"Uh, all the destruction caused was from the ensuing fight according to our records," an analyst said, shuffling through their paperwork.

"No," I confirmed. "Lance is right. Someone was there before him, there's discharge over almost every surface."

The analyst ignored me, turning back to his agent. "Are you sure, Mr Hunter, because–"

"I took samples," I said, voice firm. I tossed a small petri dish across the table, doubly protected in a clear zip-lock bag as it slid to a stop in front of the analyst. "Check for yourself."

Lance's cheek was twitching as he pressed on. "Someone was there first. Then me. Then Bobbi. Then mystery men. Then real campus security. Then the bill. It was a real farce by that point."

"Well…" Radcliffe said, not ending on any particular point. "We still need answers. And if S.H.I.E.L.D.'s sticking around until we have them, it makes sense to combine our resources."

I nearly choked.

"I agree," Hill replied. OK, now I might actually choke. "I propose a taskforce led by Bobbi."

"And Hunter," Radcliffe countered.

"Now hang on–" he began.

"We need to come at this equally if we're to make any kind of real progress," Radcliffe barked.

Lance blanched. "This is a case, not a best friend necklace we need to put back together."

I tried to disguise my laugh as a cough, but I don't think it fooled anyone.

"It's settled then," Hill said, getting to her feet.

"Huh?" I questioned.

"S.H.I.E.L.D. will open our books to you on this matter and we expect the same from S.T.R.I.K.E.," she continued.

"You will have it," Radcliffe said. "Whatever it takes to make sure Dr Calvin and what her mind can do don't end up in the wrong hands."

It felt like the meeting ended just as quickly as it started, with the screen going dark and the S.T.R.I.K.E. team clearing out in a blur of movement until it was just Lance and I left in the room, both open mouthed and staring at each other.

"Howdy, uh, partner?" he offered.

CHAPTER SEVEN

"I don't want to work with him!" I exclaimed when I was alone with Hill.

"I know," she sighed. "But it's the best thing for the mission, Bobbi."

I gritted my teeth, trying not to say something I'd regret but I was seriously peeved. I'd been given the room once everyone had bounced, but I'd thrown up the interceptors just to be safe. Being suspicious of almost everyone all the time was rarely a disadvantage in this line of work. In my personal life, however…

"How?" I snapped. "Give me one good–"

"You're the science, he's the streets," Hill interjected.

Damn it. Her one reason was actually a pretty good one. She took my pause as a victory and kept going.

"You know Dr Calvin and her work better than anyone. He knows Oxford and he knows the operators on the ground. We haven't been as clued-in to her movements over the past six months as he has and that's an advantage we can use."

"I didn't accept this mission to just be paired with another man," I huffed, knowing my battle was lost but needing to say it anyway. "I wanted to work on my own. I'm good at it."

"I agree," Hill replied. "I meant what I said the night you left. But the parameters of the mission have changed, and we have to adapt with them. There are more moving parts to this than we anticipated and, frankly, that's a concern. Who are all these stakeholders? And what do they want with Dr Calvin? Or did they already get it, so now they're just cleaning up? I'm concerned about this and if I had more resources to allocate, I would. What I have is one of my best S.H.I.E.L.D. agents and an opportunity to double our efforts that I didn't have previously."

I had been pacing, mapping a way around the long, rectangular table like the steps would suddenly solve all my problems. Now, I harrumphed into a chair.

"Go back to the drawing board," she continued. "Reshape the plan I already know you've been working through in your head and include Hunter. That's someone to watch your back now and free you up to do the best possible work you can do. If S.T.R.I.K.E. aren't our enemy, then that's an ally we didn't have before."

Hill and I ended the conversation, and I collected the interceptors, agreeing to do what I came here to do. It was as simple as that. As the window glass of the briefing room shifted from tinted to visible, I pressed my forehead against the cool surface and stared down at the people moving about like ants below. All right. OK. I could do this. And if I did it well, I'd be out of here in a week. Maybe. *Drink some cement, Bobbi.* It was a thing my dad used to say and a mantra his dad used to say to him and so on and back and forth in perpetuity. In other words: harden up. So that's what I'd do.

When I stepped into the hallway, Lance was waiting for me.

He had one foot resting against the wall, leaning against it like a bad boy in a Hollywood musical, complete with a butterfly knife he was flicking between his hands. One look at his face and I immediately felt bad. Logically I knew he couldn't have heard the things I said, but my guilt had me convinced that telepathically he'd caught the whole conversation anyway. He pushed off from the wall and gestured toward where we needed to go without a word. We were silent for several minutes, descending stairs, turning left, grabbing an elevator, turning right.

"You know, London is full of abandoned railways and old tunnels," he said finally, breaking first. "Earlier versions of the city lay below the surface, but people forget. That's what this place used to be. It was easy enough for S.T.R.I.K.E. to get a prime CBD location on real estate no one knew existed."

He was rambling. I didn't have that tendency to fill silence with inane chatter as a defense mechanism. Clint always said one of the most frustrating things about me was in an argument, I'd just sit there silent and seething. In reality, I was listening. Thinking.

"It's not about you," I said, pivoting away from his yammering and getting straight to the crux of the issue.

"I've heard that before," he replied, letting out a long breath. *"It's not you, Lance, it's me."*

"Firstly, you're the dumper, not the dumpee."

His head snapped to stare at me sharply. "How could you possibly know that?"

I made a zipping motion with my lips.

"Dying to read my S.H.I.E.L.D. casefile now," he muttered.

I smiled. "Secondly, it *really* isn't about you in this instance. I'm just Hawkeye's wife."

He spluttered, as if to cut in, but I held up a hand.

"You've seen it since the second I got here. I've been defined by who I was married to for a long time now, my own talents and achievements and skills always coming in second to his if they're not overshadowed at all. It has been a bitter pill to swallow, but I swallowed it for the sake of my relationship. That's over. And so is my ability to pretend to be any less extraordinary than I am. I didn't want to work on this mission with anyone – it's not personal – I just wanted to get back to doing what I do well *and* alone."

The click of our footsteps on the hard, marble floor was the only response for a moment and I waited, knowing he'd have something to say. I didn't like to show my hand like that, but I needed to be clear so we could begin as we meant to go on.

"For the record," he said, "I never thought of you as Hawkeye's missus. I didn't know anything about Bobbi Morse. Now Mockingbird, that's my girl."

I looked at him sideways, half expecting him to be joking but he was dead serious.

"OK, OK, I didn't recognize you out of the suit and without the platinum blonde hair – that's kinda your signature, ya know? – but I studied your work when I was a trainee. Your tradecraft, that mission in Bahrain, your versatility of assets, even the way you boomeranged that guy with battle staves tonight. I didn't need to read your file when I learned your name. All the highlights are up here."

He tapped his skull for emphasis, eyes forward.

"It's an honor to work with Mockingbird," he said, coming to a stop. "Even if she can't stand me."

I let out a laugh, unable to help it. "I never–"

"Pfft, semantics," Lance huffed, cutting me off. "We've got things we need your brain for."

He opened the door behind him, allowing me through as I stepped into a rather beautiful and intentionally outfitted testing facility.

"Lab's over here," he said, leading me toward it. "We've got this analyst out from New Zealand so the accent's a li'l funny."

"Unlike your perfectly unfunny one."

"Exactly, thank you, yes. I sent the sample you hurled in my director's face down here as soon as I could. He has been analyzing it while you finished verbally bashing me with your boss or whatever it is you S.H.I.E.L.D. women do."

The grin on my face was genuine. He'd meant what he said about Mockingbird, about me, and I'd never let him know what that meant in the moment. I'd meant what I said, too, and the fact he was already stirring and poking me again was a good sign.

"Hurled is so visceral." I cringed.

"Hey, don't apologize. You know how many times I've wanted to hurl something at that soggy grape? I'm gonna be thinking about it for weeks."

He closed his eyes, as if savoring the memory.

"Oh my gosh, hi, you guys are here!" a very specific baritone piped up. "Come in, come in, I could use another cranium."

My eyes nervously flicked towards several brains in jars that were floating in formalin solution, like silent guardians. The scientist in question was tall, around six-foot-five if I had to guess, with his hair pulled up in a practical bun that said, "I'm here to do science things, get out of my way". He was hunched over a microscope, examining one of the samples

I had collected. The other I had already sent to S.H.I.E.L.D. after doing my own very quick, cursory analysis.

"Dr Bobbi Morse, meet our leading analyst Dr Temuera Waa," Lance said with a flourish.

"Call me Tem," the subject of our conversation responded, not looking up. "See this here, see how it almost glitters under the light?"

"I noticed that, too." I nodded, leaning in. "I've never seen any kind of explosive like that before."

"Explosive? What makes you say that?" he asked, turning to me.

I noticed the young scientist's intricate facial markings, with traditional tattoos beginning on his nose and curving down into swirling patterns on his cheeks.

"Well," I continued. "Whoever was there before Lance, attempted to destroy the lab and was either interrupted or successful in the specific thing they wanted to annihilate. I assumed whatever device they let off, this discharge is what was left behind: some kind of synthetic bomb or chemical reaction."

"Huh," Tem grunted, looking thoughtful. "It has the same texture as a water-based lubricant, but if it's residue left from the initial event… interesting. I didn't think of that."

"Yeah, great, look – is there anything that can help us?" Lance questioned, bored of the science talk. "Like, this glittering goo can only be found in *one* specific Oxford laneway…"

"That's not really how it works," the young scientist mumbled.

"A direction, mate. That's all. Point us somewhere."

"I'm sorry," Tem replied, shoulders slumping. "If I find anything odd, well, odder I'll let you know as soon as I can."

"Here's my burner," I said, quickly scrawling down the details on the corner of his notepad. "Even if it's just a baseline experiment question, I'm happy to help."

He beamed at me, a toothy white smile juxtaposed against the warm brown of his skin, and clear enthusiasm danced in his eyes.

"I will totally do that," he replied. "I loved your paper on hemochromatosis being overlooked as the next step in human evolution."

"Oh," I said, genuinely touched and surprised. "Thank you. It was written in a bit of a rush, I would have loved to do another few months of exp–"

"Speaking of rushes," Lance cut in. "We have to rush off, thanks Tem! Love ya work!"

I barely had a chance for little more than a wave over my shoulder as I was dragged from the lab by my arm and pulled purposefully toward the door.

"That was rude," I said, shaking free of his grip once we were in the clear.

"Oh, I'm sorry. Did this seem like the kind of mission where we had expendable minutes to stand around talking about slime all day? Took me ages to get that stuff out of my clothes."

"I tossed mine," I laughed. "The longer it was exposed to air, the more it started to congeal."

"Ugh, can we not?" He puffed his cheeks like he might puke. "I haven't had anything to eat since your terrible canapes."

"Terrible! To start, I didn't make them. And to finish, they can't have been that terrible the way you were monopolizing the tray."

"I was trying to monopolize you, not the tray, woman. Geez."

He shook his head with bafflement, but I was a bit baffled myself so there was nothing else to say. We came to a stop in the middle of the entranceway, the enormous space slowly starting to fill up with foot traffic as more and more S.T.R.I.K.E workers began to start their day. A few were clustered together on lounge seats, flipping through the newspaper or chatting eagerly as they ate breakfast. My stomach rumbled audibly and Lance shot me a triumphant look.

"Here's the rub," he began, his smirk telling me that his choice not to comment was a kindness. "It's nearly four in the morning. I don't know about you, but I'm starved and tired. We eat. We sleep. We come up with a plan."

"I already have a plan."

"One that includes me in it."

Damn.

"I can't be buggered driving back to Oxford right now and I don't think it's—"

"Smart," I agreed. "We should wait and see what last night shakes from the tree."

He clicked with his tongue. "Precisely, partner."

Before I knew it, he was shouting a farewell to "Daf" and we were back on his bike, beginning the seemingly never-ending ascent from S.T.R.I.K.E. headquarters. The difference between when we'd gone underground and when we emerged was significant. On the twenty-minute route to his Croydon base, I watched the city start to wake up around us as people bundled up against the cold and rushed to make their trains. I tightened my grip around Lance's waist as he accelerated to pass a double decker bus, the full London experience now nearly complete as we narrowly avoided getting turned into a human sandwich.

He'd made the right call about refueling and refreshing. It

felt like I was wearing concrete shoes as we parked down a side alley and trudged up the stairs to his apartment. It was on the top floor of a red brick, three-story building that had everything from a fish and chip shop to a newsagent making up the mishmash of places on street level. Up here though, inside his home, it was not what I expected. With the exception of the bathroom, he'd knocked down all the walls so that it was just one expansive, open plan space with enormous arched windows that looked down on to the street below. I was nosey by nature, and I loved to poke around in other people's houses, watch how they moved and operated in their own space, and this was no different. Was this a shoes off or on household? I was relieved to learn "off" and I positioned mine near his as he kicked them away with abandon.

Lance hung his jacket up in a blue locker at the entranceway, there being a series of them in varying shades running along next to it. If I had to guess, one was for weapons. Another would be basic tools – disguises, passports, cash – and the third would be gadgets. The sturdy set of locks on the reinforced steel front door and state-of-the-art alarm that he disabled once inside were the only indicators from a passing glance that this place belonged to someone in the business. He headed straight to a small but sufficient kitchen that took up a corner, flicking on lamps and lights as he went. I hovered, watching as he reached for the pots and pans he was after that dangled from hooks in the ceiling.

"Go on," he said, looking over his shoulder at me. "I know you want to."

"Want to?" I asked innocently. My tone caused him to laugh and he whipped a tea towel in my direction, urging me away.

"If I was in *your* studio apartment, I'd be analyzing the color of the walls for fork's sake. Just go get it over with. I'm making a fry up, anything you don't eat?"

"Nothing," I said, shrugging off my coat. "I'll eat everything."

There was a grunt of approval, but I was too giddy with the possibility of getting to freely poke around. There was a rack of clothes that double layered to the ceiling via a clever pulley system, along with a king bed buoyed by layers of pillows that I would have given up a battle stave to crash into at that moment. A pretty standard desk and dual monitor setup bookended the other side, along with a massive flatscreen fitted into the exposed brick wall and an L-shaped couch that could have fit at least five of me. The home gym was of the most interest, really, with a conservative selection of hand weights and kettle bells in various sizes, resistance bands, exercise and medicine balls, plus a boxing bag that hung from the ceiling. Taking several steps back, I spun into a flying kick, enjoying the satisfaction of the bag's weight against the impact of my shin.

"You bring a bird home and all they want to do is work the bag," Lance muttered from the kitchen.

"Sorry." I grinned. "Couldn't resist."

From the look on his face, he didn't seem annoyed at all, just… slightly amused. I caught my reflection in the full-length mirror against the wall, face flushed with exhilaration. Why did I apologize? I wasn't sorry at all.

There was a packed bookshelf that lined the perimeter of the apartment, higher than a person could reach, with a wheeled ladder hooked on to a rail that I immediately thought of as distinctly British. He'd fitted other, smaller shelves into the walls at intermittent spacings: a few held what I immediately recognized as expensive sneakers, others a trophy and framed degree, a few with picture frames.

My eyes affixed on the last place of keen interest, a series of wooden cubes that went from floor to ceiling and were crammed full of records. A bench seat had been built into the window next to it, making the perfect place to sit and stare at whatever was happening down below while music blasted from the speakers of a very nice and expensive record player. My fingernails ran along the spines of his collection, the alphabetical organization making me smirk at what a secret neat freak Lance "I'm too cool for school" Hunter was. Finding what I was looking for, I carefully placed the vinyl and positioned the needle. The way his head shot up when the opening chords of "Your Silent Face" began playing was all the confirmation I needed.

"You a New Order fan?" Lance asked, his hands pausing as he plated what looked like an enormous feast.

"Sure." I shrugged. "Been getting into them a lot more lately since I found out Bernard Sumner was such a science fanatic."

He grinned, watching as I joined him at the wooden work bench he used as a table. "That's fascinating."

"The Specials were new to me," I continued. "Kate Bush not so much, but throw in The Cure, Siouxsie and the Banshees, The Slits, Pat Kelly... that made quite a playlist."

"You're welcome." Lance smiled, offering me the stool next to his. "Helping Americans have taste is a pet project of mine."

"I can tell," I said, looking down at the stacked plate in front of me. He used a fork to point out everything relevant.

"Poached eggs, bacon, buttered toast, fried tomatoes, baked beans, pork sausage and some haggis on the side because I know how you lot feel about it. It's basically just meat loaf with flavor. You seem like one of those skinny chicks who can eat, so..."

"Thank you," I replied. "I'm *starving*."

It was the last thing either of us said for a while, the clink of forks and scraping of plates joining the chorus of New Order as it weaved through the apartment, creating the soundtrack of the morning. With a contented sigh, Lance leaned back from an empty plate and placed his hands behind his head. I made a point not to notice the way his biceps flexed in that position and the hint of a tattoo I could see peeking out from under his shirt sleeve.

"I suppose you think it was dumb?" he said, gesturing toward the record player.

"Actually, pains me to say, I thought it was clever," I replied. "If I wasn't looking for a pattern, I probably wouldn't have found one and it made each entry impossible to search online."

"Right? That's what I hoped." He looked discreetly pleased with himself. "Gotta admit, I consider myself clever but trying to pick through her work... it was borderline impenetrable."

I nodded in agreement. "OK, something I've been wondering."

"Shoot."

"How did you manage to teach her class?"

He chuckled. "Had Tem prepare each lecture and I'd read from it verbatim."

Ah, Elle's robotic comment suddenly made a lot more sense to me now.

"It's never an engineering professor that goes missing. I'd be useful there! It's always gotta be some niche, dangerous field. Hydra are never interested in English lit."

"Thank God," I sighed, clearing our plates. "At least you've only had to fill in for a week."

"Hey, let me do that. I make a mess when I cook."

"And I'll clean up that mess. Chef doesn't wash up where I'm from."

He looked like he was going to insist and I narrowed my eyes until he backed up, hands raised in surrender.

"Tch, all right. I'm making up the couch then."

That huge L-shape lifted up to reveal a hollow compartment beneath full of linen and cushions that gave the apartment an additional bed if needed. The sun was only just starting to peek over the horizon and Lance made it disappear completely, hitting a button that saw blackout blinds wind down into position.

"Are the windows a worry to you?" I asked. "Security wise."

"Nah, they're bulletproof. And good luck scaling them unseen in Croydon! Can't make it down High Street unbothered, no unfamiliar face is getting this far in past the locals."

Interesting.

"'Kay, couch is yours. I need to take a shower and if I come out and find you audibly snoring, I'm going to have to smother you. Sorry, those are just the rules."

"And I would deserve it." I nodded. "Couch is great."

Not only was it super comfortable, but I liked it more because there was no gentlemanly pretense. If he was invading *my* space rather than the reverse, I wouldn't have given my bed up either. I barely heard the sound of water splashing against tiles before I felt the weight of fatigue pulling at my consciousness, yanking me under into a deep, dreamless sleep. The beeping sound that woke me came too soon and I groaned, rolling over to hit the alarm I didn't remember setting.

"Turn it offff," came Lance's muffled voice from across the room. "No wake-up calls, no wake-up calls."

I agreed, but when I checked my phone my eyes went from blurry and half-asleep to wide awake.

"It's not my alarm," I murmured, sitting up. Clicking into the beeping digital square on my device, the sound went quiet as I watched six figures pour into the room at Magdalen College. They were dressed as local cops, but like Lance had pointed out with campus security, they definitely were not. The sounds of rustling blankets, a lamp clicking on, and feet padding across wood floors told me he was coming, but I didn't react as I felt Lance look over my shoulder.

"Who are these geezers?" he murmured, voice still rough with sleep.

"You don't recognize him?" I asked, pointing to a man at the back. He carried his weight more heavily on his left leg. "You gave him that limp."

"Ah," Lance recalled. We watched as the man flipped the mattress. "Does he expect to find you hiding under the bed?"

I snorted a laugh, turning back to greet his smile which was... a mistake. He was shirtless, having slept in just a pair of loose boxers so that an entire eight pack was out and rippling for me to see. It was the arms though, his shoulders flexing from where he leaned against the back of the couch and my eyes drank in every line, every curve, every muscle before I could even think about it.

"Oi, hands inside the vehicle," he chuckled, a cheeky lopsided grin making the situation even worse. "We're watching people trying to kill ya right now."

I cleared my throat, not bothering to address it but making a conscious choice to keep my eyes straight ahead. Frowning, I zoomed in as we watched them search the room.

"They're not looking for me," I said.

"Uh, I don't wanna mansplain but–"

"No, look. They're searching for Millicent Porter."

One of them had my student file up on his screen, the pink hair and glasses instantly identifiable.

"Is this a good thing or a bad thing?" Lance questioned.

"Good, I think. Look how they're searching, where they're searching. It's casual, like they were hoping to find the woman they were after but in lieu of that, c'est la vie, just a standard student room. They triggered all of my alarms and haven't even found the camera."

"So…"

"I can move about, but the identity of Millicent is unsafe. The Magdalen College room, too."

"I'm sorry about your stuff."

"Huh?"

"Your stuff." He pointed, finger waggling at the room. "You can't go back there."

"Don't need to. I packed all of my things and stashed them when I met you."

He looked confused. "Then whose stuff is all that?"

"Some from the girl before me, the rest things that I bought as set dressing, a few staged photos framed around Oxford."

"You took everything except your surveillance," he said slowly. "Because you knew they'd take the bait."

"I hoped," I replied, snapping screenshots of each man as they went about their business. Propping up the cushions behind me so I was in a better position, I quickly adjusted the contrast and sharpened each image until there were six very clear and identifiable men.

"Hello, boys," Lance purred.

"Now we'll know who we're working against," I replied,

sending the shots in an urgent memo to the S.H.I.E.L.D. and S.T.R.I.K.E. joint taskforce address. Lance and I exchanged a smile, the shadow of a new plan starting to take form.

CHAPTER EIGHT

We went back to bed, which I was incredibly grateful for because a) my body needed it and b) it would make returning to Oxford that little bit easier. Everything was easier at night, but especially easier if you could avoid London's peak hour traffic. By the time we were up, we had a hit on all six of the Mystery Men quicker than expected, largely because they were mercenaries and having accessible profiles was how these guys got work. I was showered, dressed and ready in a matter of ten minutes, Lance taking considerably longer which gave me time to post up at his work bench and flick through profiles. Scottish, Russian, Russian, German, then two Brits – all ex-various-armies – made up the list and all had currently worked as contractors for a private security firm known as FiveFourThree Solutions.

"Hey, I think I know that guy," Lance said, plucking my phone away as he passed. "Yeah, Jimmy Smithers, ex-Navy. Think he was what you lot would call 'dishonorably discharged' from memory. Heard he got into CrossFit."

"Ah yes, the natural progression to evil henchman."

"Not all henchmen are evil," Lance muttered, swiping through the other men on the list. "Some are just in it for the benefits package."

It was a lead. A vital one? Maybe. But it was better than what I had, especially after the papers I managed to get from Dr Calvin's office were largely useless, one being a lesson plan and nothing odd leaping out from what she'd scrawled at her desk. Lance plopped a backpack down on the table, carefully organized in a way that signposted his own time in the service. Every compartment had a compartment, and *that* compartment had a compartment, each one full and stocked with something useful, whether that was spare batteries or energy gel. My eyes scanned the apartment, conscious of the fact this was the first and probably last time I'd be here.

"Aw, you're looking at my place like you're going to miss it," he said, batting his eyelashes as he rested his chin on his hands. "Go on then, give me your psychoanalysis based on my living quarters."

"That's not what I…" I couldn't finish the sentence. It was exactly what I was doing. It was what I was always doing. It was what I was trained to do.

"Hey, I'm not gonna act like I didn't do it to you." He shrugged. "The way you went from barely conscious to spinning into action like a jack-in-the-box tells me that you can do a very good job at appearing cool and calm. But tightly coiled? That's your natural state."

"Tightly coiled." I flinched.

"Tightly. It's what makes you a good agent, I expect. And the fact that you meticulously made up my sofa couch without being asked tells me you respect other people's property and were most likely raised with manners, even in a crisis."

The smirk that twitched on to my face couldn't be helped. "That's quite the read."

I wasn't offended, these were compliments and, in my head, *again* I started doing that involuntary comparison. To Clint, the translation was that I was too highly strung and impossible to be around. On the second point, it was that I was "obsessive" about cleanliness. After such a long time, it was strange to hear yourself perceived through someone else's eyes and those very flaws being viewed as assets in a different context.

"Do me, do me," Lance said, bobbing up and down on his toes. "I love this game."

"Most men in their late twenties – especially in this business – live like slobs," I began. "But your apartment is an extension of the things you value, not just music and sneaker culture. It's spotless, organized, and every inch of space is used efficiently. You have cleaning supplies under your sink and even your resistance to me doing the dishes indicates that you do it yourself, you don't have a cleaner. Usually, you can't hold men to the standards of women–"

"Usually?"

"We're just better. We have to develop and grow up faster because society gives us no choice, there's no cushioning for us. Even so, this is the apartment of a man, not a boy."

His eyes twinkled. "I love this."

I tilted my head, questioning, and he gestured between us.

"I love this being our thing," he continued. "The bants."

"Bants?"

"Banter, Bobbi. Great bants. So."

"The plan." I rolled my shoulders, making an invisible checklist on the table in front of me and ticking off items one by one. "We head back to Oxford tonight. Your cover isn't blown, so you still have a class to attend tomorrow morning as Professor Falkner. We go back to Dr Calvin's lab to do the inspection we weren't able to do properly the first time because we were interrupted."

"And her office."

"Her office is a dead end," I rebuffed.

"According to you. What if you missed something?"

I glared at him. Lance smiled back. "Fine. We go over the lab together, then you can search her office and find absolutely nothing while I get an almond croissant."

"An almond croissant?"

"It's the paste. I cannot get enough of it."

"Interesting."

"We search her home address," I pushed on. "If all of those leads are fruitless, then we have six chances to get information from six FiveFourThree employees."

We sat in comfortable silence for a beat, both of us going through the logistics in our heads until Lance switched from a casual lean to at attention.

"It's solid," he said. "And there's enough variables in play that we'll have to adapt on the fly."

"Agreed." I got to my feet, ready to leave and heading toward the front door when he called after me.

"Bobbi?"

When I looked back, there was something that had changed in his face, in his gait, that gave me pause. He jerked his head, indicating that I should follow him. I trailed back to where he came to a stop, standing in front of one of the shelves that had a pair of bright blue kicks positioned on it with a slash of orange that cut up from the sole. He was staring at them like they were the Mona Lisa.

"Do you know what these are?" he asked.

"Air Jordans," I replied simply, unsure if it was a trick question.

"They're the Doernbecher Freestyle Air Jordan 8s," Lance answered, carefully plucking one shoe from the platform. "They were designed by this kid, Caden Lampert, who had Guillain-Barré syndrome."

He didn't explain what that was. I knew. It was a devastating disease. It made the body think it needed to attack itself, so a patient's autoimmune system – which should be its best defense – became its worst enemy. It was survivable if you received the best and most frequent treatment, but it was also extremely fraught because complications could eventuate from almost anywhere, from infections to cardiac arrest.

"What's not in my file is that after my parents died and I went to live with my aunt, I had one friend," Lance continued. "Just the one. Her kid, my first cousin on my ma's side, Kai."

"He had Guillain-Barré syndrome," I said, Lance's grave mood telling me where this was going.

"Yeah," he replied, handing me the sneaker. "I was a real sorry sod, thought I had it so tough with no parents but Kai… you know, no one had it tougher than him. Don't get me wrong, he was a little lad. Taught me everything I knew that would get me in trouble. I was always good at taking a punch. The handcuffs trick was his."

"I still want you to teach me that," I noted. As I inspected the shoe, I could see all the details I hadn't noticed before in my cursory sweep. Phrases like "brave" and "rock on" emblazoned at various points, along with flames and a hissing cobra detail. It was the literal and physical manifestation of what the inside of a teenage boy's head looked like.

"Kai *loved* sneakers." Lance grinned. "It's what he used to jack more than anything, which was kinda pointless cos you couldn't wear 'em around the block, you know? He wanted these. They hadn't dropped yet when he died."

"How old were you?" I asked.

"Teen," he replied, vague. "Kai was older, wanted to make it to twenty but a blood clot had other plans. After that… my aunt didn't stick around so much."

I handed the shoe back to him with the care and reverence it deserved. Lance placed it on the shelf, adjusting it *just* so until the light hit it perfectly. His hands were hanging loose at his side and I took one, fingers intertwining with his for a brief moment as I gave him a squeeze. He squeezed back. I felt like I knew why he had showed me this. In my read of him, everything must have been on the money *except* for this. He wasn't just another white guy into sneaker culture, it had meaning to him because of what he'd been through and who he'd loved. Intent.

That's what he was saying without expressly saying it. Everything in his life had intent. In the same way sticking around and sharing details of his mission with me after he'd broken free of the handcuffs was an olive branch, this, too, was his way of offering me a piece of himself that he didn't have to so I would trust him. The annoying little defensive voices in my head said, "Trust him for what? Lower your guard with a sad story so he can double cross you later?" I pushed them down, to the side, ignored them. Not often, but sometimes in this line of work things could appear exactly how they were. I decided to make a choice to believe that to be true in this instance.

"Come on," Lance said. "We gotta motor."

Locking up and trotting down the stairs, I was hit with a blast of cold, English air as we stepped out onto the street. It was just shy of dinnertime, with folks packing the pavement as they milled about to get takeaways or pick up shopping. A group of guys stumbled out of a pub in front of us, refusing to make way so that we were forced to split around them.

"Awrite, blondie?" one called after me. "You're a bit fit, innit?"

Lance was a few steps ahead of me and he paused, turning back.

"Leave it," I cautioned, grabbing his elbow and tugging him forward.

"Lookin' good in all that leather," he continued, earning chuckles from the chorus of idiots.

"Waste, man," Lance muttered, seeming like he really didn't want to leave it and walking backward now as he eyeballed the group. He made a gesture with his hands that I only caught a sideways glance at, but the ringleader's face dropped. The jackals cackling cut short and they hurried off, looking over their shoulders as they did so.

"What'd you do?" I asked, examining the smugness on his face.

"Nuthin," he responded, turning back around.

"What is that?" I asked, trying to imitate the gesture. "What does that mean?"

"Stop that." He slapped my hand down, glancing around to make sure no one saw. "You can't be caught doing that around here."

"I can't? But you can pounce about making Russian mob boss gestures?"

He burst out laughing. "Russian mob boss, ya kill me."

Lance was still laughing as we pulled up in front of his bike, it immediately standing out among all the others parked alongside it. He tossed me something and I reacted instinctively, looking down to find a set of keys in my hand.

"Wanna drive?"

I beamed.

"Eaaaaasy, Bob," he said, voice in my ear as I accelerated on to the main street. "It just rained, don't kill us please."

His hands gripped tighter around my waist when I chuckled in response, the regret in his decision a physical gesture as I slowed to a very serviceable pace. It had rained, he was right, and happily that meant a puddle had formed on the side of the road up ahead. Paused at the red light, I watched as a familiar group of catcalling jerks strolled closer. The light turned green.

"Do it," Lance urged, as if reading my mind. Hand on the throttle, I needed exactly zero encouragement as I sped toward them, positioning the bike perfectly so that a wave of dirty water splashed up and over them. They disappeared amidst the cascade for a moment, reappearing a second later and yelling wildly in shock.

"WANKERS!" Lance called, flipping them the bird as we drove on. Whatever they shouted in response, I couldn't hear through the sounds of my own laughter.

Oxford was unchanged when we returned. It's not as if I had expected it to miss us. On the contrary, the outlines of the old, ancient structures coming into view as we completed our road trip felt comforting in a weird way. They were never changing, immobile and constant. It was the world around them that shifted and evolved and turned. I felt comfortable negotiating that; knowing what kind of battlefield I was on helped dictate how I made my way through it. Turning off the main road, Lance directed me down a winding route of side streets until we were pulling up next to a boathouse on the Thames. He unlocked the door while I wheeled the bike slowly inside, wiping it down out of habit more than anything else. When I was done, I looked up to find Lance watching me.

"Raised with manners," he muttered.

"Shut up," I snapped, tossing the wet rag at him. It was a small space bordering on tiny and I was surprised he had been able to fit a bike in here along with the kayak I'd first spotted him on. I clocked the subtle camera fitted behind some synthetic spiderwebs in the top corner of the room, guessing that he probably had this place just as closely monitored as I had the dorm room. There was a tall locker up the back, exactly like the ones he had in his apartment, and as he unlocked it and switched on the lamp above, I realized it was his dress-up chest. I'm sure that's not what he called it, but when I was little that's what my mom had named mine and ever since, it had stuck with me. Whenever there was a costume party or Halloween or just an afternoon where I wanted to be someone else, the dress-up chest was exactly where I would run to. The red-headed wig and professor drag he had hanging inside was pretty different to my prized catalogue of tiaras and monster masks, but the end result was the same.

"Oh God," I mumbled, something only just occurring to me. "Please don't tell me this is where you've been living."

"Gimme a break," he huffed, slamming the locker shut once he'd properly restocked. "I just needed a safe point to change. Come on."

I followed him out of the crammed space, ducking my head under a wooden beam as I looked up to examine the night sky.

The rain had cleared the further we got out of London and above us, there was little enough light pollution that the stars actually made an impact.

"Let's go, Galileo," Lance said, gently pulling me toward the riverbank. I hadn't bothered to ask where he stayed when he was here, he just assured me he had a "safe space" now that mine was compromised and I'd left it, pressing concerns and all that. Yet that concern felt pretty damn pressing now as I watched him board a houseboat. He paused, looking back when he realized I wasn't with him.

"What, Mockingbirds don't sail?" he questioned.

"Mockingbirds don't sink," I replied, crossing my hands over my chest. "Are you sure that thing is seaworthy?"

My eyes ran from the peeling paintjob to the bow, which looked like it sagged a little deeper into the water than the stern.

"Yeah, look, I'm not using it to cross the English Channel, am I? It floats in a very stationary, very still portion of the Thames so get on, will ya? You're causing a scene."

He gestured like there was a crowd nearby and I turned to find our group of onlookers were the feathered variety. A bank of swans sat patiently nearby, watching like they were wrapped up in our drama. As if on cue, one honked at me like it was in cahoots with Lance and telling me to get on board.

"Fine, fine, fine," I grumbled. "I'm going."

It flapped its wings triumphantly to prove the point. Gingerly, I gripped the railing as I stepped down onto the back deck. I could hear Lance humming inside as he moved through the interior, a whir of electricity sounding before fairy lights flickered on. I squinted, taking a moment to adjust, but as I looked around and through the plastic sheet that enclosed this outdoor space, I realized now it appeared just like any other houseboat on the river. There were close to a dozen that I could see, all with their own sets of white or rainbow string lights signaling that this place was lived in and loved. I peeled off my motorbike gloves as I made my way inside, looking around at the weirdly shaped but cozy space. What it lacked in width it made up for in length and – most importantly – warmth. Tracking down the narrow hallway, I followed the sound of banging and clanging that told me Lance's location. He popped his head out of a doorway at the end.

"What do you think?" he asked.

"I prefer your apartment," I replied, honest. It was bigger.

"Girlfriend, you're telling me! Rented this place off an old geezer who was very specific about not taking down any of the pictures on the wall, even though they hang crooked and give me the creeps."

I nearly jumped as I followed his gaze, a glowering deer threatening my life through canvas in a painting that hung at an ungodly angle.

"But," he continued, "a houseboat is very easy to defend, you have multiple exit routes if you need them, and I like the idea of being able to chug along to a new spot if I need to."

"Or the swans hold you hostage."

"Yeah, bit hostile those are. Mind the one with a scar on its beak. He's from the ends."

He gestured behind him, offering me a peek into a small but serviceable room with a freshly made bed pressed up against the wall and a chest of drawers that had an arched mirror with lightbulbs affixed to it like I was backstage at a community theatre production.

"Your room," he pointed, turning back to the darkened doorway directly across from it. "My room. Next door down is the bathroom, shared I'm afraid, and the kitchen-living room combo you passed on your way in."

Part of me had understood what the living arrangement would be, but it was one thing to understand it in theory and another entirely to be standing awkwardly across from each other in the hall. It was like the idea of us sleeping a few meters away from each other for an indefinite amount of time had just crossed Lance's mind, too, and he shifted his weight from side to side, as if waiting for me to say something.

"I, uh, should probably go and get my things," I said, relief crossing his face as I gave him an out.

"Yeah, yeah, totally. Where are they exactly?"

"Stashed," I replied, not giving him the precise location.

"You need a lift or–"

"I'll run," I interjected. "I could do with the miles."

He nodded, ducking out of the doorway to make space for me as we oddly negotiated the hallway. Closing the door, I changed into the only other fresh clothes I had with me – exercise tights, sports bra, thermals and windbreaker. I closed my eyes for a minute. No, this was not ideal. I stretched my body, my long limbs able to brush against one wall while my foot touched the other. This was a secure and safe base of operations with a teammate I thought I could trust. So why was my impulse to dash out the door and just keep sprinting? I followed that instinct, the effort to keep my steps measured as I headed for the glass sliding door considerable as I blurted a goodbye and leapt to shore. Usually I would warm up, but I curtailed the additional seconds it would cost me as I let my body take over.

Oxford's tracks and trails were only slightly less busy in the evening than they were during the day and I blended in easily enough, looking just like any other person desperate to hit their daily step count. It would only take me ten minutes to navigate my way to the gym where I had secured the bulk of my possessions in their locker room, but I curved wide. My legs found their own rhythm and the sharp pulse of my heart settled into something more manageable. Therapy was compulsory for all S.H.I.E.L.D. agents, but I didn't need to call my therapist to analyze what was happening to me. I was having a freakout. *Lance would call it a wee freakout,* I thought, mentally snapping at myself.

I had spent probably a year living with a man happily, followed by several more unhappily. It had taken time and trauma and tears, but I'd had to leave my marriage and the home we'd built together behind. The swift adjustment to living in my Burbank bachelorette pad wasn't hard, which was a very obvious sign that Clint and I should have ended things long ago. I was happy and content because I chose my space, I chose my walls, and I chose myself. Now it felt like several steps backward, even though logically I knew being stuck on a houseboat for lord knows how long with Lance wasn't that but… this Mockingbird felt caged. In lieu of being able to fly, the next best thing was sprinting through the night.

CHAPTER NINE

It was well past midnight when I returned, drenched in sweat. It was a preferred state, if I was honest. My suitcase had straps that you could unzip along with a little waterproof hood, so tracking back to the houseboat I looked like a backpacker who miscalculated their luggage allowance. Lance was pretending to be asleep, remote resting on his stomach while scenes from *Bend It Like Beckham* played in the background. I flicked some droplets of sweat at him, getting precisely the kind of reaction I expected as he leapt up.

"Ugh, gross!"

"It's just wet salt," I grinned, trudging down the hallway toward my room. "We should go to Dr Calvin's tonight."

I didn't wait to hear his response, dropping my bags and monopolizing the bathroom as quickly as I could. Wiping steam from the mirror, I could see the excitement rushing in the veins on my face. My skin was flushed. My eyes were excited. My body was charged with the promise of forward momentum.

"Physical exercise isn't a substitute for therapy," Hill had told me once, but we'd been in a hand-to-hand combat class at the time, so it really undercut her point.

"Ha," I said to myself, triumphantly. My victory was short-lived as I proceeded to hit every funny bone and limb against the constraints of the small space as I got changed. Lance was waiting for me, upright and perched on the edge of the table as I emerged in a plume of steam.

"You OK in there?"

"Fine."

"Cos you're all knees and elbows, sounded like–"

"Let's go, Lance," I snapped, clapping my hands. "No time like the present."

I was at the door when he grabbed my arm, halting my progress. "Why now, Bobbi?"

"What do you mean, why now? It's night, it's quiet, no one will be around. What difference does tonight or tomorrow night make?"

"Lab first, office second, then Dr Calvin's cottage. That was *your* pla…"

His sentence trailed off, understanding crossing his features.

"You already went to the lab," he murmured, the realization hitting him. "Without me."

"No, I went for a run. Hence the sweat and the luggage I came back with and… and–"

"And?"

I was usually *such* a good liar. "Fine! I went to the lab."

Lance stared at me, hard. He said nothing, which was somehow worse. Instead, his dark eyes saw right through me like I was cling wrap.

"I saved us a trip, what are you mad about?"

"We were going to go together."

"Yeah, well… I was fidgety. I needed something to do."

"OK," he replied, voice flat. Neutral. He got to his feet, holding open the sliding door of the houseboat for me. I was expecting a fight. When I didn't get one… I blinked. Stepping out after me, Lance locked up then marched off into the night. Our gaits were usually evenly matched, but I had to jog to catch up with him as he hit a sloping laneway that took us towards Donnington. It was only a fifteen-minute walk to get where we needed to go, but we made it there in ten tense minutes. Calvin's cottage had once been part of a larger farmhouse that had been split into four separate residences that all sat at the end of a lane with overgrowth on all sides. I bet from inside there, you could imagine you were in the country.

Wordlessly we moved into position, separating and picking our way through the tree line on opposite sides of the lane until we were right up near the fence. The other three residences were occupied, one had its lights on and even though the other two were dark, smoke was snaking from their chimneys. There were no alarms. No fancy security measures. Nothing more complex than some locks that I could pick in a matter of moments while Lance watched my six. *If* he watched my six. Right now, he was ignoring me as we crouched behind the last cover we had before we'd need to sprint across an exposed space to make it to the front door.

"You haven't asked if I found anything," I whispered, not able to take it anymore.

"Would you tell me if you did?" he replied.

OK, he had me there. He picked up a nearby stick, tossing it into the path we intended. Nothing. No motion sensors or lights flicking on. I went to speak, but he took off. I hissed under my breath, left no choice but to sprint after him and to the door archway. He had a weapon drawn, eyes sharp and alert as he looked out to the lane. He left a space for me at the lock; I had the picks I needed in my hand, ready to go, and I clicked on a small flashlight. Placing it between my teeth so I could work with both hands, I felt him move behind me so that if anyone was looking in from the road the small beam of light would be blocked by his body. Pulling the metal out from between my teeth, I clicked off the flashlight. The sound turned Lance around, who looked down with surprise.

"That was quick."

"Much as I'd like to say I'm that good," I whispered, pushing the frame of the door with my gloved hand. "I'm not that good."

The whole lock stayed in my grip. I glanced up at Lance, who slowly and purposefully clicked the safety off his weapon. Someone had been here before us. Retracting my battle staves from the holders at my thighs, I held position as Lance crept forward first. Once he was inside, I moved after him and carefully shut the door behind me as best I could. With an annoying mix of the outside light source and the shadows inside the small cottage, I had what I jokingly called "dusk vision". It was essentially an eye patch that I could slide into position, giving me enough illumination in one iris while not restricting the other. It was the best I had, given my properly equipped – and cute! – pink glasses had been destroyed.

I watched him connect his own S.T.R.I.K.E. tech and we shadowed each other using a two-point person technique that was standard operating procedure anywhere. I cleared one room, tapped him on the shoulder, we moved on and he cleared the next. The cycle repeated. The cottage only had two bedrooms, with Dr Calvin using her living room as a huge office instead, which told me she didn't have many visitors. Or friends. The place had clearly been searched, with the searchers making no attempt to clean up after themselves. If you peered in through the outside windows, nothing looked amiss but once you were inside it was obvious.

"We're alone," I said, finishing a scan for any additional surveillance. Nothing.

"I can't tell," Lance mumbled. "Is she just messy or has this place been searched?"

"It's not usually this bad," I noted, inspecting the half-open drawers and papers strewn about. "The place has been searched."

"The real question is, did they find anything?"

"Hmmm. No slime though." I held a gloved finger up so he could see the layer of dust I'd been able to wipe off the bench. Different people? Or a different device?

"Split up," he said. "We can cover twice as much ground. Together."

I could have imagined the extra spice he threw on the final word. It might have been there. It might have been my guilty conscience. It had been a split-second impulse as I completed my loop of the town, running in a wider circle than I needed to so I could add some distance and make certain I was alone, unmonitored.

We'd agreed to wait, to go and search together. Yet as the New Biochemistry Building had become visible in the distance I just… couldn't help myself. I wanted to get ahead, to cross that item off my list, and yeah, work alone. I'd done all the recon already for the catering gig, so I took the service stairwell where I needed to go, slipped past the patrolling guard who strolled the floors much too casually, and examined the laboratory space that was even more destroyed than it had been when we'd first found it. It had been taped off, most of the room cleaned of debris and wiped down, so there wasn't much left to find if there was anything there to begin with.

Part of me wondered if the lack of discovery was karmic retribution for doing this alone. I'm sure Hill wouldn't have cared, maybe even encouraged it, but the longer I sat with the choice the worse I felt. And that annoyed the heck out of me. With a sigh, I was just about to give up on the search of Calvin's bedroom as I flopped down on to the mattress. There was an ornamental light fixture above my head, like a chandelier but cheap, and it was new. Everything else in this cottage was old, from the fireplace to the light switches, but this looked like it had been made in the last decade, so it stood out. Getting my balance on the mattress, I clicked on the flashlight and examined the details more carefully. The faintest square shape could be made out among the plaster, the work barely visible as I pressed my fingers against it.

"Lance," I said, voice low. I knew he'd hear me and sure enough, I sensed his presence.

"Here." I looked down to find his beloved butterfly knife extended toward me.

"Thanks," I replied, gratefully taking it. I ran it along the outline of the markings, loosening the fixture, then used the light itself to lift it from the ceiling. A shower of plaster and probably asbestos fell from above me and I coughed, wobbling on the mattress. Firm hands steadied me, Lance's grip secure against my thighs until I stilled.

"You right?" he asked.

I didn't answer. My focus was on the dark square above us leading to a hollow in the ceiling.

"Bobbi?"

"I do not wanna go up there," I groaned.

"No kidding. All you have to do is watch one scary flick ever and you know it's a bad idea."

"I have to go up there."

He was muttering under his breath now. "I'm invisible. I talk and she doesn't even hear me."

"That would make you mute," I said, looking down with a smile. "Not see-through."

"Oh, so you can hear me to correct me?"

I handed him the light fixture by way of response. He patiently placed it to the side.

"I'm trying, Lance," I said when his eyes were trained back on me. "You've met me at a weird point in my life when trusting anyone, let alone someone else in this business, is really hard for me. You've given me ample reasons to trust you and believe that we can work together as a team. I shouldn't have searched the lab without you. I did. And I didn't find anything. I'm… sorry."

He put his hands on his hips, scrutinizing my words as much as my face. "You know, my boss told me to do the same thing first opportunity I had."

"And you didn't."

"No," he said. "I didn't."

I bit my lip. My out was right there, but so was honesty and trying to course correct the mess I'd already made.

"Hill didn't tell me to go," I mumbled. "I made that call on my own."

I expected to see disappointment on his face, but instead it was the opposite. "Director Radcliffe didn't ask me to go."

"Seriously?"

"Nah, just wanted to offer you an easy way out and see if you'd take it."

"Rude!" I huffed, slapping his shoulder.

"Hey, you didn't though! So, ya know, means I know your apology is sincere even though it looked like it took you more effort to say the S word than it did to fly kick my boxing bag out of the ceiling."

I shook my head, my attention moving back towards the hole.

"Besides," he pressed. "I feel like you're trying to clear your burdens before a demon pulls you into that crawlspace and feasts on your soul."

Swearing under my breath, I shone the flashlight up there in the hopes of scaring away any monsters.

"The power of Christ," I whispered, assessing the distance. With two test springs, I threw my weight behind it and used the bounce of the mattress to propel me through the gap. I couldn't spring too high, however, as I'd knock myself out against the wooden beams of the roof. It was enough to get my torso through and I threw my arms out quickly to stop my descent. My biceps and forearms strained as I leveraged my butt onto more secure ground, pulling my legs through afterward and feeling thankful for years of arm dips paying off.

"Aight?" Lance called. "See any possums?"

"I hate the British," I snapped, quickly scanning the dark space for any demons, possums, insert other creature here that could be wanting to eat me alive.

"It's cute, you being claustrophobic."

"It's normal. Most people are afraid of small, dark, creepy, *confined* spaces."

There was nothing up here to be afraid of, though. The light bounced from empty wooden beam to empty wooden beam, the hole leading to a triangular recess. *No,* I thought. *I know you, Wilma.* Not a chance did she go to all that trouble building a fake light only to disguise a handy storage compartment in case of spontaneous hoarding habit. Flashlight between my teeth again, I carefully moved into a crouched position. I moved slow, conscious of the fact I could fall through the ceiling given the age and condition of this cottage.

"You all right up there?" Lance asked, just the top of his head appearing as he struggled to peek though.

I removed the metal cylinder from my teeth. "Hunky dory."

Moving the light beam lower, I concentrated on searching closer to the opening. Dr Calvin was barely over five foot, she wouldn't have been able to get this in place without using a ladder and even then, not very far. She was a thick woman, crawling around up here was out of the question, so if it wasn't directly near my feet then…

"I found something," I said, concentrating on the mark in the wood.

"What is it?"

"A scratch, I think."

"Roof possums."

"I'm about to roof possum you in a minute," I muttered, tracing the line with my finger. It skipped one beam, then the next, until–

"Got ya."

There, stuck above my head, was a plastic binder.

"How the hell did some old duck get that all the way up there?"

"By being a clever old duck," I said, straining to grab the corner and pulling it down. "She used magnets, look."

Handing Lance the folder, he examined the two small circles that were glued to the rear. I turned back to check the rest of the other unreachable crevices just to be sure, but I'd found the only thing that there was to be discovered.

"Coming down," I called, barely a second before I tucked my hands at my sides and jumped back through.

"Ah!" Lance cried.

My sudden impact caused both of us to bounce, a tangle of limbs and joints as we fell back onto the bed completely ungracefully.

"Geez, Bobbi! Give me some warning before you double bounce me out of the cottage we're supposed to be *sneaking* into," he huffed, breathless as he rolled around beside me.

"What do you think 'coming down' was?" I laughed, my head resting on the lace pillows as I looked up at the dark, square hole above me. Dr Calvin wasn't a lace person, so these must have come with the place. I tried to imagine her here, fastening her secrets to the ceiling, knowing they were safe as she slept soundly below them. Wherever she was, if she was even still alive, she wasn't safe anymore. The dark thought made me frown and I tried to push it aside.

"A foot ladder," I said, imagining how she did. "It would be low enough and stable enough to get her to the ceiling. The ceiling recess was already there, she just spruced it up. I bet that curtain rod has a hook. Glue the north poles in place, wait, then glue the south poles to your binder and you're done."

My finger was in the air, tracing an outline of the woman as I imagined her doing it exactly as I dictated.

"You're right," Lance said, sliding the fabric off the curtain rod near the window. He held up the end, which had a visible hook. "She didn't trust anyone to hold on to her secrets."

"She trusted science," I replied.

The crunch of gravel under tires drew our attention, a car slowly driving down the lane and toward the cottages. It was a cop car, lights off, and Lance grabbed my hand, pulling me upright off the bed.

"We've gotta bounce," I hissed.

"Enough bouncing!" he snapped. "Playing bouncy castle with you is what probably brought them here in the first place."

He was so peeved, I couldn't help but giggle as we darted through the cottage and headed for the back door. He was right, of course – a neighbor was standing in the rear garden with a flashlight, looking for signs of a break in. She wouldn't find them out there, but once inside… well, no point cleaning up a mess we only half made. The bathroom was the best bet and we crammed inside, shutting the door behind us. I listened while Lance worked, shimmying the latch undone and bracing himself on the edge of the ceramic bath as we waited for the right moment.

"Are you the one who called, ma'am?" an officer's voice could be heard saying.

"Oh yes, I live next door. Wilma at number four is away visiting family right now, but I swear I could hear sounds coming from her place. I thought I heard it last week, too, but everything looked fine from the outside, so I didn't make a fuss."

"We'll have a look right quick, ma'am, best you head inside."

"Do you have spare keys?" the other officer asked.

"No, sorry. She keeps to herself mostly, so I don't have anything like that."

"Not a worry, we'll get to it."

Slippers scuffing over concrete heralded her departure and

we strained to hear the officers back and forth with each other, before finally deciding they'd try the main door. Probably just kids mucking around was their consensus and as they tracked back to the front of the cottage, we slipped soundlessly out the back. Lance landed first, the folder zipped up tight in his jacket, before turning back to help me as I squeezed out.

"Yeah, it has been broken into, O'Leary," an officer said from the front. "Might need to get the dogs in."

The moment we were sure they were indoors, we darted for the cover of the overgrowth. We were barely a meter in when I heard twigs snapping and leaves moving in a way that told us we weren't the only ones there. I had a second to turn to Lance before I felt the press of a weapon against my neck. He already had his hands raised, a gun pointed square at his chest. Panting, eyes wide, I tried to think. Police were already inside. These weren't cops. But they were at Dr Calvin's house and they hadn't been there when we'd gone in. Those additional seconds were what I needed for my eyes to adjust to the darkness and realize it was just these two. I liked those odds.

Lance gave me the smallest shrug and I dived directly at him. He pounced at me and we swapped places, crashing into the opposite assailants and wrestling to take them to the ground. Surprise was always a great ally and it meant I'd caught my guy on his side, moving fast to roll over him and pin his arms by wrapping my legs tightly around his body. Locking my elbow under his neck, I held him there in a rear naked choke hold and waited, every inch of me straining to hold him in place as silently as possible. Eventually, his limbs started to loosen and go limp. I held on for a few additional seconds after he lost consciousness, just in case, and Lance came to stand over me, hands on hips.

"You gonna buy him a drink first or…?" he puffed.

Blood was trickling from the side of his mouth and he wiped it away, looking delighted. He crouched down, securing the guy's hands together with zip-ties while I slipped out from under him.

"Some of us have stamina," I replied. Hopping up, I stayed in a squat as I watched the cottage through the trees. The cops were inside and I guess that was enough to cloak the sound of our struggle. Yet we couldn't stay here. Lance's guy was still awake, gagged and zip-tied, and I retrieved one of the hair clips from my efficient ponytail. I moved slowly, making sure the little light there was caught on the metal as I held it to the flesh under his chin. He stiffened.

"Any sound that's not a direct answer to my question will be your last," I told him. It didn't matter if it was a lie, he just had to believe me. He nodded. Slipping down the gag, I pressed the sharp end of the clip harder for emphasis.

"Who do you work for?" I asked.

"C… C–"

"Cadenza Industries," Lance supplied, holding up an ID badge from the body of the man he was searching. He gave me a quizzical look that told me he had never heard of them. I had.

"It's a dummy corporation," I said, narrowing my eyes as I turned back to my interview subject.

"For who?" Lance questioned.

"Advanced Idea Mechanics," I replied, holding the stare of the man in front of me. "A.I.M. Isn't that right?"

"We're just scouts," he rushed out. "They sent us ahead to find out if Dr Calvin was alive or dead."

Just like us, I thought.

"Why now?" I questioned. "She has been missing for a week."

"The p-police report," he stammered. "They didn't care until it said her lab was destroyed. That implied there was something to destroy."

"And if you found her, what were you supposed to do?"

"Extract her. It's better if she works for us than anyone else."

"And take her where?"

"Bobbi."

I gagged the man at Lance's warning, looking up as another police vehicle arrived. This one was different, a van, and I could hear the barks from the back.

"Dogs," I whispered.

"I know," Lance snapped.

"Our scent is all over that cottage."

"I know. But not *just* ours."

"Most recently ours," I replied. "If it's hounds, then they trace the most dominant scent which is–"

"I know how scent tracking works," he huffed, thoughtful for a moment. Moving in a flash, he bonked the head of the man I'd been questioning against the tree. His eyes fluttered shut and he slumped, unconscious.

"I had more questions," I said.

"And you can ask them later," Lance noted, quickly typing out an alert to the taskforce on his device. "I've flagged that the locals will have two incoming A.I.M.… agents? A.I.M.ers? What do they call themselves?"

"Their leader is known as the Scientist Supreme."

He snorted. "Seriously?"

"Lance."

"Ahem, sorry. S.T.R.I.K.E. will intercept them for us and

we can question them later. Right now, we need to leave them here. The dogs will find them fast. And if we untie them, it will look like they're the ones who broke in."

We did so fast and quiet, Lance having already stripped them of key identity documents and weapons that could make this look more serious than it was. It would just be two guys in the woods nearby, dressed like burglars, and hopefully making some noise to alert the dogs to their presence once they regained consciousness. The perfect patsies.

"We need to take a roundabout route back," I said. "Muddy our scent just in case."

"Follow me then," Lance responded, springing up.

We set a steady pace, moving alongside each other as if we were jogging rather than running to escape law enforcement even though we took more side alleys than I thought it was possible for one city to contain. We raced down this lane, we jogged up those stairs, we ran under that bridge, we hurdled over that fence.

"Talk to me about A.I.M.Y. Winehouse," he said, the request coming out between puffed breaths as we moved.

"You've never dealt with them before?" I asked, casting him a sideways glance.

"No, but it's clear from your expression it's not good."

I huffed in agreement. "Not good because they're smart adversaries. Brilliant scientists, geniuses in some cases, who put their work and advancement before everything else. They'll sell arms to fund their experiments, make a profit from dangerous technology without a care regarding who it's sold to so long as they can use it to fund their own ambitions."

"International scientist terrorist types," he summarized much more succinctly than I had. "Got it."

"But," I pressed, taking a few additional gulps of air, "this isn't entirely bad."

The sound of laughing and music and heels clacking against concrete told me we were back in the heart of town, but Lance didn't stop. Instead, we slowed to a walk.

"And how's that?" he questioned, his voice low.

"Because they were investigating her disappearance as well," I replied, counting on my fingers as I outlined the points. "Which means three things: they weren't responsible for her abduction in the first place, they don't have her currently, *and* they believe there's a good chance she's still alive."

That last detail was vital. As I felt a surge in my chest, I realized it was the first time I had allowed myself to hope. Dr Calvin might be OK after all. I might be able to get her out of this alive.

"Fourth thing," Lance offered, interrupting my optimistic thoughts with a contribution of his own. "They don't have whatever she was motivated enough to hide."

He patted his chest where her hidden folder was zipped up tightly for emphasis. I gave him a hopeful smile as I felt sweat drip from my brow. We passed under what I thought was another bridge at first, but this one was not to cross a river. It was more of an enclosed skyway, connecting two adjoining buildings while pedestrians passed by on the cobblestones underneath.

"The Bridge of Sighs," Lance said over his shoulder.

"That's in Venice," I replied, wondering if he was making this up.

"The sequel, then: *2 Bridge 2 Sighs.*"

I barked a laugh and was so busy gawking at it that I nearly missed him as he turned down a passageway no bigger than the width of a table. My shoulders scraped against the moss that clung to the damp, brick walls as I followed him toward a growing ruckus. He scooted around a black, iron fence and past a chalk sign that told me were at the Turf Tavern.

There was a boom of noise as I ducked my head, crouching under the low doorway to slip inside and amongst the blanket of music, chatter, and clinking glasses. Jolly was the first word that came to mind as I fell behind, taking it all in. There were a few students tucked among the white beards and newsboy caps of the locals, but I immediately understood why Lance had brought us here. Even *if* the dogs were able to track us this far, they'd get no further than the Turf Tavern. Too many people, too many scents, and too much history packed into close quarters. We'd be perfectly and absolutely lost among the fray.

"Here."

I looked up to find Lance pushing a black, frothy pint toward me. Taking it and nodding my thanks, I downed the first sip of Guinness with a steely smile. He led me towards a table tucked in the back, where we settled in and people-watched.

"One drink," he said, having already demolished half his pint. "It would be noticed if we didn't."

"Well then, for the sake of the mission," I replied, gulping my own. He was watching me carefully, assessing, as I self-consciously wiped the foam mustache from my lips. "What?"

"Do you know why I brought you here?"

"Besides the obvious," I replied, and he shrugged with concession. "This is a historic site. In 1954, it's where future Australian Prime Minister Bob Hawke set a Guinness World Record for consuming a yard glass of ale in eleven seconds."

I was straight-faced, serious, but I couldn't hold it for long as his eyes narrowed at me. I laughed, pointing to the sign above his head that proclaimed the odd fact.

"There's another about Bill Clinton over there" – I gestured – "but I can't read that far."

"Aussie politics aside–"

"I have a breadth of interests."

"–this was Inspector Morse's local."

"Inspector Morse? The fictional character?"

"Yeah." He beamed. "This was his local. Now from one generation's Inspector Morse to another..."

I blew a cloud of foam at him, chuckling as he flinched. "So immature."

We finished our pints, a close call averted, and Dr Calvin's secrets pressed between us. They would have to wait. It was my shout.

CHAPTER TEN

"Ugh," I groaned, sitting up in bed and wincing. It took me a moment to get my bearings as I stared out the window, the fog of sleep taking its time to abate as I tried to remember where I was. Sunlight glinted off a water view and the gentle rocking brought me back to my senses. Houseboat. Oxford. Guinness.

Rubbing my face, I threw my legs over the corner of the bed. A shower. Clean teeth. Fresh clothes. Morning skincare routine. Just cross those four things off the list, then worry about everything else later. Lance was already gone, a note stuck to the door of his closed bedroom door that simply said "9AM class". When I emerged from the bathroom, I felt considerably more human as I demolished a banana in two bites and drank at least half my body weight in water. Better.

I yanked his note off the door as I passed, holding the thin paper in my hands. Why was this annoying me? It was so short. Barely two words. I was just about to drop my towel and change when a red flash whipped by the window.

"What the…"

I reached for the shotgun I'd put under my bed, fingers

inching closer when a green flash shot by and I yelped. It was a rower. I'd made unflinching eye contact – while half naked – with said rower. I pulled the blinds shut quickly, blocking out the view from the river and laughing at myself. Wiggling into a blue turtleneck sweater, the vibration of my phone alerted me to a new message. Lance.

"Classes cancelled. Meet me at the Vaults and Garden café for lunch."

Hmmm. He said classes, not class, implying multiple. Yet he didn't say why. I checked the time then assessed the route I needed before heading back to the kitchen in search of coffee. Any coffee. I thanked the caffeinated lords and S.T.R.I.K.E.'s budget because there was a small yet completely serviceable espresso machine that I was able to get acquainted with. I inhaled deeply from the bag of powder, savoring the essential morning aroma. I foamed the milk while basically bouncing on the balls of my feet. And unsurprisingly, I burned the tip of my tongue as I hastily took a sip once the steaming coffee and frothy milk were combined.

Leaning against the bench, fingers warmed through the ceramic mug, I bashed out a quick text update to Hill on last night's activities and revelations, receiving a thumbs up emoji by way of response. I smirked, Hill never being the overly verbose type. My stomach dropped as I looked up at the clear, plastic folder waiting on the table. Had Lance looked inside already? Did he know what was in there? If our situations were reversed, I would have already looked and I felt like he knew that. Why did this feel like some kind of test?

It took everything I had to walk away from the temptation, but I left the folder where it was. Slipping my headphones in, I called Jen's number as I headed for the back deck and wiggled into the bench seat at the table there. It was just past 6AM in New York, but I knew she'd be up.

"Yellow," she huffed, answering on the second ring.

"You're at the gym, aren't you?"

"Rain, hail or gamma ray induced shine."

"What machine you on?" I asked in my most annoying sing-song voice.

"Lat pulldown," she grunted. "It's nice to hear your voice. How's the southern hemisphere?"

"Har har, you're not getting a single bite from me."

"Damn it. Hill was just as opaque. Well, hope you're having fun wherever you are. I've got no updates on the Squawk Eye front."

I nearly choked on my sip of coffee. "Oh my God, you've been spending too much time with Tig."

"She's here now, actually. Tigra, it's Bob." I heard a muffled shout in response, my guess being that she was in full sprint on the treadmill. I liked the idea of the two of them hanging out.

"I'm not calling about divorce stuff, I'm calling about…" I hesitated, glancing inside to where I knew the plastic folder sat. "I don't know anyone here to give it to me straight. You're my go-to pulse check."

"Everyone knows people in the southern hemisphere don't have pulses," she responded. "Hit me."

As carefully as I could, I recapped my situation using a fake name for Lance and vague details about where I was and what I was doing. I trusted Jen with my life, but protocol was protocol, so I made sure not to give anything away. As I spoke and sipped and spoke some more, I watched the busy waterways populated with people making their way up and down the Thames.

"I apologized," I continued. "And he said he accepted the apology, but still… why do I feel so crappy? It didn't seem like that big a deal in the moment."

"Because he was honest with you," Jen responded, a metallic clang punctuating her point. "Multiple times, personally and professionally. And at your first opportunity to reciprocate, you didn't."

"Mmmm," I mused, draining the last of the warm liquid in my cup. "Listen, I've got another question for you that's nothing to do with personal growth."

Jen barked a laugh. "Avoidance, but go on."

"That RICO case you brought against A.I.M. a few years ago—"

"A case I lost, let me remind you."

"You won in the Supreme Court of my heart and mind."

She snorted down the line. "If only that was legally binding."

"Do you think you can send me the files?" I asked.

"I can send 'em to you, but even digitally that's a lot of files. You after something specific?"

"Shell companies," I mused. "Dummy corporations active or inactive. Anything that you tied to them."

"Now *that* I can do. A.I.M. had plenty. Has plenty. Your private email?"

"Yes, please."

"I'll shoot it over to you tonight."

I was about to thank her, our conversation having reached its natural conclusion, but Jen was not one to let things get by her. It's what made her such a great lawyer and such a frustrating friend. She wouldn't let you slip away from the tricky stuff.

"Your partnership with this mystery partner doesn't seem

like an antagonistic one," she said, seamlessly picking up the thread of our earlier subject. "If it was a tête-à-tête situation, then you would brush it off and bound forward like you have in the past. You're feeling guilty because he keeps extending olive branches while you're burning down the tree."

I knew precisely why I had needed to call Jen in the moment. She was verbally knocking the lighter from my hands.

"You like this person," she said, a statement of fact.

"I do. They're really good at their job, they're funny, I'm trying to trust them and it's just… easy."

"Ah, there it is."

"There what is?"

"You're not trusting the ease, babe. You're so used to difficult difficult, lemon difficult, that you're panicking in the face of something that should be very straightforward."

"Speaking of ease, can you just tell me the answer? I feel like I've shown you all my work, just skip to telling me what to do."

"You got any branches?"

By the time I was powering up High Street to meet Lance for lunch, I thought I had some idea about what that branch could be. When I turned down the path, my breath caught at the sight before me. Clusters of tables sat on either side of a stone walkway that led directly to a perfect view of the Radcliffe Camera in the distance. Its iconic, spherical shape drew a string of tourists towards it, and I could understand why, it took an effort to draw my eyes away as I stepped inside the cafe. The name of this place made a lot of sense, too, with the building's vaulted ceilings looking like the structure went all the way back to the fourteenth century at least. I was still admiring the architecture when Lance spotted me positioned outside and under an outdoor heater as I craned my neck upwards, drinking in everything.

"I see you found your almond croissant," he said, nodding at the pastry in my hand.

My eyes snapped to his, smiling as I took in his Professor Falkner get up. "What, no kilt?"

His lips twitched under the fake moustache as he took a seat, ordering a sandwich from a passing waitress.

"Egg salad?" I flinched. "Brave."

"Some of us can hold our Guinness."

"I held multiple pints, thank you. Carried them from the bar to our table and back again. Barely spilled a drop."

His eyes danced with amusement and I looked away, thinking about my conversation with Jen while trying to work up the courage to begin another one.

"You like it here," Lance said, matter-of-factly. "The romance of a little garden café in a historic university town."

"Couldn't have put it better," I replied, picking at a leftover almond shaving. "Of course, the romance of the place is really ruined once I start thinking about how historically I wouldn't have been allowed to pursue an education here, let alone step foot on the premises."

"Mood killer," he smirked.

"What happened to classes?"

The smirk dropped. "Everything has been moved back to digital learning following a faculty member's death."

"Not–"

"No," he said, shaking his head. "I would have told you straightaway. The dean. Found dead in his bathtub this morning allegedly. You met him."

"Pinky?" I asked, flashing back to the rude man with the rude attitude.

"That's the one."

Lance's sandwich arrived and he got busy eating, leaving me with my thoughts which were all deeply suspicious.

"I know," Lance said, words muffled by his mouthful. "I don't like it either."

"That doesn't bode well for Wilma."

"I thought that, too. She goes 'missing', except nobody knows about it. The dean is murdered, but it's made to look like an accident. Were they in whatever this was together? And if you're willing to kill him, why not leave her body to be discovered as well?"

I held up a hand, closing my eyes as I tried to slow down his conclusion jumping. "Because she's the better scientist. No disrespect to the dead, but maybe what was wanted from him he couldn't deliver and she could. Or maybe she's at the bottom of the river and they're just buying time between corpses. Maybe it has something to do with the A.I.M. pair we intercepted."

"They were taken into S.T.R.I.K.E. custody this morning."

"Great! When can we interrogate them?"

He winced. "They were transferred to London."

"What?" I asked in disbelief.

"Radcliffe wants to do the interrogations there this afternoon. Says we're free to 'submit questions.'"

"Submit! Questions!" I was fuming.

"Bobbi, I hear your rage against the machine and I relate. Believe me. He's a meddler, so we just have to let him meddle because we've got to choose our battles here."

"They better record that interview. I want to see every

second of it. I want to know the timeline of where they were that night. Did they kill the dean?"

"And do they know what happened to Agent Grist?"

"Come again?"

"Before me," he said. "The S.T.R.I.K.E. agent who disappeared."

"OK, what happened there?"

"If I knew the answer to that…"

I flicked some icing sugar at him.

"Truce." He smiled. "He was a junior agent monitoring Dr Calvin when she first started working here years ago. It was just remotely at first, but once a month he would do a day trip to Oxford, assess on the ground, and submit a report. Then he never came back."

"He just vanished?"

"Without a trace. Submitted his report that everything was normal, hopped on the train back to London, never arrived."

"That's some real Louis Le Princery," I mumbled. "You were assigned in his place?"

"Six months ago. More of a monitoring assignment than anything else, especially when the investigation into his disappearance came up with zilch. There weren't enough resources to free me up and come here until she went missing as well."

We fell silent as a bubbly waitress took our plates. "Can I get you two anything else? Coffees?"

"No, thank you." I smiled. "I'm a one cup a day girl."

"Oof, such restraint!"

"Two English breakfast teas," Lance said. "Milk on the side."

"You got it!" Her ponytail bobbed with enthusiasm as she bounded back inside. My lip was curled, I knew it.

"You've been here how long now?" he asked. "I haven't seen you drink a cup of tea once."

"I'm not a tea person," I said.

"That's cos American tea is trash. No flavor."

"Right," I scoffed. "And the nation that colonized the world for spice but refuses to use any in its food knows everything about flavor?"

An elderly couple passing by caught my words and gave me a disapproving *tut tut* as they shuffled on. I rolled my eyes. The waitress returned with our steaming mugs of underwhelming black water, and I watched as Lance took over. He poured in one sugar, added milk in increments, stirred, added a bit more, then removed the bag. He slid the cup across the table toward me. I'd never taken such a carefully observed sip before and I did my best not to gag out of sheer politeness.

"Mmmm," I said, patting my tummy. "Delicious."

He raised his eyes to the heavens, like I drove him mad, which was probably true. "Give me enough time and you'll be heading home with a box of Twinings under your arm."

I was determined to finish the stupid cup now, so I sipped slowly and fidgeted with the cuff of my sweater.

"Right then," he said, with a satisfied sigh. "What's next?"

"I have ideas about that."

"Course ya do. You're all twitchy."

"First, we need to find a library."

He barked out a laugh so loud a pigeon nearby took flight in a huff of annoyed feathers.

"If only Oxford had a few of those." He grinned.

"Specifically," I replied, leaning forward. "I was thinking that one."

Lance followed where I pointed, turning around in his chair

until he was staring at the focal point of the whole city, really: Radcliffe Camera.

This had once been a library built for science, but "Rad Cam", as the students I eavesdropped on had called it, had been long since been converted into one of the main reading rooms for the Bodleian. It had key volumes of interest to us and everything else was walking distance close by in the Gladstone Link, an underground library that connected this space to the more famous Bodleian Old Library. Comparatively speaking, this was one of Oxford's newer buildings, opening in the 1740s which made even the Vaults and Garden café a few casual centuries older. Still, I felt the hallowed weight of history pressing down on me as we walked inside. Our footsteps were a muted echo as the sound evaporated into the dome above us, light pouring in through windows that entombed the building in a permanent glow.

"Did you know–"

"Oh god, is this where you tell me something about J R R Tolkien?"

Lance spluttered. "Why would you say that? Do I seem like a hobbit guy?"

"I believe the term is 'short king energy.'"

"I'm six foot!"

"OK," I said, dropping my voice lower. "Frodo."

He shook his head in despair, mouthing the word "Frodo" to himself as he led us deeper into the building. I tried to resist the urge to stand in the center of Radcliffe Camera and just spin around, arms outstretched, while going "weeeeeee". But it was hard. Lance steered us up a staircase and through an aisle that was seemingly endless, the many alleys and laneways of Oxford replicated in this structure except the bricks were books. We emerged on the other side in an empty area comprised of one long, T-shaped wooden table that was perfect for our purposes. There was absolutely no one else around.

"What I was going to say," he continued, watching as I pulled the folder he must have known I'd have with me out of my bag, "was they filmed scenes from *The Saint* here."

I had been lifting sheets of paper out when I paused. "The Val Kilmer movie?"

"The masterpiece."

"Huh."

"Huh? What does that mean?"

I smiled, unfolding each document as I went. "A high-tech thief and master of disguise who uses the names of saints as pseudonyms. I can see why something like that would appeal to you."

"Obviously using the names of British rockers is cooler."

"Way cooler."

I actually didn't disagree there, but our bickering reached a ceasefire as I finished laying out everything that Dr Calvin had gone to immense trouble to hide in that creepy ceiling recess. I had spent years working with this woman, had gotten to know her strengths and weaknesses and quirks. I felt a pang as I saw a reflection of them laid out before me, while to most people it more than likely looked like little more than lines and numbers. Yet this was Wilma, and her presence was right here where it always was: in the work. Lance was quiet, his intelligent gaze running over every marking and line before us.

"What am I looking at here?"

"Blueprints," I answered, his look of "duh" causing me to quickly fill in the blanks. "Specifically, schematics for everything one would need to build a functioning, state of the art laboratory."

"These are lab blueprints?"

"These are blueprints for *three* labs," I corrected, waggling my fingers. With a steadying breath, I dipped my hand into my jean pocket and retrieved the olive branch. My olive branch. I placed a set of old, janky keys down on the table in front of us. Lance looked across at me.

"And those are...?"

"A set of three keys," I answered. "I found them the night we met, once I got back to Magdalen. They were sewn into the lining of Dr Calvin's lab coat. The search of her office was fruitless, and I only grabbed her coat on a whim, but later I could feel the uneven weight."

He picked them up, doing the same thing I had done and examining the differences in each key. "You've had them the whole time?"

"I have," I said. "But I didn't know what they meant or what they could open until I saw the blueprints. I think each one correlates to one of the labs, but I don't know where they are or how to find them."

I sighed, feeling like I was doing a terrible job of explaining myself. I tried to let my mask drop, it being something I found actively hard to do because I was so used to maintaining it to protect myself and protect my work.

"It's not easy for me to let people in," I said, voice quiet. "Especially at the moment when I'm incredibly defensive and that's not a 'you' problem, that's a 'me' problem. It becomes an 'us' problem when it impacts the work, like it did last night."

"Bobbi," he replied, putting down the keys as he came to stand in front of me. "You already apologized."

"It didn't feel like... enough."

"It was. You meant it. I believed you. I thought the pub was a clean slate."

"To my memory, yeah."

He was holding me by my shoulders, I'm not quite sure when that happened, but he squeezed just slightly to make sure I was looking at him. His eyes were crinkled with a smile and sincerity dripped from every pore.

"That's why I left the folder. I thought you could get some work done on it while I was gone."

"Oh. *Oh.* I thought that was some kind of test."

"Literally how?"

"To see if I had the willpower to not be sneaky and peek without you."

He laughed, stepping back. I could feel the spot where his hands had been and I missed the flash of warmth there.

"I'm not that guy."

"All right," I exhaled. "Let's just say what we mean from now on."

"Deal."

"Deal."

He held out his fist. I bumped it.

"So," Lance began. "I'm no architect, but each of these blueprints are *very* different. They're designed to very distinct specifications, which should make them stand out but in reality is meant to make them blend in."

"The magnets," I murmured, thinking about how Dr Calvin had hidden these very plans in plain sight... if you knew where to look.

"If you had to build a secret lab – let alone three – there's few places better to do that than Oxford. This city is full of hidden passages, secret alleyways, buildings with forgotten chambers. I think these labs are hidden within places that already exist."

I could see where he was going. I could understand the logic. The practical logistics, however, felt overwhelming.

"Oh-kay," I started. "How do we find these buildings? There's absolutely no text at all that points to, say, Blenheim Palace."

Lance frowned, his brow creasing as he thought. "No, but I think Blenheim Palace isn't far off. Look at the keys." He picked them back up, laying them flat on his palm. "What's the first thing you notice, master lock picker?"

"They're old," I said, stroking the metal of one. "None of these keys look fit for locks made this century. And they're completely different."

"Perfect," Lance smiled. "You're perfect."

He pulled out a chair, settling into it and I followed suit. In his disguise as Professor Falkner, he carried a small leather satchel around – a staple academic accessory – and he retrieved a paper notebook and pen, the tip hovering above a line as he turned to me.

"What's the very latest date on each key?"

"Mmmm, nineteen hundreds for this one," I said, pointing it out. He drew a little symbol that looked like a crudely sketched version of each key, then scrawled my estimated ages next to each. "This one looks like the eighteenth century because of the grooves, see?"

"No, but continue."

"This one is the oldest by far, sixteenth or seventeenth century."

His pen highlighted a range of dates. "There you go, there's our net. Buildings in Oxford within this date range are what we're looking for."

"That's a range of four hundred years, Lance."

"Yes, but in a city that is home to the oldest English language university in the world. When you think about it, that's quite specific."

There was a glint of mania in his eyes that was eerily familiar. It reminded me of Wilma so viscerally I caught my breath. It's exactly how she looked when an idea would take hold, *really* take hold, and there was no stopping her until she saw it through. It's what made her a genius, but it was also what caused her downfall the first time. Lance checked his watch.

"This place shuts at 9PM, so we've got a solid eight hours to try and make a dent. What do you say?"

"I love a late night study sesh," I replied.

"You pick a blueprint, I'll pick some books."

He was gone in a wave of tweed and cologne, leaving me to examine the trio of puzzles in front of us. Of the three lab blueprints, one was split across multiple levels. It was thin and narrow, with a metallic spiral staircase in the center that meant you had to ascend or descend to get to the other half of the laboratory. A real pain in the butt for any scientist, but probably a secretly good way to stay fit. Another had a very distinctive curving shape, the space looking like a crescent moon if I squinted my eyes and stood above. The final one was the most ideal, just a long rectangle that looked like it could be anywhere to me. I wanted that one least, which was perfect because Lance called dibs when he returned with a stack of volumes in hand.

"Why would you fight for that one?" I questioned.

"I think this marking indicates stone," he replied, tapping the paper. "Maybe sandstone. And with that much surface area, I'm thinking underground."

There wasn't anything left to do but get started. I went with the multi-level lab, which I guessed had the most recent key given the layout and materials outlined in the blueprint. Where he had managed to source this, I had no idea, but Lance had five volumes related specifically to historic locks and keys. The most useful to me was a chapter titled just that, by J A MacCulloch, and contained in the *Encyclopedia of Religion and Ethics* volume eight. Published in 1915, it aligned most closely with my timeline and the brutal truth of it was there was no easy hack.

I tried Googling old keys and even did a reverse image search, but no dice. The internet's hunger for oddly specific and ancient keys was minimal, so the road to success was paved by turning one page at a time, minute by minute, hour by hour, until I started to narrow down my search. By the time an old man who looked more like a poltergeist than a human being swung by to tell us the library was closing in half an hour, Lance looked defeated.

"Not to be dramatic," he said, face flat as he lay on the table, "but my plan sucks and I have nothing."

I patted his elbow sympathetically. "There, there."

"You look smug."

"That's because I am smug."

He sat bolt upright. "You found something."

I swiveled the book I had open in front of me so he could see it, popping a key right next to an illustration of one that was almost identical. The grooves were different, as was the metal it had been forged in, but it was specific enough it had set me on track. Flipping my laptop open, I navigated back to the page I'd last been looking at and sat it on top of one blueprint. The outline of a classically old but not *super* old building was on screen and I traced the shape with my finger, Lance's eyes following as I mimicked the same shape on the blueprint.

"Hello, laboratory one," I smiled.

CHAPTER ELEVEN

Pitt Rivers Museum was unlike anything I had ever seen. I guess a part of me thought that since it had been so hard to identify the location in the first place, this portion of the assignment would be easy. I was utterly and brutally wrong.

From the outside, it looked manageable. I mean, sure, it was an enormous, Victorian neo-Gothic building that seemed to spring out of an expanse of flat, green lawn that led up to it. But I could *see* it. I could see from the blueprints where Dr Calvin's lab might fit, the multi-story structure making more sense now when I viewed the location as a whole, rather than just a fragmented piece.

Lance had glanced at me smugly and I had smiled smugly back. Idiots. We had taken the night, revising and double-, triple-checking that my conclusion was right. He was the former engineer after all, so his ability to overlay the lab design with the blueprints we could find of Pitt Rivers Museum was integral.

"It's in a corner," he said, after muttering to himself for several minutes about meters as he measured calculations across the table on the houseboat. We'd brought Tem in for backup, Lance telling me he had the best ear for creaks out of anyone he knew. When I'd asked what that meant, he'd simply shrugged and said, "Holes in the plan, anything wonky." His face was on screen, the laptop perched on my knee where I had sprawled so the young doctor had the best possible view.

"And that's helpful why?" I questioned.

"The place is one long rectangle, innit? So we only have four corners to search for whatever secret access point Dr Calvin put in place. Only problem…"

"What?"

"That's going to take time."

"It's a museum. People don't exactly rush through and if Dr Calvin has been coming and going undetected, then it must be discreet enough."

I was buoyed with hope and couldn't help that it came through in my words and actions. Three secret labs *to me* communicated three opportunities to find Dr Calvin alive and well in any one of them. She was always a work first kinda lady – to the detriment of everything else – and the idea of her cottoning on to a prospective kidnapping and dipping before they had a chance to grab her was a happy one to me, at least. Because of the stakes and the science, I had been cautious about a positive outcome. Now, in my utmost fantastical version of how this could all resolve itself, we'd strut into one of her hidden workspaces to find her hunched over a microscope with strands of gray hair escaping her messy bun. She'd look up, eyes twinkling as she considered the woman I'd become rather than the girl she knew. With a quirk of her lips, she'd say, "I wondered when you'd show up, Barbara."

Like I said, a fantasy. Yet maybe not that far from a reality. There were doubts and niggling voices of dissent at the back of my mind, but I pushed them down as I watched Lance. He was spinning a pen between his fingers, quite a skillful move as the plastic dipped and danced across his digits like it was programmed to. His brow was set into a hard line.

"Do you think we need a distraction?" I prompted. "A diversion?"

"We could just break in after hours."

I scoffed, spinning around the page of research I had been reading about this place online. "It has almost the entire archaeological and anthropological collections of the University of Oxford on display there, Lance. More than half a million objects. Their security is gonna be a little tighter than the New Biochemistry Building. And, while we're at it, however good we think we are, we haven't made it in and out of anywhere undetected yet. Some of that is bad luck, but some of it is down to other variables that frankly I don't want to take a risk on if we don't have to."

"Ah, guys," Tem said quietly.

"Life is risk!" Lance huffed.

"Unnecessary risk! I'm the American, you're not supposed to be the cowboy here."

"Guys!"

The young doctor's New Zealand accent was like a knife through our back and forth. Both of our heads snapped toward the laptop screen.

"I have an idea that requires minimal variables," he offered.

"Go ooooon," Lance purred.

"But you'd need to get me off base and in the field with you. There's no other way."

Lance snapped into action, making the calls he needed to while Tem talked me through his plan. I wasn't the only one who'd been reading up on the place, with his research leading him to Mākereti Papakura, the first Māori woman to ever study at Oxford. She passed away in the 1930s, with a collection of her personal items donated to Pitt Rivers Museum, along with photographs, genealogies, and notes for her thesis on Māori culture, which was published posthumously.

"They've been industry leaders in decoloniality," he said, analyzing my blank expression. "Returning stolen stuff."

"Ah."

"Engaging with Indigenous representatives, rewriting labels so they're authored by community, removing human remains."

"Aaaah."

"Right! So if I ask for a private tour of Mākereti's taonga, that minimizes your variables and buys you time."

He was right. He was so, so right and this was the perfect solution to get us in and get us out with as low impact as possible.

A huge grin spread across my face. "If you were on this houseboat right now, I would kiss you!"

"Aye?!" Lance grunted, ending his call at the worst possible moment. I was too elated to care.

Tem looked amused as his gaze darted from Lance to me and back again. "Save the pash rash, but while I'm here…"

"Name it," I said, slamming my hand on the table for emphasis. "Anything you want."

"A body-ody-ody, please."

I tilted my head with confusion.

"He wants to examine the dean," Lance translated. "Done,

mate. Bob's right, whatever you want. You're doing us the favor."

Tem pumped his fist with excitement. "Yes! Love an autopsy."

That's what had turned our duo into a trio: a late-night brainstorming session morphed into a private tour of Pitt Rivers Museum the next day when it closed at 5 PM. Tem had given us instructions to "dress respectably" and I hadn't known what that meant until I met him at the train station, his frame statuesque in a tailored suit and wide-brimmed hat.

"Love the color," I breathed, admiring the fabric.

"Pounamu green," he smiled, tapping the carving that hung around his neck in an identical shade.

"Hope you're not gonna perform an autopsy in that," Lance said, arms crossed as he leaned against a pole. I whacked him on the shoulder. "Ow, what?"

"He looks great!"

"And I don't?"

"You look like Conor McGregor on the red carpet," I said, response measured. "Would it kill you to wear socks?"

"That's not the menswear look, love," he replied, adjusting his lapel.

I rolled my eyes, hopefully covering how much I actually did appreciate his look. He was in dark burgundy fit, ankles exposed in a pair of very Oxford lad loafers, and a black turtleneck underneath his matching suit. He was dressed as himself, no Professor Falkner costume, and it made me wonder what he got up to in his downtime in this city and who he got up to it with. My own ensemble had been the result of a last-minute panic run to Zara, a shop I had never been to before and I was afraid to return to after witnessing women descend rather violently on a fresh rack of trench coats in varying shades of beige. Thankfully, I'd been able to leave unscathed with a jumpsuit in a beautiful, rich blue and a pair of black pumps. The excess of fabric had the dual benefit of keeping me warm and making my movements look dramatic as the flared cut *swooshed* with my steps.

When we'd been greeted by one of the head curators and brought inside, we clearly looked the part and that's all that mattered. Well, maybe the way Lance glanced at me when he didn't think I was looking mattered a little bit, too. We entered through the Oxford University Museum of Natural History building, Lance and I staying silent after the brief introductions to allow Tem to do his thing and he was thinging. He was nodding enthusiastically as the curator spoke, leading us into the now closed space as the interior of the museum opened up.

"She had been completing her Bachelor of Science degree in anthropology at the Society of Oxford Home-Students when she passed," the curator said. "At just fifty-six, too, a ruptured aortic artery."

"Such a tragedy," Tem replied, sincerely. "I was thinking of visiting Mākereti's grave while I was in town."

"Oh yes, you definitely should. It's over at Saint Andrew's Churchyard, which was Oddington Cemetery back then."

We had come in through the center of the gift shop, a small set of stairs leading down to the ground floor while balconies wrapped around the space, creating three distinct levels. The curator was about to turn left, but she paused, looking back at us.

"Your friends are free to wander, if they like?"

Oh my God, I loved this woman. I bowed my head graciously and Lance muttered his thanks.

"There's lots to look at and I'm in no rush to pick Dr Waa's brains here," she continued. "Please, take your time."

"I'll text you when we're done," Tem said, holding up his phone. "Now, all the Māori artifacts were donated after her death?"

"Mmm, that's right," the curator said excitedly, leading Tem through a maze of cabinets and displays until I couldn't hear them anymore, let alone see them.

There was looking for a needle in a haystack, then there was this. It was *beyond* overwhelming as every single inch of space was occupied with something, even the ceiling! I craned my neck upwards, looking at the wooden boat that was suspended above us and the colorful banners that fluttered ever-so-slightly in a draft, each one depicting a different culture from around the world. I swore.

"I know," Lance sighed next to me, reading my thoughts. "It's hidden in a corner, so let's start there."

"Three levels, four corners at each," I said, shaking my head. "The task has already tripled."

"Come on."

He took my hand, leading me to a staircase of marble, glass and chrome that took us to the upper gallery. We split apart, each of us taking a side as we followed a path between dark, wooden cabinets that had carefully itemized drawers with gold labels. Inside each one, glass made the preserved objects visible as you passed between thousands upon thousands of years of culture. Nothing was arranged via region and period, it all appeared to be organized typologically depending on how the objects were used, which is how my first corner spanned

from beautiful Native American renderings of butterflies and
thunderbirds to tools used in Pasifika tattooing traditions.
One of the men framed in a huge, wall-sized painting had
markings almost identical to Tem and I wish I had more time
to linger. Yet a potential keyhole was what I was searching for
and as I cradled the object in my hand, searching desperately,
there was nothing that came close.

"Anything?" Lance asked, coming up behind me.

"Nothing," I said, shaking my head. We had started in the
middle without discussing it because it made the most sense,
the ground floor having easily the most amount of traffic and
this the second least amount. It did, however, provide more
privacy than I was expecting with the view from below partially
blocked in long stretches due to the suspended displays.

"Up then," he suggested, and we made our way back to the
stairs, looking down at a mountain of history below us. Tem
and the curator were far off in their own corner, him pointing
out something to her through the glass. She reached for her
own pair of keys, going to unlock the cabinet and donning
a pair of handling gloves. *Good work,* I thought, sending the
positive energy toward him in a wave. Lance and I peeled off
again, him taking the two right corners while I took the two
left. My side was marked by a towering totem pole, which
began on the ground floor and stretched upwards across all
three levels at the center of the museum. I paused, reading
the label that told me it was from northern British Columbia,
Canada, and a place called Star House on Haida Gwaii. There
was a cabinet of other items from the same region up here and
in one of the corners of interest, but it didn't lead anywhere.
The opposite side was full of masks, and I nearly moved right
past it before stopping. The latch on this cabinet was different,

the whole fixture being constructed into the corner at a hard right angle. I felt that familiar surge of excitement and hope shoot through me. *Wilma.*

"Who do you reckon that big purple guy is?"

I had been so focused in my examination that I jumped, not hearing Lance approach this time. Turning around, I followed his gaze upwards to huge, tribal shields that were hung across the length of the ceiling above us. These stood out because of the figure hand painted on them in various poses, in some cases holding guns and in others bookmarked by skulls.

"The Phantom," I replied.

"You what?"

"The big purple guy." I pointed. "The Man Who Cannot Die. The Ghost Who Walks."

"How do you know that?" He frowned, like I was teasing him.

"Firstly, because I spent some time working out of the Western Highlands in Papua New Guinea. He's everywhere there, like their Captain America."

"Huh." Lance examined the shields with new interest.

"And secondly, it's written on each of them."

He tilted his head to the side, getting a better view. "That's not Andrew Lloyd Webber's mate at all."

I snorted, turning back to the matter at hand. With a steadying breath, I inserted the key. I sensed Lance tense beside me, drawing a weapon as we both listened to a chain reaction of metallic clanks. With a subtle blast of air, the cabinet popped up and open. It was just an inch, an incremental space, but it was the equivalent of a very weird door creaking wider. I slipped out of my pumps, bare feet flat on the carpeted floor as I held the shoes in my hands and crept soundlessly forward.

I let Lance go first, his body disappearing into the dark space. I positioned both heels at the entryway. I couldn't see a mechanism you would turn to exit this place, so my concern was that it would lock behind us and we'd be trapped inside. Maybe that's what happened to Dr Calvin?

As my toes made contact with the grated steel floor beneath me, lights flicking on as we slowly moved further inside, it became abundantly clear that was not what had happened to her. We were on the top level just like in the blueprints, the entirety of the space not much wider than the inside of a car but circular. In the center, a spiral staircase descended to the ground floor. Even with his conscious movements, the pressure of Lance's heels echoed through the cylinder like a very creepy cathedral. He used hand signals to indicate that he was taking the middle floor. I nodded, inching past him and retracting my battle staves to examine the ground floor. From the freezing inner temperature to the cobwebs I had to swipe away to clear a path, it was clear no one had been here in quite some time. My fantasy scenario slipped away from me like the whisper of a chilled breeze running through this place.

"It's empty," Lance called from above me, his clanking footsteps drawing closer as he made his descent. "Someone worked here, but we have no way to tell if it was even her."

"It was her," I said, standing in one spot as I stared at a case of empty specimens. Mice. They had been mice once. Some of the Perspex cases were empty, just a bed of hay remaining, while others had tiny, white skeletons inside. The subjects had either died from the experiments or been left here to starve. It was cruel, but if you were leaving in a hurry you wouldn't prioritize your failures. Some had been taken because some had contained useful data. Those niggling doubts niggled just a little bit harder, but I kept my thoughts to myself. For now.

"Just when I thought this place couldn't get creepier," Lance said, standing beside me.

"Dr Calvin always started with mice," I muttered. "She said they were easier to get and analyze than almost anything, especially once they banned the use of dogs."

"Dogs? Like, puppies? No, don't tell me."

"Knife," I said, holding out my hand. He gave it to me and I worked fast, prying open one cabinet after the other. Wiggling my fingers into a pair of gloves, I plucked bones from each of the skeletons left behind, bagging them separately.

"Cute habit you have there." He cringed as I returned the blade.

"They were her model systems. The bones might retain data, give us some kind of clue about what she was doing and why."

"If you say so. I had an ex who was big into taxidermy and I promised myself I would never march past that red flag again."

I smirked, not able to generate much more than a laugh as I scanned the ground floor space. Beneath the steel grate, something was shimmering and I clenched Lance's arm. He followed my gaze, posture tense before he relaxed. He grabbed one of the mice bones I had left behind and dropped it through the gap. There was a soft splash and I felt the droplet hit the soles of my feet.

"Water," he said, sounding impressed as he crouched down and lifted off a portion of the floor. "It's flowing, look. It must run below the museum and connect with one of the rivers. Explains the cold."

"Explains the power," I replied, looking around the space with new eyes.

"How exactly?"

"The facility we ran Project Gladiator out of was next to a swamp in Florida," I explained. "Ill-advised for swimming, but she chose it specifically because she could utilize hydropower to cut down energy and electricity demands on our already overrun grid."

I pointed out various mechanisms to Lance, cords and cables and connectors.

"Extra clever here," he noted. "You run no risk of surging, you're completely separate to the building's power, an unusual bill is not how you're going to be found out."

I checked my watch, noting that we'd been down here for five minutes already. We were tight on time. We worked as a team, quickly going over the space to make sure we hadn't missed anything that could be useful. It seemed as if she'd taken most of it with her, the work bench largely clear except for dirty beakers and half-empty bottles of chemicals you could buy anywhere. Moving up to the middle level, it had a whiteboard that wrapped around the lab in a curling shape. Whatever had been scrawled on there was now rubbed out. Rather hastily, mind you. I could make out a few symbols in the top righthand corner where it would have been hardest for her to reach.

"I checked the desk, the drawers, filing cabinets and everything but there's no paperwork left," Lance said.

"Alcohol."

"Yeah, I could kill for a Negroni Sbagliato."

"No," I sighed, "isopropyl alcohol. Take pictures of everything here, I'll be right back."

I could hear Lance spluttering a response behind me, but I also could hear him doing exactly as I asked and taking the shots as I raced downstairs. On the ground level of the lab, I searched among the remnants of supplies that had been left, eyes lighting up as I found the bottle and grabbed the roll of paper towels. Lance lowered his phone as I returned, eyeing what was in my hands.

"What…"

"It's an old trick," I said. "To try and get an overused whiteboard clean, like *really* clean, professors would scrub it down with toothpaste because the erasers are only good for so long."

"Oh-kay."

"It doesn't really work, at least not as good as isopropyl alcohol of more than ninety per cent."

I showed him the label on the bottle, but he was still confused. "So, what? We're gonna do her spring cleaning for her?"

"She didn't have time to erase everything properly, look. In the corners her work is still there, which means the chemicals in the marker are still on the surface enough that when they react to contact with this–"

I wiggled the bottle for emphasis.

"–they appear like the negative of a photograph for a few seconds, before disappearing forever."

His eyes widened. Now he got it. Lance raised his phone, camera ready to go as I unscrewed the bottle. There wasn't as much fluid left as I would like, but it would have to do. I moved slowly, pouring it from the top of the whiteboard and working my way around the arching space until I was back where it started. I let gravity do the work for me, the alcohol dripping down in inconsistent streaks. There was still a bit left and I spat into the bottle, mixing my own saliva with the remaining droplets as I shook it and then started splashing all of the dry patches on the board. The audible clicking of Lance's phone was going off, firing every two seconds as Dr Calvin's work illuminated in an almost neon blue around us. My pocket vibrated and I looked down, seeing a text from Tem.

"Wherever the hell you are, hurry up," it read. "I'm stalling but we're heading up the levels now."

"We've gotta go," I told Lance.

"It's already fading anyway," he replied. "This is everything we're gonna get."

I tossed the bottle and we jogged up the final staircase, my eyes level with his boots as we ascended straight up and through the middle of her lab. Propping my shoulder against the door, I retrieved my pumps and listened while slipping one foot in at a time. I nodded and we crept forward, back out into the gallery, and sealed the hidden laboratory behind us. I could see the curator and Tem's backs across the other side of the platform, and I hurried to press the cabinet closed as gently as possible.

"Ah, there you are," the curator chirped, the rustle of her voluminous skirts heralding her arrival. "I see you found one of our pride and joys."

Lance beamed. "Absolutely! I love–"

I watched his eyes dart sideways to one of the labels.

"–Japanese Noh masks. These are from the Kongo Noh School, yes?"

"That's right! We have one of the biggest collections in the world – some fifty-two!"

"Wow," Lance breathed, bending closer to the glass to inspect. Tem widened his eyes at me over the woman's shoulder and I winked. I could see the faintest shadow of relief slump into his shoulders. Thanks to Lance's ability to make small talk with seemingly anyone, I didn't have to add much to the conversation as the curator walked us out.

"That represents a total of over a hundred hours of conservation work, the one conservator did it all," she explained. "She said some masks took forty-five minutes, others took upwards of twenty hours."

"Incredible," Lance replied, so believably I thought he might actually be interested. "Listen, thank you so much for having us here tonight. I know we were just the hangers-on, but we learnt so much inside your four walls."

I smirked, nodding in agreement while Tem shook the curator's hand.

"Tēnā koe," he said, bending low to make eye contact. "It really meant so much to me."

"Absolutely, any time." She beamed.

We made our way back through the connecting buildings, the cluster of students growing more frequent as we trekked closer to the center of the university.

"You know," Tem said. "It really did mean so much to me."

I looked across at him, visibly able to see that he was being truthful, and I gave his hand a squeeze.

"I'm glad," I replied.

"And I'm glad," Lance began, about to say something that I'm sure would ruin the moment, "that we were able to get what we were looking for without having to spend the rest of the night running for our lives."

Huh. That wasn't as bad as I was expecting. The three of us were side by side, gold columns stretching up next to us as we headed toward a connecting hallway that seemed to stretch on forever because of the mirrored walls. We looked like off-brand Powerpuff Girls as I examined our reflections, Lance in burgundy and me in navy, both of us bookending the much taller Tem in the middle in his glorious green suit.

"And looked hella good doing it," I noted, earning a laugh from Tem and a cocky "yup" from Lance.

CHAPTER TWELVE

Much as I would have loved to call it a night there, it was impossible. We had a real lead and limited time to capitalize on it for once, instead of feeling like we were always playing catch up to whoever our mystery adversaries were at any one moment. Plus, S.T.R.I.K.E. was particularly sensitive about any time Tem spent away from the office and in the field: the most obvious sign that even at twenty-two years old, he was a valued asset.

First, we ate dinner. It sounds superfluous and silly, but it was actually critical. Oxford was overflowing with enemies we couldn't keep track of and every time we did something visibly public – like visit Pitt Rivers Museum – there was a chance we popped up on someone's radar. And if we were being monitored, then our cover would hold. So we took our visiting friend from out of town to a local landmark, according to Lance.

"Really?" I muttered under my breath. "Cause this just looks like a bike shop."

"It's The Handle Bar, thank you very much," he replied,

gently elbowing me. He conferred with one of the staff, who led us to a table for three that was positioned precariously under a penny-farthing hung from the ceiling. In fact, all manner of bikes from all manner of eras were displayed about the place, with tables tucked among them and a cute little vase of fresh flowers at the center of each one. A soundtrack of ice cubes smashing against chrome came from behind a corrugated iron bar that was whipping up cocktails. Strategically placed lights fitted into exposed beams gave the whole venue an intentional but subtle kind of ambience. I was so busy looking around that by the time I was done, Lance had taken the liberty to order for all three of us.

"I love this place," Tem said excitedly, tapping his hands on the table with glee as a trio of enormous cocktails arrived in front of us.

"Three Smokey Handles," the waiter said with a flourish.

Tem leaned in, about to take a sip from the tropical-looking drink when he paused. "Wait, what's in this?"

Lance had already slurped down half of his and was crunching an ice cube between his teeth. "Mezcal, pineapple juice, tequila, fresh lime, aperol and sugar. Lotta sugar. Bobbi has a sweet tooth."

I tilted my head, intrigued. How'd he know that? He gave me a wink.

"It's unprofessional to drink on assignment, right?" Tem asked, nervous.

Lance and I didn't even need to look at each other before we burst out laughing.

"Unprofessional?" I asked, wiping away a tear from under my eye. "Some would say it's absolutely required."

"Absolutely," Lance agreed, clinking his glass against mine.

An array of plates started arriving almost immediately and I didn't realize how hungry I was until I surveyed the mix of tapas that left very little room on the table for anything else. The others were clearly just as starved as I was, digging in without hesitation as we made our way through a variety of small plates.

"Try this," Lance said, sliding two skewered meats on to my dish. "Korean spiced lamb lollipops, garnished with pickled watermelon and gochujang mayo. Best thing on the menu."

I groaned in agreement, the meat juicy and packed with flavor as I tried to take semi-human bites and not just annihilate the whole thing. He looked as pleased with my reaction as if he'd made it himself.

"Does that make up for the BMX above your head?" he teased.

"Maybe," I replied, wiping my mouth.

"Worst accident I ever had was on a BMX," Tem said. "Broke both my wrists."

"That's nothing," Lance responded, holding up his wrist and pulling back his cuff to reveal a long scar. "Had to fight this Wolverine wannabe once who stabbed me with a fork. A fork! Let me tell ya, you never want to see your radius outside your body."

"Now did that require a metal plate?" Tem asked, not horrified at all as he leaned forward with interest.

"Two!" Lance said, swallowing a cabbage parcel. "What about you, Bob? Worst injury on the job?"

"My marriage."

I replied so fast I didn't think about it. Tem was in the process of finishing his cocktail and choked on a sip. Lance looked like he was holding in a laugh, his dimples twitching with the restraint.

"Worst injury on the job…" I said, musing.

"You've been in a coma a few times," Lance offered, revealing just how closely he had read my file. Probably re-read it, too.

"Eh, who hasn't?" I shrugged. "Besides, you never remember that."

"That's due to a serious brain injury," Tem mumbled, looking around. "Where's the bathroom in this place?"

"I daresay hidden behind a tricycle," I replied, while Lance pointed in a direction that was actually helpful. Tem excused himself and we were left alone, the small space of the venue actually being felt for the first time as I realized how close we were. Our shoulders were touching, our knees brushing against each other under the table, none of it even registering in my psyche until now because it had felt so… comfortable. *Easy,* Jen's voice said in my head. The silence felt loaded and I struggled to fill it, playing with the wooden kebab sticks left on my plate instead.

"Oh, I know!"

Lance looked like he had been about to say something, but my exclamation cut him off. "Perforated ear drum and a broken jaw."

He looked unimpressed. "That doesn't seem that bad."

"You wouldn't say that if you'd had either, let alone both. I got hit in the side of the face with debris after a bomb went off. The pain was so unbearable, it was like it was right in my skull and there was no way to make it stop. You just had to ride it out."

"Which side?"

"Left," I replied, stilling as he reached up. He brushed a strand of hair back behind my ear slowly, as if inspecting the damage. My breath caught as his fingers slowly trailed down the side of my face, following the path of my jawline. We were so close together. Too close. Yet I was frozen, unable to move as his gaze finally met mine, our faces only inches apart. A chorus of happy birthday across the other side of the restaurant snapped me out of it and I straightened up, Lance withdrawing his hand almost reluctantly. Tem had been returning from the bathroom and halted where he stood, watching us, and he quickly pretended like nothing had happened. *Because nothing had happened,* I told myself. If I could have imagined my consciousness, she was swiveling around in a chair right now and giving me a look that said "girl". I was a spy, it was often my job to lie to others, and I used to be able to convincingly lie to myself. Not quite sure when I lost that.

"What's the time?" Tem asked, awkwardly retaking his seat.

"Almost time for night shift," I said, watching his eyes light up.

Lance smiled, but it felt strained to me. He called for the check.

The hospital was only a short, ten-minute walk and we stopped in a public restroom to get changed into boring black slacks, a white blouse and black overcoat for Lance and I, scrubs for Tem. He required an additional few minutes to disguise himself as he removed his hat, fingers working expertly to pull his long hair back into a perfect braid. I got to work on his face, covering his moko with concealer while Lance decked him out with all the flourishes: stethoscope around his neck, monogrammed white coat over his body, ID pass affixed to his top pocket. When we were done, sadly none of the things that made Tem stand out remained, which was of course entirely the point. If someone was asked, he'd be remembered as just another tall, young, aspiring doctor completing his internship.

"Don't be nervous," I said, noting how incredibly nervous he looked. "You just follow Lance and I in, where we go, you go. Before you know it, you'll be in your happy place: the morgue."

"I'm just really bad at lying," he said.

"You were great at the museum!"

"That wasn't a lie, though. I really did want to see Mākereti Papakura's work."

"And you really are a doctor," I repeated, trying to psych him up. "Dr Temuera Waa. Med student. Seeker of knowledge."

"If things go according to plan, you won't even have to open your mouth once," Lance added, patting him on the shoulder.

"Really? Because if it comes down to it, I can do a Russian acc–"

"No Russian!" Lance and I said in unison.

I shot him an amused look. "The simpler, the better. You've got this. We've got this."

Both Lance and I knew that wasn't for certain. Nothing was in this business. The important thing was that if Tem believed that, he'd project that same energy as we stepped through the staff entrance to the hospital. The idea was that Lance and I were supposed to look like cops, heading to the morgue and being accompanied by a junior doctor, which was a perfectly normal thing to be doing. Lance nodded at a security guard passing us and the woman nodded back, nonchalant, while we pressed on through a set of sliding glass doors. I scrutinized my cover up job on Tem under the fluorescent lights, but it looked passable as we took the emergency stairs down to the basement level. The route we had chosen had minimal exposure to security cameras and avoiding the elevators was a crucial part of that. The morgue was just like any other, this part of a hospital always avoided by those who had an option to be elsewhere.

Night shift was just about to start, so we had a thirty-minute window between one coroner and morgue attendant finishing and the other duo starting. All we had to do was look like we were meant to be there as Lance pushed open the metallic swinging doors and led us inside. You never quite got used to the smell, not of death per se but of disinfectant so sharp and strong, it stung your nostrils. I always associated one with the other now. Lance took position at the entrance, guarding and keeping an eye out. Tem headed straight for the sink, washing his hands and pulling on his gloves. I made a beeline for the freezer, scanning the name written on the outside of each metallic square as I looked for the dean.

"There you are," I muttered, crouching down. He'd been stacked near the bottom and with a heave, I tugged open the door. Hit with a blast of cool air, I slowly pulled the handle of the steel tray his corpse was placed on. There was no point moving the body, we didn't have time, so whatever examination Tem was going to do had to be done right where he was.

"Ugh," Lance said, watching us over his shoulder.

"I didn't pick you as squeamish," I chided.

"Not squeamish," he corrected. "Just didn't wanna see the dean naked."

"Ah yes, all those famously clothed autopsies," Tem muttered, joining me beside the dead man. He had a clipboard in hand, flipping pages as he read the report.

"What's the cause of death?" I asked.

Tem's brow was furrowed. "Suffocation."

"In a bath?"

"They found no water in his lungs, meaning he was already dead before he went under but there's no signs of foul play so… suffocation. Possible heart attack. Says here he was found only ten minutes after his estimated time of death."

I examined his fingertips, which were blackish blue but also pruned enough that it would indicate he'd been in the water for a while before he croaked. Tem grabbed a pair of pliers, working as quickly as could be warranted as he removed the staples in the man's chest from the previous autopsy. I knew exactly where he'd start and I watched as he inspected the chest cavity.

"Any signs of trauma to the heart?"

"None."

"What about a stroke?"

"No bleeding on the brain either, unless it was a TIA – a transient ischemic attack – and the damage didn't fully show up."

"For the record," Lance called over to us, "you do *not* have time to crack open a skull, Tem."

"Technically someone else already did that for me," he said under his breath.

"Any weird bruises?" Lance offered.

"Any bruise can be weird post-mortem," I responded. "A seemingly normal bruise while you're alive can manifest horrifically in death because of blood flow."

Even so, I checked all the usual places that might show signs of a murder meant to look like an accidental death. His neck was stiff, and it took a sickening crack to tilt it back, Lance visibly shuddering as I examined under the man's chins. Nothing unusual. No ligature marks or signs of forced choking. I checked his shoulders and chest thoroughly, too, places that could have been used to hold him down under the surface once he was unconscious. Clear. No bruises, no hand marks, no impressions.

"Hold up," Tem said, leaning forward as I went to move the neck back into place.

"You see something?"

"I don't know," he murmured, turning away to grab a cotton swab. "It looks like there's fluid in his nose."

"Embalming fluid?"

"Maybe," Tem responded. I watched as he inserted the swab into the dean's nasal cavity, wiggling it around to grab the most amount of sample possible.

"Ten minutes," Lance called. "But we should be gone in five if we don't wanna push it."

Tem held the end up to the light, eyes narrowing at the sticky wetness there. I took the clipboard, leaving him with an additional hand to bag the sample. I snapped images of the report and returned it to where it had been found. Tem cleaned up, I slid the body back into the freezer, and we did a quick once-over of the space by examining where everything had been via an image I had snapped when we first entered. It aligned.

"Let's jet," Lance ordered.

We marched in the direction we'd come, the *ping* of the elevator echoing just as we neared it. We broke into a swift dash, darting past the doors and to the stairwell as the sound of air whooshing heralded their opening. I caught the handle, holding it *almost* shut so it didn't slam behind us and give away our presence. Backs pressed to the white walls, puffing, we listened to the idle chatter of the next shift as they switched out. The voices grew quieter and quieter before disappearing into the morgue itself and our trio let out a collective sigh of relief.

Once we were out of the hospital, we split up to take roundabout routes back to the houseboat. Lance went with Tem on foot, whereas I jumped on one of the dozens of bikes for hire that were littered around the city. It was nice to decompress as I cycled, looping around the university precinct before joining the crowd on wheels who were following behind each other like a line of ants. The bike path ran parallel to the River Cherwell and I pedaled around joggers just like they had me when I used this track on my first morning in Oxford. In an ideal scenario, I'd have headphones in my ears just like every other carefree adult cyclist on this track. Yet I wanted to utilize every sense I could, just in case, and hearing a gun shot in the distance could mean the difference between me getting clipped or taken out completely.

In lieu of music, I had my thoughts and a space where they couldn't be avoided anymore. There were a series of things bothering me and on their own, they were small. Yet together... I pondered the keys Dr Calvin had sewn into her lab coat and the secret labs they opened. I thought about the magnetized schematics she'd hidden. Even Lance spotting the mechanism she'd used to power the Pitt Rivers workspace and keep the siphoned electricity off the grid. It was sneaky. All of these things were sneaky. The Dr Calvin I knew had been an open book. She wasn't sneaky. Where had she learned that skill? With a start, I realized exactly who had been the educational model. She learned it from me. From us. From S.H.I.E.L.D.

It was an uneventful ride, and I was grateful, because it felt like there was enough going on inside my head. When I dismounted the bike and left it at one of the allocated stations, I could already see the lights on inside, so I knew the boys had beaten me. Mounting the dock, a motion sensor beeped to alert those onboard to my presence. Lance stuck his head out and beamed at me as I joined them.

"So glad you're here," he said, extending a hand which I took for balance I didn't need. "I just found your pseudonym playlist."

"*Your* pseudonym playlist, to be precise," I corrected. The closing chords of a Janet Kay song were fading as I joined them.

"Whatever. I added some others."

"Excuse you."

"Trust me, you'll like this one." He paused dramatically as a woman's very British, very London accent made a statement about little girls being seen and not heard. The second she finished, raw guitars shredded through the speakers and – most surprisingly – an accompanying saxophone.

"*Oh bondage, up yours!*" Lance sang, doing an atrocious air guitar accompaniment. "*Oh bondage, no mooore!*"

Tem had his face buried behind his hands, laughing. Breathless, Lance bounced toward me. The grin that I felt spreading across my face was unavoidable. He looked like an idiot, and he absolutely couldn't care less so long as Tem and I were tickled. A warmth flared in my chest for a brief beat.

"What do ya think?" Lance puffed.

"I love it," I giggled. "Despite your best attempts, it rips."

He pumped a fist triumphantly. "Knew it. The one American with taste."

I flopped into the seat next to Tem, slowly beginning to unpack items of note. "Who is this anyway?"

"X-Ray Spex," he replied, turning the volume down to a manageable standard. "The proto-British punk band with a proto-punk hit."

"I'm so glad I gave you collaborator permissions then." I smiled, turning to Tem. "Mouse bones."

"Um, thanks?"

"I don't have the equipment to analyze them properly, but when you head back take them with you? Obviously these specimens were failures but–"

"It could still tell us what she was trying to do," he said, finishing my thought exactly.

"Bang on."

It was late, but we would lose Tem in the morning on the train back to London so neither of us wanted to waste any additional brain power while we had it. Lance got to making coffee, I got to spreading out everything of value on the table. Tem sourced the interrogation video of the A.I.M. agents. Radcliffe did the interrogation himself, so I was conscious not to criticize as I was uncertain about his and Tem's relationship. But it was hard. His style was seemingly to bore them – and us – to death. By the end of the forty-five minutes' worth of footage, there was little there that we didn't already know except for the fact they weren't anywhere near the dean's residence at the time of his death. They hadn't even arrived in Oxford yet. We'd gotten lucky or unlucky, depending on your perspective, by running into them during their first active foray. I fiddled with my coffee mug, revising everything we had so far with the others.

"After years trying to claw back her career, Dr Wilma Calvin finally gets a plum posting at Oxford University in a field she's a world leader in," I began. "Then she vanishes against her will."

"That's an assumption," Lance said. "I don't think ruling out the possibility that she voluntarily vanished is wise."

Hearing him voice my own internal worries caused a frown to settle on my expression. I held my tongue, not quite ready to admit that he might be right. Thankfully, Tem came to my unknown rescue.

"Maybe," Tem mused. "But this is an impossible job to get. I can't imagine she'd leave an opportunity as rare as this."

"And second chances are even rarer," I said. "Voluntarily or not, she disappears, but it's made to look like she's attending to family matters so the police, S.T.R.I.K.E., S.H.I.E.L.D., are all none the wiser for as long as possible. Except we're on to it straightaway and so are you guys."

"We were on to it first," Lance murmured, taking a diplomatic sip.

"*Wut-evah*," I replied, in my best impersonation of him. "The time that bought with the cops has probably run out now after they investigated the break in at her cottage."

Lance grimaced. "Whoops."

"And now they cannot get hold of her."

I let the chain of events hang in the air for a moment, giving everyone an opportunity to ask a question or raise a point I'd missed. When they didn't, I pressed on.

"Rewind," I said. "Before all of that, Dr Calvin begins working on a project in secret. It's not something she wants the university to know about."

"But it's likely she had help from someone at the university or at minimum, they had knowledge of her activities," Lance added. I didn't follow.

"Why?" I asked.

"The location of the first lab, for starters. Everything is being done and woven into the tapestry of Oxford."

"You think the dean was helping her?" Tem questioned.

"Or forcing her," I countered. "So she makes blueprints for three hidden labs–"

"Four," Lance interjected. "Sorry, not to interrupt but four labs total. Three hidden. Her laboratory at the university was destroyed, so I think it's safe to say it was being used as well. The others may still exist because whoever else is searching for them hasn't found them yet."

"Right." I nodded, liking the way he was thinking and getting into the groove of it. "She has custom labs created, hides the plans in her attic, hides the keys in her lab coat, and continues her work in secret until…"

"I show up," Lance says, starting a list. "You show up. Someone else shows up minutes before us, destroys the lab or finds whatever they were looking for in it. FiveFourThree Solutions shows up. A.I.M. shows up. The dean is murdered, *allegedly*. We uncover the first hidden lab, leftover experiments performed on mice, and whatever formulas she had on that board."

"What formulas?" Tem asked.

"On the whiteboard in her lab," I said hurriedly. "Don't worry about it. I can handle that aspect, you just concentrate on the model systems and dead man's snot."

I felt Lance's eyes on me, but I didn't meet his gaze.

"Did you get anything from the goo glitter bomb?" he questioned.

"Lance," I scoffed, half-appalled, half-amused.

"Oh, I'm sorry. Is science slime more acceptable to you?"

"Nothing yet," Tem responded. "I'm working on it, but I'm also working on it around every other analysis I have to perform on every other stupid assignment that's not this one."

The way he huffed made me think he wasn't playing favorites because he liked Lance and I the most – obvs – but this was his favorite assignment because it was the most interesting. I reached into my bag, tossing him a packet of make-up wipes so he could remove the concealer I'd caked onto his face.

"Is there something we can do about that?" I asked, eyes darting to Lance. "Ask for this case to become Tem's number one priority?"

He looked strained. "I think I might have played every card I have when it comes to that particular hand. Getting him here was the last favor I had banked. It *might* sound better if there's a request from an adverse ally."

A smirk twitched into place. "Oh, reeeeeally?"

"A suggestion that S.H.I.E.L.D. scientists could be flown over to assist if this case wasn't a priority, well... that would certainly force them to assign *someone* to it full time."

He was jerking his head at Tem so aggressively I was worried for the state of his neck muscles.

"I'll call Hill." I smiled, getting to my feet. Stepping out onto the back deck and closing the door behind me, I let out a long exhale. I was a list maker. I liked to know what I had completed and what was left to be done. I had joked before about the comas, but the truth was my brain didn't work like it used to. In some capacities, it worked even better: I had incredible recall and an ability to hyperfocus on tasks. In others, I could forget little things – things I never would have previously. My mother had always been opposed to the idea of me working at S.H.I.E.L.D. and I was partially grateful that she never had the chance to see me actually hurt in the line of duty. It had been during my first rehabilitation that I was encouraged to use the idea of lists, written or mental.

"No point crying over milk you don't even have to spill," he'd said, in one of those bizarre comments that were so distinctly him but also so distinctly profound the more you thought on it. "Take the strain away from your head, write it down or verbalize it, then you have one less thing to occupy that impressive noggin.'"

He'd weakened the point by tapping on my head like it was hollow, as I'd sat there in the hospital bed fuming. Listening to Hill's dial tone, I already felt better addressing where we'd been, where we were at, and where we were left to go. There were two labs left to locate. Results to wait on. Enemies to duck. And the thing I was most reluctant to do: scrutinize formulas that had defined so much of my past.

CHAPTER THIRTEEN

The second Tem left, the sky fell apart. Quite literally. We had barely made it back after taking him to the train station when the air rumbled above us, the gray clouds swirling into black as if they wanted extra attention. By the time we stepped foot onto the houseboat, hard rain quickly transitioned to hail in an attempt from nature to do the absolute *most*.

"I don't want to even voice this," I said, half-yelling so Lance could hear me over the storm. "But how much damage can this old girl take?"

"Don't you worry about *Linda*!" he shouted back. "She's a tough, blousy broad."

He tried to casually lean against one of the kitchen cabinets to illustrate his point. Unfortunately, his weight was more than it could take and a handle snapped off with a hollow *crick*. The golf balls of ice didn't last long, thankfully, growing smaller and smaller as the minutes ticked by. From the back deck, I watched them splash into the river at a rapid *plop plop plop* until it transitioned into a steady but heavy downpour.

"See?" Lance said, approaching from behind me. "Nothing to worry about."

He threw a crochet blanket over my shoulders, clearly having watched me shiver through the oversized knit I was wearing and making a choice not to tease me about it. A mercy, really.

"You named the boat *Linda*?" I asked, smiling as he blew warm breath onto his own hands. Aha, so I wasn't the only one who found it freezing today!

"It already has a name," he noted. "But it's half underwater, half peeling off at the front so the only letters I could make out were L, N, and A."

"*Linda* it is."

"*The Lindas want you to open the dwoar*," he quoted, giving a Boston accent his best shot. I laughed at how bad it was, Lance following me inside as I stared down at the devices in front of me. Laptop, print-outs of the whiteboard, the dried papers from her office, even an old notebook of mine I'd maintained during Project Gladiator. I sighed deeply, and picked up a pair of S.H.I.E.L.D. handcuffs Lance had been trying to teach me to break out of the same way he had. It had become my Rubik's Cube and I started fiddling with them.

"The longer you put it off…" he murmured.

"I know, I know."

"What are you so scared of finding in there?"

Something I already knew in my gut. I didn't say that, though. I just tightened the blanket around my shoulders.

"Aight." He stirred, clapping his hands together. "It's bloody Baltic out, so we're not going anywhere today."

"Oh, you're making a call for both of us, are you?"

"Yup." He nodded, the set of his chin stubborn. "You're

gonna park yaself in that corner window seat, the best lit and comfiest on board, do your science thing until it's done."

"My science thing," I muttered, incredulous.

"I'm gonna crank the heat so your sensitive California girl temperature gauge doesn't frost over. A cup of tea will be made. Snacks will be placed. And we don't do anything of physical consequence until tomorrow."

I really, really liked the sound of that. "And you?"

"I've got two more keys to find labs for," he replied, gesturing to a stack of books on the counter that looked oddly familiar.

"Lance, did you steal books from the library?"

"No! I borrowed them... for a prolonged period."

I shook my head in disbelief, having no idea when he had managed to smuggle what had to easily be a few pounds' worth of literature out of Radcliffe Camera while I was none the wiser. He had shifty skills they didn't teach you in the academy.

"I've got something else you could take off my plate," I offered.

He looked surprised at that, an admission that I needed help. He couldn't realize how much just yet.

"Of course," he replied, eager. "Anything."

I had the list ready to go and handed it over to him. "See if any of the names here are listed as financiers of Dr Calvin's research at Oxford. Or anywhere, really. Did they sponsor an event she appeared at? Pay a speaking fee? We're looking for a connection, big or small."

"All right," he murmured. I could see the question in his eyes, a few of them actually, but he didn't press. He was willing to trust me. I held out my fist and he bumped it, our non-verbal way to agree that we had a deal. Bundled up like a burrito, I settled in and opened my laptop. Negotiating my way through my own thesis files, I opened the ones I thought would be relevant and diverted back to the print-outs from the lab at Pitt Rivers Museum.

I thought I recognized Dr Calvin's handwriting, but it had also been ten years since I worked with the woman and it paid to be certain. Thankfully, I had examples to consult in a series of images taken from a happier time. I couldn't remember who it was that had taken these, but a cluster of a dozen images catalogued scenes in the lab from when we had been running those initial tests. It was someone from S.H.I.E.L.D., but that's all I could recall. Dr Calvin was beaming, her fervor almost leaping off the screen as she looked up at the man towering next to her: Professor Theodore Sallis. We all called him Ted. He was tall and dark and handsome and carried himself in a way that always made me think of Christopher Reeve for some reason. There was a classic classiness to him.

And then there was me, working under them both. They were the project leads and I was the laboratory assistant, perfectly placed to balance duties as a scientist with Dr Calvin, my PhD supervisor at the time, and duties as an agent of S.H.I.E.L.D. Standing behind the two of them, holding a binder packed to the brim, nineteen-year-old me looked like she was way out of her depth. I was, not just because of the curtain bangs I told myself I could pull off in the Florida heat or the Seventies frames that I was sure would make an eyewear comeback. I didn't think I knew everything back then, but I wholeheartedly believed I could. I was an earnest and enthusiastic sponge desperate to soak up knowledge.

Pulling my eyes away from my younger self and the professional friendships that were all about to fracture, I zoomed in on the whiteboards behind us, enhancing the image so I could see the work clearly. It was easy to tell whose side of the board was whose, with Dr Calvin and Ted sharing space harmoniously. I searched for the small foot ladder at the edge of the frame, its positioning telling me the left whiteboard was Dr Calvin's. At a glance, the handwriting looked not just similar but identical. Although someone's handwriting would change over the years, the movements in which we communicated didn't. The shape of her sevens were the first thing that leapt out, the angle extra sharp and precise as she drew in one swift movement. I compared her k's, the next obvious letter, which were done in two movements, and even her division symbol was specific. The dots on either side of the line were not circular, they were like slashes that I knew came from the feverish pace at which she worked.

"Here."

Lance's voice pulled me out of the past and I looked up to find a steaming cup of tea placed in front of me along with two cookies.

"Have a cuppa and a Hobnob," he said.

"What did you call me?"

"The biscuit," he cackled before disappearing down the hall. Soon, I could hear music playing from what I was now thinking of as our playlist. The Cure became my soundtrack as I munched and sipped, a fan of biscuits and a growing fan of the tea. I could never let him know either fact, I thought stubbornly.

With so much of Abraham Erskine's original research destroyed and corrupted, Dr Calvin's mission – as assigned by S.H.I.E.L.D. – had been to not only recreate the Super Soldier Serum of her predecessor, but to make it more compatible with the human body. With the exceptions of Steve Rogers and Isaiah Bradley, the results had been so varied and unpredictable on other human subjects. A formula was half of the goal, a consistent and stable formula being the true aim. She had been making progress toward both during my time, but it was a lot of pressure: pressure she ultimately couldn't handle. As I re-examined the formulas, I felt a pain in my chest. Switching between the photos, my notes, and the screen, it was immeasurably hard to see a recipe of your own failures outlined right before your very eyes. Mine. Hers. Ted's.

It began with manipulating small parts of human biology. Once that was achieved successfully, then you moved on to the next cell and the next and the next, stacking them on top of each other like a deck of cards formulated out of DNA. The problem had been each time we moved on to the next stage, say enhancing body mass or improving endurance, the previous stages had to stabilize as well. We'd get four elements figured out, then the fifth would corrupt the second. You'd need to go back and figure out why, and once you tweaked that, then the third would shift and onward into infinity.

"It's scientific snakes and ladders," I had said at the time, hunched over a series of test results with frustration. Ted's laugh was always like a sonic boom, his demeanor serious from the outside but his secret super-power being levity. No matter the roadblocks, the challenges, he was a relentlessly and annoyingly positive problem solver. That feeling in my chest tightened further and I leaned back, closing my eyes against the sensation.

"Bobbi?" Ted asked. Except it wasn't Ted.

"Bob?" Lance's hand on my shoulder snapped me back to the boat, the now, the present. "Are you all right?"

"I'm fine," I said, angrily wiping a tear from the corner of my eye that betrayed my verbalized sentiment.

"Oh, OK." He shrugged. "You just looked incredibly upset crying in the corner but hey, what do I know?"

I laughed. "Get stuffed."

"It's what all the girls say," he said, sliding in next to me with something in his hands.

"Did... did you make a charcuterie board?"

"Yeah, don't worry about it," Lance mumbled, placing it down. "Little bit of pâté, some quince paste, few cold cuts, some soft and smelly cheeses."

"Yum," I replied, my mouth watering as I reached for a slice of salami artfully positioned into the shape of a rose. He swiftly slid the plate out of reach. "What the heck?"

"Talk to me," he cautioned. "And then I'll give you a sliver of double truffle brie."

I groaned. That sounded so good, minus the talking part. "You're bribing me with food."

"Correct."

I let out a long, uneven breath.

"I know you didn't want Tem to look at what we found on the whiteboards in the lab. And those companies you had me look up? Cadenza Industries was on that list."

I was quiet.

"They're tied to A.I.M., aren't they? All of them."

I nodded. "They were from a friend of mine who has more experience dealing with them than I do, but I wanted you to look at them because..."

"Why?" he asked, voice gentle. "Why not just tell me what I was looking for?"

"Because Dr Calvin has made mistakes in the past and I didn't want you to judge her. So have I and I didn't want you to judge me."

"The past is the past," Lance huffed. "It shapes us, but it doesn't make us. None of those companies came anywhere close to her work, by the way. There are no A.I.M. connections."

"Good," I said, sighing with relief. "I... I was worried I couldn't be objective enough."

"But you trusted me to be?"

He ran a hand through his hair, frustrated but not giving up. There was understanding there as he saw the truth in my eyes.

"Don't tell a soul cos my job would be on the line, but whatever you say doesn't leave *Linda*. You can trust me, Bobbi."

"I don't know if that's true," I murmured.

"Why?" he questioned, looking offended.

"You're easy to like and that's..."

"Annoying?"

"Scary."

He held my gaze, unflinching, and I returned it. I could do it, I could just lean across and grab him, kiss him like I wanted to, and leave the truth somewhere that was else. Distract us both.

"Why would you say that to me?" Lance asked, voice soft as if he knew exactly what I was thinking and was trying to resist the urge to do the same.

"Because you're not gonna like me much after this story."

His fingers nudged mine, just a pinkie, slipping between digits and grasping my own. A tiny but significant sign of support. *Drink some cement.* I gently pulled my hand away, using it to bring up the old photos that had been so painful.

"Whoa," he said, eyes widened as he immediately clocked a younger version of me in the frame. "Look at you! Baby bombshell!"

I whacked his shoulder, smiling, and steeled myself. "Director Fury commissioned Project Gladiator over a decade ago now. The intent was to recreate Super Soldier Serum, with Dr Wilma Calvin and her right-hand man Professor Theodore 'Ted' Sallis the project leads. They worked on various S.H.I.E.L.D. contracts over the years so had the clearance and experience. I was appointed as the lab assistant because I already had a relationship with Dr Calvin as I got ready to defend my thesis–"

"And you'd been recruited by S.H.I.E.L.D.," Lance acknowledged. "The perfect gal on the inside."

I nodded. "Technically I was still in training at the academy, but I thought this could be my Agent Starling moment, you know? They knew, of course, that was the whole point, having someone present whose allegiances were perfectly balanced. At least to start. The first year we made steady, gradual progress with our model systems, but Dr Calvin didn't think things were moving fast enough."

"Model systems?" Lance quizzed.

"Mice and rats we used to test the formula as it moved through each progression. This was the kind of project that wouldn't just make someone's career, they'd go down in history, and I started to sense that was weighing on her, and on Ted. They were in an evolving relationship personally and professionally, but it was fracturing, like everything else. One day I came in and the vermin had been replaced with pigs."

Lance handed me a cracker loaded with cheese. A carrot dangled. I accepted, munching, swallowing, then continuing.

"Pigs are closer test subjects to humans because we shared a common ancestor millions of years ago, genome similarities, you know?"

"No."

I smiled. "It meant that she was moving in that direction faster than I thought was wise," I said. "Or ethical. I raised my concerns, but both she and Ted disagreed and ultimately they had veto power. It was tough, it wasn't going well, and I... I snitched."

"Snitched?"

I hated that word but there was no other. "Officially. I flagged it with S.H.I.E.L.D. in my weekly report and they paused the whole project. Dr Calvin was furious, she knew the information had come from me. She said I'd gone behind their backs, betrayed their trust and betrayed science, all so I could wear a cape."

"Ouch."

"She said she was ready for human trials in a month and now that was ruined while Project Gladiator was on ice. I'd successfully defended my thesis by that point, but Ted threatened to retract his and her support. Publicly."

It was easy to remember exactly how that felt at the time. Panic. I was panicked and emotional and upset by the confrontation, something I'd had little experience with until that point. I was the good girl, the one who sat idly by, listened and learned while my parents yelled at each other. It had felt similar to their divorce in a way, finding myself wedged between two parties: science on one side, S.H.I.E.L.D. on the other. The subject of kids had always been a sensitive one between Clint and I. He wanted a brood. I didn't. He called me selfish and career-focused, but it was a moot point. I think we both thought the other would come around to the opposite point of view, yet I was never going to yield. Aspirational posters be damned, I knew the reality.

Men could, but women couldn't have it all. I couldn't have the career I wanted, the relationship I wanted, and have a kid, let alone several. And the whisper at the back of my mind adding to it all was I never wanted a child of mine to feel the way I had: like they had to choose.

"Project Gladiator wasn't just put on ice," I continued. "My remarks had raised several red flags and while it was paused, S.H.I.E.L.D. started to look more closely at Dr Calvin's own reports. She had been fudging data. Getting to the same solution, but blurring all of the work to get there so it appeared that they were further along than they were."

"Why would she do that?" Lance wondered out loud.

"So the project wouldn't be taken off her," I guessed. I'd never really been able to answer that question for myself. "To buy more time. Anyway, it got halted indefinitely. And she seemingly took the news of Project Gladiator's termination well, which should have alerted me immediately but..."

Lance rubbed my shoulder. "You can't be expected to know what's going on in someone's head, Bobbi."

Fury had said the same thing to me once. "I should've, though. I worked more closely with her and Ted than anyone. They were fighters and I should've anticipated that they wouldn't give up that easily. And they didn't. There was a twenty-four-hour window before the lab would be dismantled. Dr Calvin and Ted went there and locked themselves in."

"Oh my God," Lance breathed.

I could see it now, the red security alert going off and telling me that the lab had been penetrated, my heart dropping when I pulled up the CCTV footage and saw the pair of them on the monitor.

"I called it in. I was the closest to the site and I was the first agent there. I didn't wait for backup, I thought I could get inside and talk them out of doing what they were about to do. By the time I got in, Ted was partially strapped down and Dr Calvin was about to administer the first and only dose they'd managed to prepare. If S.H.I.E.L.D. wouldn't let them do human trials, they'd do it themselves."

Lance huffed next to me. "A villain story as old as time. That's why you had me look into A.I.M. You didn't want to believe she could be working with them, but the evidence told you we couldn't rule it out after we ran into those eejits."

"Right," I agreed. "Except I did manage to talk her out of it back then. I begged, pleaded, and she lowered the syringe only for Ted to snatch it out of her hands and administer the dose himself."

I shuddered involuntarily, the sound of his screams echoing through my skull as he thrashed against the restraints that held him in place. Lance pulled me to him and I let him, craving the sanctuary he created between his arms. It was a false god, but I worshipped it as I breathed him in and stayed still while he held me to his chest.

"We tried to help him, to save him…" My voice broke. "Then S.H.I.E.L.D. arrived and you know how that goes."

"Guns blazing," he said, chin moving against the top of my head.

"Basically. Dr Calvin tried to save her data, save her friend, save her work, and the agents triggered a kill switch she'd built in, in case the space was ever raided by Hydra. It went wrong, the lab exploded, everything was destroyed. Ted's body was never found. I was in a coma for two weeks. Dr Calvin's whole life blew up in her face, literally."

It was the simplest summary I could manage. Necessity required me to gloss over several relevant but tangential details that I just didn't want to get into with Lance now or maybe ever. That whole period of my life felt like one big, open wound and exposing it fully was terrifying. I left out the part about how I threw myself into work at S.H.I.E.L.D. and in the lab because my mother was in the hospital fighting for her life while in a coma. I didn't mention that during this time Dr Calvin was double- and triple-checking her files every week to make sure her doctors hadn't missed anything. It wasn't essential to explain that when I woke up from my own coma after the lab was destroyed, I needed to put myself back together, piece by piece.

"It was a miracle no S.H.I.E.L.D. agents were killed and Ted having died at his own hand was the only thing that kept Dr Calvin out of prison," I said, voice thick. "I gave testimony in support of her, telling the internal review board that she had made the right choice in the moment, changed her mind, but with the surprise of the agents it threw her into a panic."

"That's why she couldn't get work in the US after that," Lance noted, elements of the story he had now clicking into place.

"Yeah. She kept her freedom, but she basically had to start again. The details of Project Gladiator were only known to those with level three clearance at S.H.I.E.L.D., which made things not as bad in academia, I guess. If they really knew everything, then she would have never worked again anywhere. She was still marred with Ted's death though.

For her to get back to a teaching position of note at a place like Oxford, I can't imagine how hard she would have had to work."

"Not as hard as you."

Lance's response was quiet, like he was saying the words to himself rather than to me and I closed my eyes for a moment. It was so, so easy to just stay in this moment, say nothing else, and just enjoy the sensation of his hands running through my hair. The sensation of being held, comforted. The sensation of being heard. The sensation of not having to be the tough one for a second, of being able to break just a little and those cracks not being a thing that someone ran away from. All of that, however, was temporary. It couldn't last.

"I can't imagine why you would think telling me that story would make me like you any less, Inspector Morse."

I smiled, burying my head deeper and listening to the rumble of his laughter at my reaction.

"You did the right thing and how they reacted to that, everything that imploded after, that's not on you. Respectfully, that's on Dr Calvin."

Slowly, I pulled back from him and sat up. My arms were still wrapped around him, his around me, and I wasn't willing to let that go just yet.

"That's what she said," I whispered. "I later learned she came to the hospital every day while I was in a coma and then when I woke, she came just once. To apologize. To tell me that it was all her fault, that she should've listened and that she was blinded by her desire to do something great, something truly memorable. She said her ambition killed Ted and it nearly killed me. She'd never let something like that happen again. If she got her freedom, if she got the opportunity to work, she'd never even steer close to that field again. Wilma kept her word."

Lance's stare was far off, his gaze fixed on the river outside and a slight frown creasing his dark eyebrows. He looked like he wanted to tell Dr Calvin that she could jump into said river, but was trying to be sensitive of my feelings. I cupped his face with one hand, angling it toward me so he could see how serious I was.

"That's how I know she's being held against her will," I said, watching as surprise danced on his features. "She promised. She would *never* resuscitate Project Gladiator or anything close to it, not just because she was forbidden to, but because it cost her everything. Her life. Her career. Her love."

"Then what's all this?" he asked, gesturing to the paperwork on the table. I felt my mood darken.

"It's Project Gladiator," I said. "Kind of, because this has some of the same basic scientific principles but it's different. It's evolved. The work is not just Dr Calvin's, it's combined with someone else's and the baseline is way off."

"Bob," he said, thumb running under my chin. "Speak to me like someone who failed their A-levels in chemistry and biology."

I huffed.

"Aced physics and math though," he quickly added.

"This is her handwriting," I began. "These are her calculations and they correlate with her earlier work. But she's not alone. The mice weren't her only model systems and I don't know where the rest of her information is coming from, but if I had to guess it's the same person who's holding her against her will and providing the resources to see this through."

Lance still looked uncertain, but I was sure. He could hear it in the steel of my voice, see it in the hardness of my stare.

"Well, then," he said, perky. "Lucky for you I found the next lab. Cheese?"

CHAPTER FOURTEEN

The key to, er, the key was its oldness. That's what had cracked it for Lance, who had just quietly been working away in his room, unbothered, while Kirsty MacColl sang about not being a London girl. It was the most distinctive of the three and was reminiscent of your classic skeleton key: big loop at one end, long shaft with a ridge, and small iron teeth that dropped down at the opposite end. It was from the sixteen hundreds and unlike the Pitt Rivers Museum laboratory key, this one was residential.

"From there it was just a matter of narrowing the pool," he said, smearing pâté on a cracker as he explained. "It needed to be publicly accessible, so a grand house, local, and from the seventeenth century. Chastleton House wasn't just the top of the list, it was the list."

He shuffled the blueprint of the second lab to a more prominent place on the table and slid my laptop over to his side, fingers confidently flying across the keys.

"Please." I smirked. "Go right ahead."

"Naw, thanks, babe," he countered. "I will."

Chewing as he worked, with a few clicks he navigated his way to a website that had its own set of blueprints.

"Because it's a Grade I listed building and has been owned by the National Trust since 1991, everything I needed to verify it was online already."

"Gosh, I love the internet," I murmured, leaning forward as his fingers pointed out the similarity in the structures to me. "What's that bit there?"

"A false wall, if I had to guess. And the best part?"

"Please tell me it's in a library."

"It's in a library."

"Ha! I could kiss you!"

"Please do."

He said the comment so quickly, so carefree, I couldn't be sure if he… well, he meant it. Lance was an outrageously flirty person and I, in contrast, tended to overthink everything. It was like the words just rolled off his tongue and I panicked to fill the silence.

"Do you think we have to pull out a book to reveal the hidden chamber? Ah, this is so cool! I've never gotten to expose a secret bookshelf before."

My mood was slowly starting to shift, in part because of the cheese I kept shoveling into my mouth and in part because it felt like a proper, tangible path was before us.

"How are we getting in there? Pose as tourists? You could pass for Italian. I could be your goomah."

"Much as I'd enjoy that," Lance began, tapering my expectations. "Chastleton House is closed to the public for the next week."

I slumped "Ugh, another break in."

"It's closed because there's the high society wedding of Lady Davina taking place in two days' time."

I perked right back up. "I could be high society."

"Oi." He frowned. "Where did the 'we' suddenly go?"

"It vanished right after the 'oi you wut guv'nr'."

"That's not how I sound *at all*."

I wasn't listening, instead I was searching for info about the incoming nuptials and assessing the leaked guest list that had made its way to a low-level tabloid. Among the details listed were the catering company, boutique florist and celebrity wedding planner.

"Two days isn't a lot of time," I mused. "But this is a big event, so it shouldn't be too hard for us to slip in as waiters or something."

"No."

I looked over at him with surprise, fingers hovering above the keyboard.

"When I met you, you were dressed as 'the help'," he said. "We're not doing that this time. Also, this is a high society wedding. You're about to see Britain's class system in full swing and let me tell you, for something like this you'd be so busy running around following orders or getting blocked from that part of the building by some toff that you'd never get a chance to slip away. If we go as waiters, that will get us in, but it will not get us access."

"What's your suggestion then?"

"We go as guests."

"*Lance*," I scoffed. "I think two people who weren't invited by the bride and groom would be noticed pretty bloody quickly."

"Bloody," he laughed. "You're sounding like me. And please, you're telling me you knew *everyone* at your wedding to what's his face?"

A felt a slow smile creep up at the hint of jealousy I heard in his tone. "You know his name. And yes, actually, I could name every single one. We eloped. It was just us and an Elvis impersonator. This list of invitees has a different type of king on it."

"The king of France doesn't count," Lance scoffed, batting a hand. "You've got it all wrong. This is the perfect kind of wedding to infiltrate because there's five hundred guests. I counted! We'll just be the fourth cousins everyone pretends they remember."

"Mmmm," I groaned, clicking back to the online article. I scrolled down, looking at the images of the people who would be attending.

"Come on," Lance whispered. "I'll wear the kilt."

I laughed. "Please don't."

Chastleton House might have been the scariest thing I'd had to face since I got here, mainly because I was having to face it in stilettos. The towering example of Jacobean architecture looked like something out of a BBC miniseries and I couldn't help but be impressed as a procession of finely dressed wedding guests made their way toward it. The route was down a long, pebble path that was really testing the ankle dexterity of Britain's elite as women clutched desperately to the elbows of their partners for stability. The past few days of storms had shifted, making way for clear blue skies that would look beautiful in the wedding photos. The memory of how crisp the air was that day would be quickly forgotten.

For all his bragging, Lance had actually lived up to his own hype and managed to get us on the guest list by hacking the wedding planner. There was a rom-com plot in there somewhere, but I'd save that brain space for nutting out the specifics when I had hours to kill on a stakeout. Turns out, there was a wait list of potential guests sitting in a spreadsheet, desperate to be tapped into the metaphorical ring in the event of someone else pulling out.

"Celeste, there must be absolutely *no* empty seats," Lance said in an affected voice as he'd read one of the emails from the couple. "I will not stand for looking out and seeing gaps in the crowd on *my* wedding day."

"Yeesh." I winced. "That's a demanding bride."

"Try demanding groom." He grinned. "And those demands will be met, my lord!"

We were added to the top of the waiting list and twelve hours later, the couple's distant relatives Mr and Mrs Waller were forced to "regretfully" inform them of their inability to attend due to unforeseen family circumstances. On their end, they'd unexpectedly won an all-expenses paid holiday to the Maldives in a competition neither of them could remember entering. Yet the prospect of a tropical vacation was immediately much more appealing than attending a boring wedding in Oxford during the backend of winter. The invite was extended to the bride's very distant and almost forgotten fifth, maybe sixth cousin on her mother's side, Mr Dakar. He cut a fine, sharp figure in a classic Tom Ford tuxedo jacket and trousers, the dinner suit a shimmering pool of black fabric that was only broken up by the crisp, collared white shirt underneath. I'd told Lance he looked like the fanciest penguin I'd even seen.

"Thank you." He smirked, adjusting his small, black bowtie with a flourish. "It's the same suit James Bond wore in *No Time to Die.*"

"Ugh," I groaned, rolling my eyes and making a specific gesture in the air. "You just had to ruin it."

My own outfit was a joke that only I got, but I snapped a selfie and sent it to Jen knowing she'd find it funny, too. Lance looked at me like there was nothing hilarious about it. Floor length velvet in ice blue hugged my athletic frame, a slit beginning at my ankle and spanning midway up my thigh. The gown cinched at my waist subtly, the fabric coming up high on my neckline, covering my collarbone, with long sleeves that ran down to my wrists. The money shot, however, was the back, which was covered in a gray overcoat for now. It was harder than I expected, dressing for an event like this while also keeping in mind that despite the exuberant costs covered to heat this place inside and out, the sun would set soon, and the temperature would plummet even further. Warm air billowed from the entrance to Chastleton House as we stepped inside, the women dramatically shimmying out of their thick furs and readjusting their strings of pearls and diamonds in the enormous Baroque mirrors that took up much of the entranceway.

"Invitations, please?" a man in a top hat – an actual top hat! – asked us, and Lance handed them over. "Thank you, Mr Dakar and–"

"Miss Summers," Lance answered for him. "My fiancée."

"A very warm congratulations to you," he said, dipping his head respectfully. "Please head right through, there's canapes and champagne in the Best Garden."

He and Lance did that British head bobbing thing and I slid out of my coat, handing it off to a nearby assistant. I heard Lance's breath catch as he caught the view from behind, which was the most dramatic part of the dress. The velvet rolled over my shoulders and then plunged right down in a sharp V that ended just above the arch of my lower back. My hair was parted to the side and pulled into a messy, low bun that took way more effort than the tutorial I followed online had promised. Lance was standing back from me, mouth slightly ajar, and I couldn't help myself. I did a small spin, giggling as I took the arm he extended, and we strolled forward with the others. He didn't say anything. I had literally left him speechless, and it was hard not to be buoyed by that kind of power as a woman sometimes.

"Who are Mr Dakar and Miss Summers?" I asked, voice barely more than a whisper as I leaned in.

"Huh?" He looked dazed, as if my question after minutes of silence had brought him out of a stupor.

"Come on, I know they're from some band that you've no doubt already added to the playlist."

"Oh." He blinked, falling quiet as he thought. I looked above us, examining the detail on the curved ceiling as I waited for an answer while following the flow of people around us. We turned a corner and suddenly the *best* garden was before us, waiters positioned near the open doors and offering flutes of champagne as we stepped out of the house. A sea of cocktail tables dotted the immaculate lawns, each one draped in white silk and a bouquet of flowers spilling over the side, wrapping down the column until blending in with the spongy grass below. There was a ten-piece band tucked against the side of the house, performing a cover of Earth, Wind and Fire's "September" to a cluster of swaying guests who were already fighting the urge to find a dancefloor.

"The Bodysnatchers," Lance said, regaining the ability to speak as we posted up at a table off to the side. "Nancy Summers was the founding member and Rhoda Dakar was the lead singer of an all-chick seven-piece British 2 Tone ska revival."

"There ya go," I said, patting his shoulder supportively. "Knew it would be something."

"They used to tour with The Specials in the late Seventies. I put a track in the playlist that will appeal to your sensibilities."

I arched an eyebrow, suspicious.

"It's called 'Ruder Than You.'"

I laughed, throwing my head back in a way that made me feel young, reckless, carefree. The reality was I had a lot of cares and few of them were free, but when you got a moment of levity in this line of work, you took it. I caught Lance watching me over the rim of his glass, his usually dark eyes having a warm texture to them today.

"Aren't you two a beautiful couple!"

A woman with a huge beehive of gray hair was hobbling over to us, held up by a stoic gentleman in an offensively brown suit. Her accent was posh but the poshest thing she did was hold out a bejeweled hand for Lance to kiss. I curtsied, I guess? I panicked and just lowered my knees, an amused glance from my "fiancé" causing me to stumble ever-so-slightly.

"Now who are you?" she demanded to know in that nosy way old ladies did. "Friends? Family? Heavens knows there's too many of both here, hmmm?"

"It's a big, beautiful wedding," I said, smiling politely.

"I'm a distant cousin," Lance replied, hand snaking around my waist as he pulled me to his side.

"On the groom's?"

"On Lady Davina's."

"Oh, you must be Mr Havisham."

"Dakar, ma'am."

"Dakuuuur?"

"Although my mother did love playing croquet on Sundays with the Havishams, rest her soul."

"Such a sweet woman," I agreed, patting his hand. "Loved a scone."

Lance's mouth twitched and he quickly took a sip from his flute.

"Yes, well," the old lady murmured. "Everyone loves a scone, don't they?"

"Indeed." I nodded. "Absolutely."

I was running out of small talk, but thankfully someone began announcing that the ceremony would begin in fifteen minutes, and could we do our best to make our way around the side of the estate. I tried not to let out a sigh of relief as we joined the crowd, some being able to take seats that had been lined up in perfect spacing, while others stood at the rear. That's where Lance and I parked ourselves, hidden safely in the throng but still able to see the arch of the altar which was – of course – decked out in more flowers. The "Bridal Chorus" started, a sea of heads turning to "oooh" and "ahhh" as flower girls began making their way down the aisle.

"Is that what your wedding was like?" Lance whispered, attempting to poke the bear. I would not be poked.

"No." I smirked. "It was much less…"

"Grand?"

"Floral."

I could see him chewing the inside of his cheek, desperate to ask more but fighting the urge.

"How long does this usually take?" he asked, the bride having made her way to the celebrant and joining her line of bridesmaids.

"It depends."

He looked pained, head snapping to face me. "On what?"

"On whether they do a reading, have friends recite a poem–"

"A poem?" he whined.

"You're a grown, adult man," I chuckled. "This isn't your first wedding."

"Yeah, but the weddings I go to are usually fun. All these rich society people make me uncomfortable." He fidgeted with his pocket square, which was made from a piece of fabric I had snipped from the lining of my dress. Desperate times.

"I couldn't tell," I murmured, but I did know what he meant. The window to the library was annoyingly in sight from where we stood at the back of the crowd. Our mission was right there, yet we couldn't just sprint to it and get in and out. Sure, there were a lot of people here to provide cover in numbers but that also meant a lot of eyes. And after our deep and meaningful on the boat, Lance and I wanted to be careful. More careful, that is, so when we eventually got to Dr Calvin, we had a chance to get her out of this alive and as unscathed as possible. We had to be patient and wait.

That meant enduring the ceremony, which did indeed have *several* poems. That meant clapping and cheering when they were pronounced legal spouses. That meant mingling while the wedding photographs were taken. That meant making small talk during the dinner and being relieved when the crowd hushed for speeches. That meant being patient as the sun set, the drinks flowed, and everyone got looser and looser. The dancefloor ballooned after the first dance, spilling away from the temporarily laid wooden floors to the surrounding lawn and garden. It was nearly time for Lance and I, but first he asked me a question.

"May I have this dance?"

I hesitated, looking at his extended hand for a moment.

"Because if you don't say yes, I'm pretty sure that bloke leaning against the side of the building is going to ask you," Lance said, subtly jerking his head. I followed the direction of his gesture, spotting the man in question who winked at me through a plume of smoke. "And I heard in the little boys' room that he's a Saudi prince. I can't compete with that."

"You don't have to." I smiled, getting up and taking his hand. He didn't lead me to the dancefloor, however, he took me to the lawn that was dotted with a small cluster of couples. Mounds of immaculately sculpted hedges stood like silent guards around the space. Their shapes were big and bold, even in the darkness not penetrated by the light spilling from strategically placed lanterns. I couldn't say I hadn't imagined how his body would feel against mine and I tried to suppress a contented sigh as we fit together perfectly. We took slow steps as we swayed in time with the music, my arms forming a comfortable loop around his neck while I rested my chin on his shoulder.

"Your British accent is really good, you know?" Lance said. We were far enough from any prying ears that we could drop the charade and slip into our natural tongues. "You do posh well."

I smiled. "Ice queen."

"What?"

I leaned back so he could hear me more clearly. "Ice queen. That's what he calls me."

"Barton?"

I nodded. "It was even on the record in a mediation for fu–"

My teeth bit into my lip, the word fizzling out in my mouth as I let it go like a deflated balloon.

"You can say it," Lance responded. "You don't have to stop yourself talking about him. I can't imagine how much this whole thing must suck, so if letting it out helps…"

"It doesn't, actually. Attending a wedding while going through a divorce doesn't make me want to stack my pockets full of rocks and run into the Thames. I love weddings. Wish I hadn't had one, but–"

"Why did you?"

"Impulse." I shrugged. "It was important to him, the tradition of it all, even though we didn't have a traditional ceremony or anything. I'm a child of divorce so I was reluctant, but if someone keeps on and on about it, eventually it wears you down. And relationships are about compromise. They only work if each of you are willing to bend or it breaks."

He looked thoughtful at that, hands wrapping around me just a bit tighter whether he realized it or not.

"You've never had anyone to bend with?" I asked. "Or break?"

He grinned, dimples punctuating that absolutely devastating smile. "Bit of both, actually. Maybe too much."

"Really?" I smiled. "You love hard and fast."

Color flushed his cheeks and his eyes shifted from mine to the wedding party across the lawn.

"Lancelot Hunter. Is the L word making you blush? *You*?"

"I–"

"You're an international spy," I hissed. "Get a grip."

"Then let's do international spy things! Ditch the slow dancing and do a salsa."

He threw his body back, spinning away from me dramatically before moving his legs quickly and rotating his body in a rather terrible attempt at the classic Latin dance.

"Get those hips away from me," I gasped, laughing so hard I hunched over as I struggled to breathe. "Away, away."

Laughter was booming from him as well as he spun back, sweeping me up in his arms and pulling me to him as our cackles mixed together in harmony. We fell back in rhythm easily, swaying and stepping. Lance's fingers were warm as they brushed against the skin of my exposed back, gently running down my spine and leaving a trail of goosebumps in their wake.

"Ice queen," he said softly, shaking his head in disbelief.

He spread his fingers wide, taking up as much surface area as possible, making contact with as much of my skin as he could.

"You're warmth, Bobbi. You're light and shimmering and glitter and…"

He stepped back, holding out his arm and I spun under it, the light catching and reflecting against the texture of the velvet. He brought me back to him, cradling me against his body, and I stared up at him, feeling giddy.

"You're not an ice queen," he said, his words light but his face deathly serious. "You're a diamond."

I felt it. And for once, I decided not to think. I cupped his face in my hands, pulling him toward me. I heard the murmur of surprise escape his lips just before I covered them with my own. I let myself get lost in Lance for a moment, just a moment, and him in me as my fingers slipped into his hair, tangled amongst it, and held him to me in the same way I was gripped to him. It was like sherbet exploding across my lips, my tongue, my spirit, as I gave up restraint and kissed Lance like I meant it, *really* meant it.

We separated after what could have been minutes, probably

was, and only because I needed to breathe. His own breath was shaky as we pressed our heads together, taking a moment but needing several. Lance's thumb ran over my bottom lip, tugging ever-so-slightly as I met his gaze.

"Lancey Boy?!"

The voice cut through our self-made sanctuary like a knife and we jerked apart. Lance looked around in the direction it had come from, zeroing in on a man in a navy tuxedo.

"Lancelot Hunter! I knew it was you!"

My stomach dropped as I realized where I recognized him from.

"Jimmy," Lance said, voice flat. "Jimmy Smithers."

CHAPTER FIFTEEN

Lance released me, stepping toward the man he had once served with eagerly. The man who now worked for FiveFourThree Solutions. The man who had been part of a group that raided a room at Magdalen College, looking for Millicent Porter.

"Jimbo Smithers," he said, forearms gripping each other. "How the heck are ya, buddy? How long has it been? Seven years? Six?"

It shifted into one of those bro hugs that was more about chests bouncing off each other and arms slapping shoulders. It looked friendly. It looked casual. It looked like nothing more than two long lost mates getting reacquainted. Yet I knew Lance. From the comments he'd made about Jimmy Smithers, it was clear this guy didn't know Lance well if he thought they were friends. Everything from the stature of his shoulders to the barely visible strain on his face told me how he was really feeling. The subtle way in which he positioned his body in front of me, sticking close to Jimmy, and blocking his view of where I stood. I shifted, giving this man my back as I fidgeted with my hair and tried to look shy.

"Six years, I reckon," Jimmy said. "You are looking sharp, my man. A right proper gangster!"

Lance's laugh sounded hollow. "I don't know about that, mate, I don't know about that. Where's the missus? Shelley about?"

"Nah, daffy bint left me. Took the kids. Fled to Scotland."

"Fled" was an interesting choice of word, I thought.

"So you riding stag?"

"Here working, bro."

"Working? You in the band?"

Jimmy's laugh was grating, unexpectedly high-pitched and immediately something that got on your nerves.

"Private security, Lancey Boy. It's where the big money's at."

"Now who would be dumb enough to hire you, eh? What are you supposed to be securing?"

"Ah, just rich you-know-whats at this kind of thing. Swear there's no real threat, just makes those low-level royals feel important if there's someone with a piece trotting around."

"Ha, I bet."

"Speaking of, this isn't usually your kind of scene. You on the job?"

"A different kind of job…"

They fell silent and even though I was looking away, now pretending to examine a nearby rosebush, I could feel their eyes on me like heat sensors. Jimmy let out a low-level whistle, like I was a racehorse that impressed him. I intentionally ignored it.

"You always loved rich girls," he said.

"Always," Lance chuckled. "Speaking of, I better get back to it. Can't leave a dime waiting."

"Not when you're a seven," he replied, slapping hands with Lance.

"You in town for long? We should catch up for a pint before I head back."

"Bro, totally. Would love that."

"Give me your number. Great, we'll link up."

"Looking forward to it, Lancey Boy, looking forward to it."

"You gotta retire that nickname," he fake-laughed, his voice moving closer and closer towards me until I felt a hand on the small of my back.

We snuggled into each other affectionately, and watched Jimmy's back shrinking smaller and smaller as he headed to his post around the corner of the house. It was a good thing we did, as he looked over his shoulder and offered Lance another small wave.

"Rich girls, huh?" I said, smile strained.

"You gotta know, everything just said–"

"Please," I murmured, turning to adjust his bowtie. "My skin is a lot thicker than that. You maintained your cover and that's all that's important. Well, that and I'm a dime apparently."

"An eleven," he replied. "How high does the scale go?"

I tapped his chin. "Focus. How screwed are we if FiveFourThree Solutions are here?"

"I don't know that they are," Lance said as we began to make our way back to the main bar. "Shall we do a circuit?"

"Sure, honey."

I planted a kiss on his cheek and we split up, moving in opposite directions as Lance went to get us drinks and I went to the bathroom. I took the long way. So did he. When we met back at the table, we had information.

"I think he's freelancing tonight," Lance said, sitting down beside me with two beverages neither of us were going to touch. "I couldn't spot any of the other video stars."

"Me neither. Just him. Still…"

"I agree."

We looked at each other, hard. If things were going perfectly to plan, I would have waited another half an hour before we moved. My eyes scanned the crowd and people were messy. They were laughing and dancing and falling over each other, but there was still an element of class to it. There was still civility. The benefit of even just thirty more minutes would be that Jimmy's job would be less security and more people management by that point, his main task keeping his clients out of trouble. It would keep him distracted. If it was just him.

"No time like the present," I said, getting to my feet. Lance followed me, both of us discreetly emptying half our glasses on to the grass, linking arms and giggling as we cut back toward the house. We took a wide berth, out of Jimmy's line of sight and away from his post. Slipping in through one of the side entrances, we were just another couple of tiddly patrons.

"Oops, sorry there," Lance apologized, brushing against a waiter. He placed his now empty glass on the man's tray, patting him on the shoulder. "Appreciate it."

The words were slurred just enough as we made it past the kitchen and into the main entranceway where some of the older guests were lingering. We pretended to linger too, leaning against a wall right next to a darkened hallway that was roped off. Lance nodded, keeping his eyes on the guests, and I stepped backward over the barrier, creeping into the darkness completely. I moved fast, tiptoeing so my heels wouldn't make a sound against the hard floors. Lance would make his move when he could; until then I had to travel quick and quiet: left, right, down a set of stairs and left again. The library door was at the end and I rushed towards it, crouching down as I fished the flashlight out of my purse. I clicked it on, slipped it between my teeth, and removed my picks from the purse lining. By the time I had the door open, I heard two mouth clicks behind me which I knew was Lance's signal. His hand lightly touched my shoulder and I stayed low, pushing the door open with a steady creak.

A glow from the lamp far in the corner was the only source of light as we slipped into the space, closing the door behind us. This looked like the kind of library that came with a butler, free of charge. It smelled like woodsmoke and the overwhelming vibe of the place was leather, mahogany and wood. There was also not one bookshelf, but dozens. My eyes scanned the sheer number of volumes in awe, noting that this would have been more impressive to me if I hadn't spent the past week in some of the most beautiful and expansive libraries in the world.

"Hey, Engineer Eddie," I mumbled. "Any hint as to which bookshelf is hiding the false wall?"

"Not a bookshelf."

His tone turned me around quickly and I groaned. "Oh, come *on*."

One whole wall had been split, the bookshelf small on this side to make way for what looked like a historic art installation made of locks. It was similar to a family crest, I guessed, with locks from all different periods seemingly set into the very wall itself.

"Hiding in plain sight," I breathed, taking the key from Lance as he held it out to me.

"Over to you, Key McGee."

"I hate you," I mumbled, shining the flashlight over the layers of holes that all went to nowhere *except* one. But which one? "You start at one side, I'll start at the other."

Lance followed my orders and we fell into a rhythm, analyzing one, moving down, then the next, and so on until a row was completed vertically. Then we'd pop back up to the top of the line of locks and start again. It was just guesswork, though. We eyeballed and kept moving because there was easily about a hundred locks here and we didn't have time to try the key in each one. We knew roughly what the hole should look like and if the period aligned, we'd pass the key back and forth between each other until, finally, right near the center, Lance thought he found the right one.

"This is it," he said, his face over the hole. He took my hand, holding it in front of the tiny shape. "Feel that?"

At first, no. Then I concentrated, frowning as he released me and grabbed the key.

"Air," Lance supplied. "Just the faintest air flow."

He was right. The lock was also old, slightly wider than some of the others, and fit the time period we were looking for. He inserted the key, twisting the iron slowly until a satisfying, mechanical *clunk* sounded and we stepped back. The whole art piece lifted from the wall, revealing an entrance that was wider than it was tall. I went to slip out of my stilettos and wedge them between the door, but Lance stopped me.

"Keep your shoes on, we don't know what's down there. You can't just be bare footing concrete in a six-hundred-year-old secret chamber."

He pulled several volumes from the shelf behind us and I winced, watching as he used those precious books as a doorstopper. We moved forward, ears straining for any sound as we hustled as quietly as we could, heads crouched, through a short tunnel that sloped down almost immediately. There were moisture catchers positioned every few steps, but as I crouched down to examine them, I realized they were overflowing. There was a slick of water steadily dripping down the walls, too, creating a soothing trickling sound despite the distinctly unsoothing nature of the situation.

"No one has been here for a while," I whispered. When we entered the lab, that suspicion was confirmed. This looked like a small, stone chapel that had been converted as best it could with curved benches fixed into the walls and shelves towering upwards filled with vials in various colors. There was just the one whiteboard here, the portable kind that could be transported on wheels, and it was positioned low to the ground. Like Pitt Rivers, this place had been vacated, too, but much more haphazardly. My eyes fell on a small cot in the corner, barely more than a foldout bed with a tangle of blankets and a tiny space heater unplugged from the wall.

"She slept here?" Lance questioned, gaze focusing on the same detail.

"She must have been freezing," I murmured, my own breaths visible in the icy chamber. If it was brisk outside, it was nothing compared to in here, which was so deep in the bowels of the grand house that no warmth seemed to penetrate. It was the horrid combination of damp, drafty, and downright freezing which only gave credence to my theory.

"No one would work here of their own free will," Lance said, voicing it.

"I agree. Let's hurry then: you snap and I'll search."

His camera began clicking quickly as he hurried, and I tried to match his pace. There were no mouse bones left or any sign

that Dr Calvin had been experimenting on living subjects
this time and my eyes passed over the whiteboard, working
quickly. The formula had been finessed here, with whatever
she had learned from her model systems leading to a tweaked
recipe as I examined her handwriting. She had made her way
closer and closer to a solution. Maybe. What she believed
was a solution anyway, but I wasn't so sure. There was still
stacked instability, yet she was proceeding unhindered. It
was neither smart nor safe, but outside of the constraints of
S.H.I.E.L.D. – and if your life was on the line – I guess you
didn't have to worry about that so much.

Yet this space left me with even more questions. It was clear
Dr Calvin had been here too, but when exactly? Why have
several labs and move between each of them, voluntarily or
otherwise? And what was the inciting reason for each move?
I couldn't grasp the motivation behind it, but the answer felt
close. I flipped the whiteboard over, looking at markings there
in handwriting bordering on illegible. I didn't recognize it.
There was just one, enormous silver light illuminating the whole
space and it looked like an oven ventilator. It probably worked
better as one, too, as it did little to chase away the shadows
here and I kicked on the portable worksite lamp at my feet for
additional visibility and gasped. It was just in slicks, but it was
clear enough to me that the same substance from Dr Calvin's
lab at the university was smeared on this whiteboard. It made
the calculations look like they were frozen in amber. We'd had
to bring minimal equipment with us, minimal weapons, too, so
we could pass all the security checkpoints, and I cursed under
my breath at not having a kit with me to get a sample. But did I
need to? It looked the same and using a pen to run through the
sludge, it had the same texture and same distinct lack of scent.

"Bob."

I looked around the whiteboard, finding Lance staring down at an opened drawer. I trotted over, peering down with confusion as I processed what I was seeing. It was a deconstructed gun – a Glock .84 – with the parts fragmented and separated from each other in a cushion of foam.

"What do you think?" he asked.

I shook my head, moving to the next drawer and pulling out a deconstructed revolver. "I honestly have no idea."

The drawer below that had a Mk 2 grenade and a Mills bomb, the British equivalent of the hand grenade, each pulled apart and broken down like they were part of a mechanical autopsy.

"What does this have to do with Project Gladiator?" he asked. "Was it tangentially attached to the weapons division?"

"No," I replied, shaking my head. "I mean, in the way that proposed subjects could become a human weapon, but not in the literal cocking of a shotgun sense."

"This is so strange. This lab is almost nothing like the last one."

"Different sites, different facets of the project," I murmured, my eye catching on a rusted portion of the stone wall that stood out. It was a tall rectangle and with some help from Lance, we were able to yank it open and reveal a stone shaft that spanned upwards, seemingly endless, with a cable running through the center and disappearing into the dark. There were disintegrated chunks of wood below and I picked one up; it almost turned to sand in my hand with the applied pressure.

"It's a dumbwaiter," he said.

"Don't call me that."

Lance chuckled. "Not you, that. It's what servants would use to move food between levels back in the day. This chamber must have been actively used, at least in the beginning."

I stepped away, this not providing the answer I was hoping for. "Look for targets, something that could be used for practice."

"So your old mentor's Rambo now?"

I huffed. "No, but you have all these broken-down weapons *here* and not at Pitt Rivers. Why? Not enough space to fire there. You'd be heard. And why not use them to escape your captor?"

"I don't know about a homemade range, but what about these?" Lance held up a series of clear blocks that had bullets encased inside. Their trajectories had been frozen in gel and I turned to a huge sink, something I had written off as being for personal hygiene, but it now had new meaning. It was filled with what should have been clear, smooth gel in almost a jelly-like texture.

"Ewwww," Lance said, using a broom handle to poke at the chunky lumps that went right to the brim. I rattled the plastic cylinder next to the sink, recognizing the label and the chemical.

"You need to mix this powder with water and stir continuously until the color shifts from cloudy to clear," I told him. "Then you have a five-minute window to preserve whatever you like inside: bugs, body parts, bullets."

"This is the target practice?"

"Mmmm. Except left unattended, it turns into goop."

"It looks like what was in her lab, doesn't it? Is that where it could have come from?"

There was nothing harmful to the cocktail and I squeezed

a slimy chunk from the sink between my fingers. "No, this is different."

"Look, I'm no scientist man, but it seems exactly the same to me."

We didn't have time to argue this point and I went to turn back, take one final sweep before we left, when I froze. Jimmy Smithers was pointing a gun squarely at my chest. And he was not alone. We'd had our backs to the entrance as we looked over the contents of the sink, allowing them to creep in and block our way out. I was deeply annoyed at my mistake and for getting so caught up in what we'd discovered. That error was now staring me down from across the other side of the chamber.

"Lance," I said, voice low and urgent.

"Yeah, yeah, OK, I don't get the specifics of–"

His words cut off the second he pivoted around fully, catching the same view I had: his old colleague at the center and five guys fanned out behind him. All had their weapons drawn. Lance tilted his head and I could tell he was doing the same calculations I was.

"Those the same dudes from the–"

"Yup," I interjected. The whole dorm room crew.

"Interesting. I definitely didn't see them."

"Me neither."

"Stop talking!" Jimmy shouted, his smug smile cracking at our apparent calm as we chatted back and forth to each other. "I can hear you."

"You call these guys in?" Lance asked him then, directly.

"I… What? Yes. I was freelance tonight."

"Told you," I said, whacking his arm.

"I believed you! But if I missed it and you missed it, then I would seriously–"

"Shut up!" he yelled. "I will shoot you right here, right now."

"For what?" Lance questioned. "Getting frisky at a wedding?"

He was clutching, but Jimmy's guys were dumb enough to glance at each other, questioning. And Lance was stalling, trying to give me time to find a way out of this. Or maybe he had one? Either way, the options were few. Six of them. Two of us. One exit, which somehow required us to get past all of them unscathed and out into a library where they should have stationed an additional guard if they were smart. They weren't particularly smart, however, but even then, we'd have to hope we weren't physically disheveled enough to make it back out through the house and leave the wedding unnoticed by anyone else.

"You're a thief!" Jimmy snapped. "You were breaking in here to steal—"

"Beakers?" Lance offered.

"I followed you and caught you red-handed!"

"And now what?" Lance pushed. "You're going to arrest us for being found in a secret chamber of the house, holding nothing, stealing nothing, just… existing."

"Not you," one of them grunted. "Her. She's the chicky who broke into the lab."

"Chicky," I said, wrinkling my nose.

"I'm not sure what you're up to, Lance, but I'm on to you," Jimmy growled, clicking off the safety.

"I'm curious," I said, tilting my head. "What do you think he's up to?"

I wasn't trying to be a smarty pants, I genuinely wanted to know. They didn't seem to have any clue about what we were doing or why we were here. In fact, it was becoming increasingly obvious that the only reason they'd found *this* lab was because we'd led them to it.

"Corporate espionage?" the guy who called me "chicky" said. I had my eyes on him. I also had my hands behind me, searching the shelf for something, anything, of use.

"Sorry, is that a question? Are you workshopping suggestions or…?"

"We're hired to do a job and that job is protect our boss' investment until the completion of our contract term," Jimmy barked. "And that includes making sure no professional rivals can hire someone else to sweep in here and steal it from under them. Now if you'll just come peacefully–"

I hurled a beaker directly at Jimmy, the glass shattering as it made contact and the green contents spilled over him. There was a slow hissing sound, steam started billowing from his suit and he screamed, patting himself down like he was on fire. While his teammates were distracted, I grabbed and tossed several more in rapid succession as Lance started flipping benches in front of us.

"What is in those?" he cried.

"I have no idea!"

Each one seemed to be having a different kind of effect on its target, some appearing no more harmful than water and others creating adverse chemical reactions. All I wanted to do was manufacture panic so they would start firing, which is exactly what they began to do as they re-aimed their weapons. Lance dragged me down beside him, pulling me into a makeshift fort he'd created out of the benches, the whiteboard, even a chair. In close quarters like this, with thick stone walls, if you missed, the bullets would ricochet and create an entirely different kind of chaos as they bounced from surface to surface. Whether our protection would stand up to that kind of barrage, only time would tell and Lance threw his hands over me as the firing started.

I heard their yells amongst the bullets and the debris exploding around us, chemicals erupting as well until the whole space was blanketed in a haze of smoke and dust. I risked a peek over Lance's shoulder, eyes scanning for a solution until I fixed on the one slash of color amongst all the gray. The reddish, rusted door that led right up to the center of the house. My purse was still looped around my shoulders, and I felt for the pair of gloves I knew I had in there, their padded fingers just enough to buy me some additional grip.

"I really hope you've got weapons with you," Lance said, lips brushing my ear as he spoke.

"I couldn't have a visible panty line with this dress, so where the heck do you think I'm stashing battle staves, Lance?"

He blinked, leaning back slightly as he examined my expression carefully. "You look like you have *some* kind of plan besides relying on the ricochet."

I smiled. "I knew you'd get it."

"Of course I'd get it. We're the only smart people in this dungeon."

"How good's your upper arm strength?" I asked, squeezing his biceps through the tux. "Oh, *hello.*"

"Can you feel me up another time?" He grinned, but flexed enough that I could feel it through the fabric. Searching the floor around us, trying to be careful about when I slipped my fingers out from behind our protection amid the firing, I tugged on the pale purple fabric I saw wedged between the rubble and yanked a set of gloves free.

"Put these on," I said, shoving them at his chest.

"What the hell are they? It looks someone dismembered Grimace!"

"They're cut-resistant gloves," I replied. "Every lab has them."

"Cut-resistant? Bobbi, *cut-resistant*? What am I about to be cut with?" He shook me briefly, drawing my attention back to him.

"Not cut! Just something to create a barrier between your flesh and the cable when we climb."

He followed the jerk of my head, wincing. "How long has that thing been there? I don't know if it will hold our weight."

"It will have to," I snapped. "Soon as they run out of rounds, we just need a distraction to get to the door and in safely. I'm out of schemes."

Lance glanced around, his eyes settling on something I couldn't see. I didn't like the flash of excitement I saw there. "I can get us a distraction if you buy me time."

"Done." I nodded. "The second they're out–"

A defunct clicking echoed through the space, standing out as it was the first thing that broke the previous barricade of noise. We didn't wait. Lance took off in one direction and I slipped away in the other, broken glass and shattered furniture splintering beneath me. I was glad Lance had convinced me to keep my shoes on now as I stalked toward my prey, eyes straining through the haze to see the outline of their figures across the room as they back and forthed about what to do next. I crouched low, registering the sound of a drawer opening as Lance did whatever he needed to do. I watched one of their heads swivel in his direction and I pounced, grateful for the protection of my gloved hands as I used them to spring up from below the man and kick him in the face.

"UNTFH!" he grunted, flying back into his colleague. I used the considerable bulk of his frame to flip around him, using his neck like a stationary pole as I flung my legs wide and connected with the faces of two more of his colleagues. Bracing my knee against his chest, I rode this guy to the floor and heard the crunch of debris beneath his back. A forearm slipped over my neck from behind, tugging me back and crushing my windpipe. Shifting my body to the side slightly, I threw my elbow into this guy's gut at a hard right angle and gasped for a breath as he released me with the impact. One of his colleagues charged front on, throwing a punch which I ducked, sliding underneath his swing to land a quick *pop* to his jaw. I was still short on breath so it wasn't as hard as I would have liked, but I followed up with two more body shots as I tried not to think, to just react and flow amidst the hand-to-hand combat.

"Time to go!"

I dashed away, heading for the sound of Lance's voice. It didn't look like it was time to flee, as he was standing in front of the drawers of weapons, hands flying in a blur as he slapped this piece with that piece and twisted that nozzle. He glanced up, seeing I was close, and pulled a pin. He tossed a sphere over my head, which made a *sssss* sound the entire time in a way that did *not* sound good. He already had the door to the dumbwaiter open and I climbed inside, although it was difficult to contort my lanky limbs the precise way I wanted. I leapt upwards, arm muscles straining as I grabbed the cord. It supported my weight, thank heavens, but would it support Lance's as well? The subject of my concern appeared below me in the shaft.

"Was that a grenade?" I exclaimed, looking down.

"No," he scoffed, his teeth pulling the pin from something else in his hand. He tossed it out the hatch behind him and yanked the dumbwaiter door shut. "*That* was a grenade."

CHAPTER SIXTEEN

I grunted, wrapping my legs around the cord for additional grip and moving as fast as I could. I tried to pretend this was a rope at the gym that I had to climb quicker than all the other muscle bros to hit the bell attached to the ceiling and cement my dominance. Lance's own pants echoed in the contained space and I spared a look down, impressed with how far we'd come already. We'd cleared one story at least, but not one that had a viable exit point unfortunately. The chamber was narrow enough that he had his back against one wall and legs touching the other side, taking some of his weight off the cord as he shuffled upwards.

There was a booming sound below us and I copied Lance, bracing my legs against the sides of the chamber as it felt like the whole house vibrated with the motion from the bomb going off below. Dirt and pebbles and lord knows what else rained down. Closing my eyes, I prayed that I wouldn't die in here. *Please don't let this tunnel collapse*, I begged. *Please don't let me die in this horrible space.* It was deathly quiet for a moment. Chastleton House stilled. A few beats later, shouts could be heard below us and a voice that sounded distinctly like Jimmy coughing out orders that I couldn't make out clearly.

"Bobbi?"

"Mmmm?"

"Are you OK?"

"Mmmm."

"Your eyes are closed."

"I can climb with my eyes closed."

"Then scooch, sweetheart. We're all right."

His hand reached up to grip my thigh, squeezing, telling me he was there. I scooched, my relief at finally making it to a dumbwaiter window short-lived as neither of us could pry it open. It was sealed shut, maybe bricked right over. I quelled the rising panic in my gut and proceeded upwards, having more success at the next window and narrowly avoiding an anxiety attack when we rolled out of the space and into what looked like an upstairs kitchen. Why you would need kitchens on multiple levels, I had no idea, but I was *very* grateful for the opulence as I struggled to my feet. We were filthy, our wedding attire unrecognizable under the layers of grime. Lance cupped my face in his hands, eyes running over every inch of me as he did a rapid inspection.

"Are you–"

"Later," I told him, taking his hand in mine as I limped toward the door. The hallway outside was empty, but the sounds coming from downstairs meant the blast had been felt. As we rushed toward the exit, signs of it were everywhere with thin clouds of smoke and dust hanging in the air. The charge had blown open every creak, hidden corridor and forgotten passage this house had, and wedding guests who'd been inside were filthy with the contents. It was good, because we blended in and joined the group heading toward the way we'd come in, ushers guiding us to safety as cars pulled up. Music was still playing from the gardens, voices laughing and singing and mixing with the tune in a way that told me the majority of the guests outside had no idea about was happening inside. The wheels of a cab crunched over the pebbles and Lance grabbed the back door before it had even slowed.

"Thanks, mate," he said. "We've been waiting for ages."

I folded in, Lance following behind me and slamming the door on the protests of a guy further back calling after us.

"Hey, that's my cab!" he cried.

"Silverton Boathouse," Lance said. "If you don't mind."

The driver crept out of the driveway at a snail's pace and I wanted to tell him to floor it, but I had to fight the urge. Instead, I watched the grand house disappearing behind us, the wall of gardens eventually blocking the view as we hit the main road and let out a sigh of relief. By the time we were trudging over the ramp to the houseboat, I was exhausted. The adrenaline had worn off and as Lance double, triple, quadruple checked every security monitor, I was starting to feel it. Pain, that is, all over my body as various cuts and bruises and strains flared to life. I grabbed a knife from the kitchen, using it to slash my heels so I could just slip out of them. They weren't worth saving anyway, which was a shame as I unwound the once-silver straps from around my calves. I winced as I did so, letting out a sharp exhale as I felt a cut on my back. Lance had been stripping out of his own disgusting clothes, the ruins sitting in a dirty pile at his feet as he turned toward the sound I'd made. He was just in a pair of black briefs and I tried to focus on that rather than the myriad of injuries I felt flaring to life.

"What is it?" he asked.

"It's nothing," I said, ignoring him as I continued to work at the shoes. He moved forward in a smooth blur, hands covering my own and forcing them to stop. I stilled, letting out a slow breath as he took the knife from my hands and placed it down on the bench I was leaning against. Crouched low at my feet, he gently pulled the straps free and slid one foot to the ground, followed by the other. Straightening up, he grabbed a rattling bottle of pills from above my head and handed me a glass of water.

"Take two of these."

I didn't argue. No one should argue when it came to pain meds. I slammed them back and took a long sip.

"Where?" he asked.

"My back," I sighed, his hands on my hips as he carefully turned me around. A finger pressed against the skin there and I gripped the counter for support. He handed me a pair of scissors.

"Shower," he commanded. "Cut yourself out of the dress, don't risk opening up any other wounds by trying to wiggle out of it."

"But–"

"It's a beautiful frock, Bobbi. But it has seen better days and I can't inspect the damage until you're out of it."

I grumbled something in response. I'm not sure the words were actually fully formed, but Lance chuckled like he understood their meaning. Making the shower as hot as I could stand it, I bit my lip and rested my head against the tiles as water poured over me. Lathering the soap, I did three full rinses before I was satisfied that every bit of ick was off me. I couldn't even dry myself properly, the friction of the towel causing all kinds of new issues. Moving like an old lady, I changed into an oversized singlet, something that would barely touch my skin even though my goosebumps were begging to be covered. But the houseboat was warming up, the heaters working fast, unlike me. By the time I was lumbering out of my room, Lance was waiting near the benched seat with a series of first aid supplies laid out on the table. His hair was wet, his skin now washed clean, and a pair of gray tracksuit pants hanging loose on his hips.

"Sit," he said, patting the table. I did so, an ice pack wrapped around my foot the second I took pressure off it. I had done a lot of good face kicking with that limb tonight, to which the bruising at the base of my toes was testament. There were a few minor cuts on my legs, only one that required a bandage, then mostly just a smattering of abrasions on my arms from the odd blast of debris that Lance dabbed antiseptic cream on. My back was the worst, I knew it was, because I'd worn a stupid backless gown when I should have showed up in head-to-toe body armor. Would that have raised a few eyebrows? Sure! But I wouldn't have to deal with what seemed like hundreds of little knives digging into my back.

"B, I'm gonna have to lift this up," Lance said, voice gentle. I nodded, because I knew he had to, but as I went to lift the singlet above my head he took over so I didn't have to move too much. I pressed the fabric over the front of my body, resting my head against his chest as he examined the wounds. He was silent, stoic, and I heard metallic sounds as he reached for an implement.

"There's a few pieces of stone in here from the chamber of

doom," he told me, keeping me abreast of what he was doing. "And a little bit of glass. I'm going to use tweezers to get them out, OK? While your skin is nice and soft."

I nodded, my wet hair moving up and down against his sternum as he worked around me.

"Then there's two cuts that are a bit deeper. Those will need a few stitches, but I'm great with a needle so don't worry."

He got started and my hands slipped from the fabric of my tank, not efficient enough to grip against the pain. My fingers dug into him instead, clinging, as I watched the minutes on the microwave tick past midnight.

"There go my days of wearing a halter," I muttered, the hair of his chest tickling the skin of my face.

"Don't say that," he growled. "That would be a loss too insurmountable to manage."

I smirked. "I think FiveFourThree were hired by the dean."

"Really?" Lance said, tone surprised. I knew he wanted to keep me talking, keep me distracted from the pain, and I was happy to oblige. "What makes you say that?"

"*We're hired to do a job and that job is protect our boss' investment until the completion of our contract term,*" I replied, repeating Jimmy's words verbatim. "Doesn't that seem like odd phrasing to you?"

"Yeah, but… Jimmy's odd. Clearly."

"Have you got your phone?"

"Left pocket."

My fingers were clumsy as I dug my hand in, noting just how dangerously loose those tracksuit pants were.

"Passcode?"

"1310," he said. "Kai's birthday."

I planted a kiss on his skin without thinking about it,

forehead moving back to rest against his heartbeat as I navigated my way to the FiveFourThree Solutions website. They had sample contracts online, with thousands upon thousands of words crammed into the fine print. I was patient though, I loved to read, and I needed the amusement.

"There it is," I said, triumphant. "Upon the event of a client's death, FiveFourThree Solutions are legally obligated to carry out the terms of the contract unto completion or satisfaction of the client's rightful living heir."

"A lifetime guarantee," Lance noted. "But the dean has no heir. He's a bachelor, no kids, no relatives, always used to joke about the Oliver Twist of it all."

"Everywhere they showed up was tied to the university in some way. Her lab, but not Pitt Rivers and not Chastleton House. Tonight was just bad luck. I think the dean hired them, maybe to stay on top of whatever he suspected Dr Calvin was up to. I kept wondering why she had those offsite locations and I think he's the reason. She builds additional labs outside of the university – and hides those plans – so she can work freely and without his prying eyes. He dies a few days ago and until they find someone to release them from the contract…"

I never finished that sentence, my mind tripping over a tiny detail. I tapped through Lance's phone, finding Tem's number and hitting dial. He answered on the second ring, like a legend.

"Hello?" he said, voice muffled with sleep. I was sorry to wake him, but not sorry enough to hang up. "Lance, what's going on?"

"It's Bobbi. Listen, have you had a chance to run the sample you found in the dean's nostrils?"

"Ugggh," he began, voice quiet for a moment as he thought. "Yeah, yeah, it was the last thing I did before leaving the office on Friday. I'll have the results Monday morning."

"Test it against what I found in the university lab."

"Huh?"

"I think they're the same," I said, my mind recalling the moment I'd made the connection. "There was more of it in the second lab tonight."

"You guys found the next one? That's great! Did you find anything useful?"

"Um, we did," I began. "But we weren't able to bring anything with us."

"Oh," he said, clearly disappointed. "Can you go ba–"

"Ow!" I jumped, Lance pulling the thread tight on my last series of stitches.

"I told you to stay still," he murmured.

"And I'm trying to solve the case."

"And I'm trying to *sew you up*, Inspector Morse."

"I – ugh," I huffed. "Tem, I gotta go. Compare the samples and let me know what you find."

"Of course. Are you OK? What did Lance mean by sew–"

"I'm fine, just get those answers."

"On it."

I hung up, slipping the phone back into Lance's pocket as he kept working. I was silent, entirely out of distractions and doing my best to stay stationary as instructed, ignoring the sensation of a needle weaving between my flesh.

"Don't give me the silent treatment," he mumbled.

"I'm not. I'm checking out your abs."

Said abdominals flexed with a laugh, really proving the point.

"Look at them, wow, that's great," I breathed. "They're like little, pronounced shelves. Are you sure you've drunk water lately? That's dehydration definition."

"I see the pain meds have properly hit."

He moved around to stand properly behind me and away from my prying grasp, tying off the last bit of loose thread.

"I'm a scientist," I said, closing my eyes. "You know *that I know* that's not how the medication works."

He murmured in agreement, not a proper word, just a sound as his fingers inspected each wound once more and covered the two stitched tight with plaster. I felt his breath against the back of my neck, a comfort to me as much as the knowledge that the pain was over. My body relaxed, leaning back against Lance, and he placed his chin on my shoulder, hands inching around my waist until they clasped at the front.

"It was still a nice wedding," he said, the scratch of his chin tickling my skin.

"You mean besides all the rich people you hate," I replied.

"The terrible music."

"Us getting shot at."

"The grenades."

I opened my eyes, arching my neck back to look up at him. "All the weird science."

He grinned, his face so close to mine the gesture pressed our cheeks together. "*So* much weird science. All the time. Everywhere we show up."

Running my hand down his face, I touched the dimples there. I loved those dimples. Few men had dimples anymore. When did that stop being a thing?

"I enjoyed the company though," he said, expression still amused but much more serious now.

"Suck up," I replied, pulling his lips down to meet mine. He kissed me back, the desire seeming just as urgent to him as he pulled me tighter, holding me as securely as he could without causing any more pain. I let the singlet fall away as he shifted, picking me up without a sign of strain. I wrapped my legs around his torso, attaching myself to his body like a barnacle as he carried me down the hall. This night had gone wrong in every single way it could, but as I felt Lance's heartbeat thud against my chest, I relished the sensation that one thing could still turn out *spectacular.*

"That's too much cheese."

"Hush, too much cheese! What are you saying?"

"Look, it's oozing everywhere."

"Exactly, that's what makes it perfect," Lance snapped, flopping down on the bed next to me and somehow managing to keep a toasted sandwich perfectly balanced on the plate. I wrapped the blanket around me tighter, tucking the edges under my arms in protest. He gave me a look like "really?" We both knew it wasn't staying in place much longer.

"Just try it," he said, voice soft as he planted a kiss on my shoulder. "You said you were worn out. Here's sustenance."

I cackled, looking down to see his mischievous stare twinkling up at me. "*You* said you were worn out, as I recall. *I* said I was hungry. Then you threw on Kate Bush and scampered down the hallway, excellent butt moving out of view and to the kitchen apparently."

God, that did smell good though. My tummy rumbled dramatically, betraying me, and Lance mercifully stayed quiet as I picked it up. I took a bite, holding it in my mouth for a moment because it was so hot, but I was starving. I gulped

down the lava, risking it. It took a second for all the flavors to
hit, but once they did, they didn't quit. My eyes went wide and
I took another bite, bigger.

"Easy," he laughed. "It's still scorching."

"Hoo kares," I struggled through the mouthful. "What's in
this?"

"Nothing that will make sense."

"Tell me or I won't offer you a bite."

"Mean. Baked beans, old cheddar, and Worcester sauce." I
gave him the other half of the sandwich and he pushed it back.
"No, I made it for you."

"Please," I said, licking my fingers as I finished my portion.
"I need you energized."

He was quiet for a beat. Suddenly, he took the largest and
most dramatic bite possible. I laughed, trying to wipe the
cheese from his face but somehow making it worse.

"Oh my god, you're an animal," I cackled, repositioning
myself as he rolled on to his back. Pillows propped behind his
head, he threw up an arm to make a hole for me like it was
the most natural thing in the world. I wiggled in greedily,
careful of my padded cuts, and watched him eat the rest of
the sandwich. I wasn't sure if this could ever be happiness
permanently, but it felt like happiness right now and that was
enough. That was all I could handle, all I could wrap my head
around, and I wouldn't burden myself with anything further
than the next five minutes, the next ten, the next fifteen. It
had been a moment since I'd spent time with someone like
this. I was a grown adult with needs just like anyone else and
being a single woman in LA wasn't hard. This, though, the part
afterward, the bit where I wasn't sneaking out, the intimacy. I
hadn't had this in a while.

"Stop looking at me," he said, swallowing the last of the toastie. "You're obsessed."

"I am," I smiled, watching the shock in his expression. "With this album."

He rolled his eyes. "Yeah, yeah, everyone loves *Hounds of Love*."

"Best song off it: go."

"Already said it. Album's named after the best song."

"'Cloudbusting', come oooon."

"I'm changing to The Slits," he huffed, reaching for his phone. "You can hear it through the grapevine, I don't wanna argue."

I tossed the blanket away, climbing on to his lap and snatching the device before he got a chance. His reaction times were usually quicker, but he was distracted. Maybe captivated was a better word as he looked up at me like he was admiring the ceiling of the Sistine Chapel.

"I don't wanna fight with you either," I said, voice low as I turned off the music. I tossed the phone to the side.

"So don't," he replied, leaning up to pull me to him as we collapsed back into the sheets.

The best sleep I'd ever had in my life had been on this houseboat. Whether it was the stress or the jet lag or the freedom of being in a new place, I'd had deep, dreamless sleeps in this cozy cocoon on the Thames. I don't know if I ever slept better than the few hours I had that night, well, early morning technically. In one of Lance's shirts and his warm body pressed up against my back, arms lazily thrown around me, I was so content that I was confused when I stirred. Frowning, I couldn't work out what did it at first until I felt the water on my hand.

"Bugger," I murmured, raising my head as I realized that I'd knocked over the glass of water next to the bed.

"Wazit?" Lance groaned.

"Nothing, I spilled some water. Go back to sleep."

"Mmmkay."

He rolled over happily and I went to move the glass, except it was perfectly still. Upright. Stationary. It took a few additional, precious seconds for my brain to start whirring into gear. The floor was a mirror? No, it couldn't be. I reached out my hand, thinking I was dreaming, before yanking it back as I made contact.

"Lance, wake up!"

"Why? You said I could–"

"We're sinking! Get up, get up!"

"WHAT?!"

The water was seeping in so quickly and so quietly, pouring into the bedroom like black oil as we lay there in complete darkness. None of the outlets were sparking so I knew the power was off, but that meant the lights we'd gone to sleep with were out, too. We were in Lance's room, which had only one tiny window the size of a long rectangle and way up high. It was our only source of light and barely at that, it still being dark outside. The water spilled onto the bed and I shrieked, the cold of the Thames shocking every remaining part of me to life.

"Move, move," Lance said, springing to action as he rushed to the door. It wouldn't open. The handle barely even jiggled. We were locked in here, stuck in a sinking room with a window too small to fit either of us through and a door that wouldn't budge as Lance smashed his shoulders against it repeatedly. He waded to his bedside cabinet, retrieving the gun that was there and firing at the door handle. I covered my ears, the sound extreme in such close quarters, but he didn't stop until he emptied the clip. The handle fell right out, water pouring through as he yanked it open. He threw out his hand and I took it, Lance pulling me into the hallway with him as the water rose to above our hips. It was *so cold*. I couldn't feel my toes, I could barely will my legs to move, but I knew that was better than the opposite. If I felt warm, then the hypothermia was setting in. We rushed past my room and I paused at the doorway.

"Bobbi, come on!"

"Two seconds," I cried, ducking inside. "My gear."

"Forget the gear!"

"Get to the door, I'm right behind you."

I heard him splash off toward the sliding door and I paddled deeper into my room, searching for my bag. It was still hanging on the hook against the wall and I threw the strap around my shoulders, wincing as it rubbed against one of my fresh wounds. I could hear Lance tugging at the door, yelling at it to open, and I rushed out to assist him. The water was now at my chin, and I was bobbing along the hallway, not walking. My head brushed against the ceiling and I told myself to stay calm as I searched for him. There was a splashing motion and my eyes tracked toward the sound, only just able to make out an arm among the spray. Then it went silent. Still. That's what scared me the most. Was he out? No, he wouldn't have left me behind.

"Lance?" I called, spitting at the water around my lips. "LANCE!"

Nothing. I patted the outline of my bag, looking for the shape I was after and grateful that even after returning with my tail between my legs from the wedding, I had still unpacked the few things I had taken with me. Pulling the flashlight free, my nose brushed the ceiling as I took a deep breath and the water covered the last pocket of air. I dived under, clicking on the light and pushing debris out of the way as I swam forward. My heart stabbed my ribs with urgency as I caught sight of him floating near the sliding door. Lance's body was still and my own cries came out muffled underwater. Yet there were bubbles escaping his lips, tiny ones, which meant he wasn't dead. For now. I couldn't see any sign of what had knocked him out, so I pivoted to the door he'd been trying so hard on. Yet with the added assist of the light beam, I could see why he'd had no luck.

A bike lock was chained around the handle. I didn't even waste time expending the last morsels of energy I had on it. It wouldn't budge. Spinning to the window seat, the table had flipped against it and I felt despair mingling with the burning of my chest. *No,* I thought. *We were not going to die on some dumb houseboat named* Linda. Lance was shirtless, so there was very little to grab him by safely. I clutched on to his wrist, pushing off against the glass door and using the momentum to send us forward down the hall. With my free hand, I half paddled, half grabbed at anything I could as I yanked us back to my bedroom. *Sorry, Lance,* I thought, using both feet to kick him into the room and closest to the last viable window. I'd never been so grateful to be freaked out by a kayaker my very first morning here.

The boat was sinking deeper, fast. I could feel it in the pressure building between my ears as I grabbed the shotgun I'd stashed under the bed. The range would be minimal, but I had to hope it would be enough. Lance was floating dangerously close to the target, so I kneed him out of the way. I fired, the round cracking but not smashing the window. I went again, this time with success as the glass compressed with the weight of the outside river. It was like flames were licking my lungs and I felt my body cough, convulsing with air, which I knew from training meant I had about forty-five seconds left if I didn't pass out. The third round didn't work, the weapon well and truly waterlogged now.

There was nothing left for it. I bent Lance's arm around the strap of my bag, trying to secure him to me as I smashed the butt of the shotgun against the window, once, twice, three times. On the fourth strike, I felt the pressure with a boom.

I dropped the gun just in time, clutching to every part of Lance I could as we were sucked out with the water flow. The second we cleared the structure of the boat – and I was sure I had him – I started kicking upwards. My legs burned, my back burned, my lungs burned, my eyes burned as I just told myself to keep powering toward the slightly lighter gray. I punched through the surface with a gasp, throwing my head back as my mouth flew open and I tried to suck in as much air as I could. The water was cold, the outside air somehow even colder, but I didn't care as I gulped as much of it into my lungs as I could. Lance was face down and I flipped him over so he was skyward.

Shouts were coming from the shore and they distracted me for a moment. One of our neighbors had woken up as we sank and he was yelling, pointing at the bubbling black water where our houseboat had once been. Others were appearing now, lights blinking on as they woke up. There were figures running down from the boathouses and all I could do was watch with a strange, horrified detachment. It was closer to swim to them, call for help, climb on to their boats and seek sanctuary. Yet I knew safety didn't wait for us there. Whoever just tried to kill us, whoever thought they successfully had, was probably watching from that very same shoreline. I tucked my arm around Lance in the position that would keep him floating on his back best, his airways open and exposed to the fresh night. Slowly, quietly, I started swimming us to the opposite side of the Thames.

CHAPTER SEVENTEEN

The mud was like painful jelly, its cold stinging my legs as I dragged Lance's dead weight up the riverbank. *Not dead,* I snapped at myself internally. *Not dead, never say dead.* He was breathing, I'd checked, and I'd kept a finger on his carotid artery as I struggled to swim us to shore. It was faint, but it was there. He hadn't regained consciousness, but that was a concern for when I could get us up off the bank and onto the grass proper.

"Gah!" I felt the stitches in my back reopen as I tugged, my hands gripping under his armpits, yet I didn't stop. The grass was stiff with frost, and it crunched under my bare feet as we finally made it. I'd worked with the current, using the flow of the Thames to take us downstream while I gradually worked my way to the opposite shore.

I'd kept my eyes on the scene at the houseboat as I paddled, watching as red and blue flashing lights joined the yellow ones of bouncing flashlights as people searched. For us. They wouldn't find us. They'd bring in divers eventually and they'd discover *Linda* at the bottom of the river, but no bodies. The smashed window would tell them we'd made it out, but never to the surface. That was a good thing. Let them think we were dead. Let the person who had sunk us think we were dead. We weren't just yet, but every additional minute of that belief bought us time. And it was time that I needed desperately because I was running out of it.

I rolled my fingers, feeling up Lance's ribcage until I found the perfect spot for compressions. Marking it with one hand, I tilted his head back and quickly checked his airways. Then I began CPR. I hummed a song from The Specials under my breath, his favorite, "A Message To You Rudy". It helped me keep pace as I switched and blew air into his lungs, but I also hoped my terrible singing would cause him to wake with a start. Then I would have a whole new set of problems, I realized, and mentally I started making a list of them so I wouldn't freak out, so I wouldn't panic, so I wouldn't succumb to the chattering that had started at my teeth and turned into full body shudders. One, get Lance awake. Two, get Lance warm. If the river hadn't killed him, hypothermia and the shock of the cold his body had been immersed in for far too long now would. An extension of two: get myself warm for the exact same reasons. If we both froze to death, we'd be useless to help the other. Three, get somewhere safe. Anywhere safe.

The only thing we had on our side was it was still dark, with only the faintest streak of gray teasing at the horizon. Dawn was still a few hours off at least, so we weren't causing any attention on this side of the bike path and tucked in next to… My eyes narrowed, trying to see what the faint outline of that structure was. Mercifully, a badger happened to run right up to it and the motion caused the exterior lights to flick on. A rowing club. Kind of a crappy and rundown one at that, but it was an enclosed space. It would have running water, preferably hot, and hopefully towels. How long until folks started rolling up for that morning's session? Probably not long, but I'd take whatever window I could get if only Lance would just–

"Wake!" I huffed, pounding his chest.

"The hell!" I blew in a long breath.

"Up!" I slapped his face, I'm ashamed to admit it.

He coughed. I froze. He coughed again and my hands shot forward, rolling him into the recovery position as he hurled up half the river. I collapsed onto him, resting my head on his bicep as he gagged and breathed and coughed under me.

"*Thank you,*" I said, not quite sure who I was saying it to. "*Thank you thank you thank you.*" Lance's hand brushed my knee, fingers too weak to grip but it being his way of telling me he was back, he was him, he was there. I leaned onto my heels, pushing his hair off his face and examining his eyes in the low light.

"I got you," I told him. His hand found mine, fingers twisting together as he breathed heavily. "Good, take those big gulping breaths. And the second you're able, we're gonna sit upright, OK?"

He nodded, a few more moments passing before I helped prop him into a sitting position.

"Ugh," he groaned, spitting to the side. "My mouth tastes horrible."

"The Thames isn't famed for its flavor," I replied, bracing myself under him as I threw his arms over my shoulder. "We need to move, ready?"

He grunted in response. His voice was ragged, and I knew his throat would feel shredded after the past ordeal, every gulp painful. Having nearly drowned myself, I wasn't a fan. With a heave, I got him to his feet and began hustling him toward shelter. It was less than half a mile, but it may as well have been a marathon as we struggled together. The shaking had started and as his body jolted in response to the freezing cold, I had to struggle to keep us both level.

I left him on a park bench right near the entrance of the rowing club, slipping my hands into my bag and retrieving my staves. My aim was off so it took me two goes, but I smashed the external lights so badgers or burglars wouldn't be triggered by our movement. I did a lap of the perimeter, looking for the best way in and finding one via what looked like a gear shed. It only had one padlock hooked around the handle, which I was able to pick with my shaking hands. I think the erratic motion actually helped, weirdly, because I was able to get the job done without my usual kit. Unfortunately, I'd left it on the kitchen table. In the houseboat. Which was now sunk.

I tried to not think about everything else that remained in there as I climbed through the rows of stacked kayaks, awkwardly moving my body around the horizontal racks and hollow fiberglass objects. Our laptops. The print-outs. Everything Lance had brought with him. All our weapons except what I had in my side satchel, which was very little. All our tech. I stumbled down to the cement, opening the door that led from the gear shed through to the changing rooms. I marched into a shower cubicle, turning on the hot tap and adjusting it until it was a manageable temperature then I jogged out to grab Lance.

The inside of the clubhouse was creepy, with trophy cabinets and cheap dining tables dormant as I rushed past them toward the main door. There was no alarm system, and I was grateful for it, propping the entrance open as I headed back to where I had left him. He was hunched over, shivering violently, with his arms wrapped around his chest in an attempt to warm the most vital parts of him. He looked up as I approached, getting to his feet but stumbling. I caught him, looped under his arm, and we got a good pace going as we inched inside and toward the changing rooms where steam was now billowing from the doorway. He let out a long, slow groan as he stepped into the warm water.

"You all right on your own for a bit?" I asked, helping as he slid down the wall and into a sitting position. His eyes told me no, but he nodded his head like a good soldier. We'd barely survived and with all my attention on him, there was no one to watch our backs. I dashed away as much as I could with my injuries, wishing I could switch on some lights in here but not willing to risk it. First, I made it back to the riverbank. Using a tree branch, I covered the dent our bodies had made by repacking the mud. Then I followed our route to the rowing club, erasing any visible signs I could see, before clearing up the glass from the smashed lights. I dumped the broken shards in a nearby trashcan, locked up the gear shed from the outside, then slipped back in through the front door and resealed everything exactly as I'd found it.

Then I hunted for items of use, finding them when I broke into what looked like a combination storeroom and tuck shop. There were boxes upon boxes of club merchandise, and I grabbed corresponding sizes in the tracksuits, T-shirts, beanies and swimwear for undergarment support. Sadly so few rowing clubs had their own underwear lines, so speedos in Lance's case and a sports bikini in mine would have to do. I also grabbed a few of their huge, logo-laden beach towels and nearly cried with relief when I wrapped one around me. Finally heading back to the changeroom, I left everything of use on the wooden racks and checked in on Lance, who had his eyes closed as he stayed under the stream of hot water. One eye peeked open and he smiled, lopsided, as he took a look at me.

"Have I ever told you that you look amazing in a wet T-shirt?"

I laughed. OK, so he was *back* back. "You're a monster, but at least you've stopped shivering."

He held out a hand for me and I took it. "Get in here."

I let him drag me under the stream, my body shaking even harder at the shock of sudden warmth at first, before my muscles soon started to relax. Lance tugged said wet T-shirt off my body, my remaining underwear, too, and it joined his one item in a wet pile at the corner of the cubicle. He pulled me into his arms, his legs wrapping around my body and holding me there as we just sat. Naked, holding each other, and under the jet of warm water that was slowly bringing us back to life. We stayed like that until the hot water turned tepid, us having truly drained the club of its entire supply. I wasn't sorry. We deserved it. Wrapped in one of the towels, I quickly inspected Lance as best I could while forcing him to drink an entire bottle of water I'd salvaged.

"All of it," I said. "It would be so embarrassing for you to survive drowning then die of dehydration."

He seemed fine. He said he was fine. He looked fine.

"Let me see you," Lance replied, pulling my own towel away. "Your stitches have reopened. And pretty much all of your bad cuts are bleeding. Again."

I hissed as he touched one. "I know. I could feel it. There's not much of a first aid kit unfortunately, but it's got antiseptic spray so hit me with that and I can use sanitary pads."

"Sanitary pads?" he asked.

"Don't tell me you're one of those guys who gets freaked out by *periods*, Lance," I teased, looking at him over my shoulder.

"No, but how are–"

"They're sticky and absorbent. Put them over the worst cuts please."

"*Oh*, OK," he huffed with a laugh. "Got ya."

I heard the tearing of strips, the sting of the spray on my back, and the pressing of the napkins against my flesh. He had to help me into clothes, my old aches and pains flaring up by the minute, and it seemed incredibly rude of fate to have him recovering faster than I was. He'd been a proper cadaver, after all, but now he was bundling up all our bits into the trash and leading me out into the dining area, making *me* a cup of tea in a Styrofoam cup. I couldn't verbally complain though, because I was grateful. Not just for the warm liquid pouring down my throat, but for the company. He'd been the first to say it what felt like weeks ago now, yet Lance was right. We made a great team. Properly equal. I realized with a start that was what one of the major issues with Clint had been. We should have been properly equal. Yet outside of our relationship, few people had treated me that way. Then inside our relationship, his behavior had started to reflect that.

"What's going on in that big brain of yours?"

Lance's question startled me out of my thoughts, back to the present, and back to where I sat on the edge of the counter with him resting between my legs.

"Nothing." I smiled. "Just really glad you're not dead."

"That's the most romantic thing anyone has ever said to me."

I huffed out a laugh. "I hope that's not true."

His finger dipped under my chin, tilting my face to look at him. "Thank you. For saving my life. And very nearly at the expense of your own."

I placed the cup to the side, tugging on the fabric of his tracksuit as I pulled him in. I gripped on to Lance for dear life, my head buried in his neck and inhaling his fresh scent like it was a drug. I couldn't let go. I just latched on and hugged tightly, so grateful and glad that he was OK. That we both were.

"I'm all right, Bob," he murmured, planting a kiss on my head. "I'm all right."

He pulled back, creating a small amount of space between us, but not enough that we weren't touching, which I was glad for.

"We can't stay here much longer," I said, jerking my head in the direction of the lightened sky. "The first squad is here in an hour, coaches half an hour before that according to the schedule on the board."

"We need transport," he suggested. "And somewhere to lay low. We shouldn't be visible right now."

"I have an idea."

In the gear shed, at the very top of the rack of kayaks was a much older boat. I'd seen it as I crawled in, cobwebs dangling from it. I left Lance to acquire snacks, refreshments, and shoes from the lost and found. Socks were a bonus, dirty or not, but I was desperate to cover my toes. I made the boat above us hospitable, wiping down the inside and making a toasty cocoon with fresh towels. We climbed in one after the other, the outside still looking like the relic it was, yet inside we were bundled up against each other, resting and regaining our strength while we waited.

"Tell me what happened down there," Lance asked, passing me a packet of chips with a flavor suspiciously named spring onion. They were good, though. Great, even.

"How much do you remember?"

"All of it up until the door. I remember seeing it was locked, tugging, diving down and trying to get it open in between breaths and then… nothing. Waking up on the shore with you."

I munched thoughtfully. "I heard you yell. Came out and you were unconscious. I got us out through the bedroom window and that's the gist. But there was a bike lock on the main door. Your bedroom had been locked. Somebody snuck on board with the intention to kill us."

"Then why not just do it?" he huffed. "They didn't trip up any alarms and I had several, Bobbi."

"I know."

"We were unconscious, why not just kill us then?"

"To make it look like an accident," I replied. "Just like the dean. Another accidental death."

"I agree, but I don't know. This isn't Jimmy's style–"

"And what kind of condition were they left in last night to come after us?" I cut in. "We got away smooth and even we were worse for wear. They were in no state. Besides, who knew about the houseboat?"

"No one," Lance replied. "I didn't even have Professor Falkner's address linked to it, all of that went to a PO Box. I rented *Linda* under a pseudonym, there was no way it could be tracked back to me, and we *always* went roundabout routes to get home. We were careful, Bobbi. I was. You were."

The sound of a car engine rumbled closer toward us, cutting out as someone pulled into the parking lot. We listened as a set of keys jangled, opening up the main door and turning on the radio so the morning news blared as they set up. The coach.

"What pseudonym?" I whispered. "For the boat."

"Uh." Lance strained, thinking. "Lene Lovich."

"'Lucky Number'," I said, my mind flicking through the songs on the playlist in my head.

"And the superior version of 'I Think We're Alone Now'," Lance added.

I pressed my hand against his forehead, assessing. "I knew there'd be some permanent damage."

He went to brush my hand away with a huff, but paused as lights clicked on in the gear shed. We stayed perfectly still, not that it really mattered, as we were invisible and forgotten way up high. Soon the rowers started arriving, a steady audible rhythm of a car rolling up, someone shouting "hi!" to somebody else or a standard "morning, bit nippy, isn't it?"

Couldn't relate. After so much painful cold, we were snug and cozy as the roller door was hurled up and kayaks started being removed, one by one. We listened as the coach outlined that morning's session while running through a series of stretches, the clunk of boats and paddles moving off eventually growing smaller. We waited an additional ten minutes, just in case. I stuck my head up first, assessing what I could strain to see of the outside and parking lot down below. There were voices from inside the clubhouse, but as long as they stayed there it wouldn't matter.

I slowly, carefully, quietly climbed out. Perched on the now empty racks, Lance handed me my bag. I wrapped it around my body, waiting for him to join me. When he did, we dropped down fast, our descent much easier given there were no kayaks in the racks. I swung off the final bar, landing on the concrete with perfect balance and crouched low as my eyes scanned the empty parking lot. No one. There were a few cyclists well off in the distance, but it was still too early for most.

"Show off," Lance said, passing me as he marched toward a car with purpose. He clearly knew which one he wanted, and he pulled a contorted wire coat hanger he'd pinched from the changing rooms from his tracksuit. I leaned against the vehicle, trying to look casual as he slipped it between the glass of the window and started working.

"I'm so grateful for your juvenile delinquent days," I muttered.

"You should be," he said, winking as the door popped open. I dashed around the side and he leaned over, opening the passenger door for me. He leaned under the steering wheel, yanking at wires and pulling cords free.

"It's those juvenile delinquent days that mean I know a black Vauxhall Corsa is the third most common model on the road," Lance muttered, the engine rumbling to life. He pumped the clutch and we waited, idling for a moment. He leaned across, opening the glove box and quickly pocketing a few loose bills he found there. Throwing the car into reverse, he began slowly backing out of the parking lot and onto one of the nearby side roads. We only drove for about half an hour before we spotted what we wanted, Lance dropping me off at a small motel while he drove away to ditch the car. I booked a room for three days, paying in cash that was noticeably damp but – gratefully – the clerk didn't mention it.

The room was cute. Quaint. A lot of lace. I mean, the place was called Inn The Country so I'd expected as much. I caught a glimpse of my reflection in the full-length mirror. In head-to-toe cream, the only thing that broke up the vanilla palette was the maroon logo on the front of my tracksuit. It was a drawing of a cartoon narwhal in maroon. It had huge hearts for eyes and the horn made up the letter "L" on the text which read: Northside Narwhals Rowing Club Est. 1884. Tough. But to be fair, I did look like someone who had barely survived getting crushed in a tunnel and then drowning on a boat. Par for the course.

I yanked my bag off, quickly laying out every item inside it on the floor in front of the heater so I could take stock and hopefully dry them off a bit. Sure, grabbing this had nearly come at the cost of Lance's life, but he was fine now. It had been worth it. I had a bundle of soggy cash. I had several passports and documents for various identities, all unsoggy thanks to the zip-lock bag I'd put them in. I had a random mishmash of tools, from my flashlight to Lance's butterfly knife, which I couldn't remember putting in there but clearly had. A packet of quite useful hair clips. Several pairs of gloves. A handgun. Ammo, but not enough. Harnesses. My personal devices, phone and tablet, also undamaged due to their airtight and impenetrable magnetic protective case. One tactical suit, the other now belonging to the River Thames Narwhals. My staves. And the cluster of keys, two which we now knew what they opened, and one still a mystery to us. Dr Calvin's final lab.

I left everything where it was, taking just a stave with me as I pulled a chair outside and posted up out front, twirling the stave in my hands. There was no trick to this. People asked what the trick was all the time, but the trick was that there was none. I guess that's why I had first been drawn to fighting sticks in my training as a tween. They just required practice. Time. Patience. Persistence. I was spinning the stave idly between hands, deep in thought, as I watched a vanilla creamsicle peddling down the lane on a road bike. It took me a moment to realize it was Lance, a backpack strapped to his shoulders and a grocery bag in the basket of the bike. He rode right up to the door, wheeling his ride and everything inside. I could hear him banging about, unpacking, sorting. Finally, he joined me with a chair of his own.

"Where'd you leave the car?" I asked.

"Back where I found it."

I turned to him. "Seriously?"

"Yeah, it was a risk, but I figured I'd drive past and if they were back already, I'd keep going. But they weren't, so I returned it in semi-working order."

"Semi."

"No stolen car report to be filed, no flags to be raised if anyone was looking for them."

"Clever."

"What'd you book the room under?"

"Shane Bradley."

"I do love The Nips."

I snorted.

"Got us some groceries and a few essentials on my way back."

"Essentials?"

"It's grim. I wanted to go back to the boat shed, but I couldn't risk it. It's too close to *Linda* and there were still people everywhere."

"I bet."

"But when we call in–"

"No."

"What?"

"We're not calling in."

"Bobbi, we're going to have to–"

"Who knew, Lance? Who knew the location of *Linda*?" I had been sitting there for a while, pondering this exact question and had come to the same conclusion every which way I examined it.

"Hang on, you can't turn this back on S.T.R.I.K.E. What about your people?"

I looked at him, hard, waiting for him to get there.

"They didn't know," he whispered.

"They knew I was in Oxford, they knew I was at Magdalen College, but they didn't know about the houseboat. I'd never updated them on the details."

Lance ran his hands over his face, as if trying to rub some sense into his features.

"If you're confident it wasn't FiveFourThree–"

"It wasn't," he cut in.

"I agree. Then the parties who knew were me, you and…?"

Lance leaned back, closing his eyes. "S.T.R.I.K.E."

My gaze flicked back to the road, watching as a line of ducks waddled across it and into a nearby bush. There must be a creek nearby. This idyllic, country scene couldn't have been further from everything we'd been through in the past twenty-four hours, let alone what I was feeling inside.

"Whatever we do next," I began, "we need to keep it strictly between us. No S.T.R.I.K.E. No back up. Just us."

He was quiet for a beat then Lance held out his fist, knuckles scratched from where he'd tried punching the glass on the houseboat. I bumped it.

CHAPTER EIGHTEEN

We slept in shifts to start. Last time we'd thought the alarm systems and surveillance would keep us safe. They hadn't. Now we had none of that, but what we did have was each other. And that would have to do. I had to send a message to Hill, to let her know I was OK and when S.T.R.I.K.E. would inevitably reach out to see if I'd made contact, lie. Fudge ignorance. I used my own phone for that, keeping it on airplane mode, connecting to the inn Wi-Fi and sending only the briefest of messages to Hill's private line. Her reply was brief.

"Understood."

She was a rock and although we were looking every which way for enemies, Hill was someone I knew could not only be trusted but was immovable. The next thing I did – working while Lance slept – was access my secure drive. Every image I had taken on this mission I had set up by default to upload here. The blueprints might have been fish food, but I still had a digital copy. Unfortunately, I didn't have a copy of the physical books which were now destroyed as well. Lance was better at the blueprints on the final lab than I was, respectfully, and I left him to it. He could search for stonework and phrases online with a few quick strokes of the keypad, whereas it would take me hours to identify that as something of value. Besides, the only fully impenetrable and safe digital device was my tablet and that was not conducive to two users simultaneously.

If he was working on that, then I needed to be unconscious or actively elsewhere. I alternated between both options, using several hours on the first night to stake out the boathouse storage site he kept with the rest of his supplies. There was no movement. No sign of threat. But I was super cautious. He'd used a different name for renting that place – Dan Woodgate, a guy from a Camden ska band called Madness – and he'd paid in cash from a different landlord. If this site hadn't gone down already, then it likely wouldn't. Key word: likely. I was more risk averse than I had been, because I had more to risk. I left without taking anything.

I did watch though, from a distance, as the crowd that had been searching for us last night were replaced with professionals. When the sun set, the search was called off, the divers returning to land, and the tent becoming the base of operations for the night shift. There were a few passing onlookers, the usual nosy neighbors, and the occasional reporter. Yet no one who raised a red flag. When I returned, Lance looked a wreck. I might have had more visible injuries, but he was still battling unseen ones.

"You need to rest," I said, placing a hand to his cheek. "You're still recovering."

He closed his eyes, like my touch soothed him, and he leaned backward into the half-made bed. "Fine, but I'm going to tell you what I found while I rest my eyes."

"Deal."

"You go first."

"Double deal. This will be quick though."

I summarized what I saw and my hesitation to move on the boathouse. Lance agreed, questioning whether we go back at all.

"How was your day, honey?" I teased.

He smiled, looking like he was moments away from sleep. "Right here."

Lance tapped the tablet, his hand going limp. I turned back to find him dozing already, his breathing heavy as he fell back under. I was keen for sleep, too, but I was more interested in what was on the tablet. I picked it up, examining the screen. He had edited the photo I'd snapped and uploaded of the final laboratory's blueprint, inverting the colors of the lines and heightening them. He'd overlapped it onto an existing blueprint, just like I had with Pitt Rivers. I didn't recognize this place though and I had to decrease the visibility, bringing the blueprint down and this location way up. It looked like a castle. No, not looked like: *was* a castle. I switched tabs toggling to the website Lance had last been looking at: Oxford Castle and Prison.

"Of bloody course," I moaned, sounding like I'd been spending too much time with Lancelot Hunter. "Only you would pick a location like this for your lab, Wilma."

There was a dry humor to it, at least that's what I interpreted. If she was a prisoner being forced to bend to the will of her captor, she would damn well do it from a literal prison. Thankfully that prison was a tourist attraction and during set hours, on set days, just like Pitt Rivers Museum and Chastleton House, it was a very accessible place. Our path in was just a matter of purchasing two tickets, which I did in a few hasty clicks, and then finding an opportunity to get split from the tour group. Of all the destinations so far, this seemed the most doable.

I was twitchy, posting up by the window and fidgeting with the handcuffs just like Lance had taught me. He was better at this than I was, faster, even as much as I'd practiced, but the most crucial aspect was it gave me something to do with my hands while I waited. And watched. And waited some more. I knew Lance had set his own alarm for when he needed to wake and we would switch shifts so I could get some sleep, but I disabled it. Soon as it was light enough, soon as the world started waking up, I wrote him a note and I left. He needed all the rest he could get if we were going to make the tour in fighting shape. I could rely on caffeine, which I acquired after jogging to the center of town. Platinum hair hidden under a beanie, I looked just like anyone else fighting the cold of the season as I made my way through the shopping list of items. When Lance had ridden up on that bike, the backpack he had with him was stuffed with as many clothes as he could fit when he'd purchased it from a sporting goods store. That was essentially workout gear and thermals for the both of us, which was better than what we'd had – Northside Narwhals represent – but left me to acquire the bridging items. When I returned to Inn The Country, he was up and pacing the room with agitation.

"You let me sleep too long," he huffed by way of hello.

"You needed it."

"*You* need it. How much rest have you had, Bobbi? Look at the bags under your eyes."

"Hurtful. You should be asking about the bags under my arms."

I tossed one, Lance catching it and looking inside with suspicion that turned to horror. "Ugh, not tourists."

"We're just two crazy kids from America who *love* spooky castles," I grinned. "Like, oh my god, it's giving major medieval!"

"You're the worst," he mumbled, pulling out the items one by one. Ditching my own bags, I sidled up closer to him.

"That's a shame," I replied, planting a slow kiss at the base of his throat. He stiffened, his attention redirecting to me as his body reacted and he let me tug his lips to mine.

"How much energy do we have to save for this tour exactly?" he asked.

I leaned back, answering the question not with words but with actions as I tugged his T-shirt free of his body. We had a little time.

"This is humiliating," Lance sighed. I did my best to swallow any laughter I felt bubbling up. He was wearing a *Ghostbusters II* T-shirt, which had the superior logo in my opinion, complete with red scarf, matching beanie and a black overcoat bulky enough that it could disguise some rather essential items. Weapons, mostly.

"If it makes you feel better," I said, "it's hard to de-hotify you. Even in geek chic."

"Because it can't be done! You cannot sand off my edges, baby!"

"Rrrrright," I said, zipping up my tactical suit. I would have preferred my all-black one, but I hoped a local mermaid was making use of it. This black and white version was more closely aligned to my West Coast Avengers costume, minus the capelet, and I felt Lance's eyes on me as I clipped the utility belt with a distinctive "M" in place around my hips. Others had a power suit or a favorite bra that made them feel like a super hero. I had a holster for my battle staves and thigh straps to sheathe a variety of small knives. Throwing a structural, white coat over the top, blue beanie, and fingerless gloves in a matching shade, I looked like someone ready to tour "one of England's most haunted locations!" We just had one stop to make on the way: the boathouse.

We scoped it out for probably longer than we needed to, but once we were inside it was clear it hadn't been touched. No one had discovered this place and despite the camera I'd looped around his neck as a prop, I could see it in Lance's stature that he felt better the moment he was running his hands over his Ducati. Leaning against a bench with amusement, I watched as he loaded two handguns and attached them to his person.

"Where are you going to affix a third?" I asked as he searched for a spot.

"It's my little .22 caliber. I love this guy."

I held up my hand. "Give me. I'll keep it warm for you as a treat for finding the third lab."

He looked delighted as I clipped it to my waist. We cleared the whole space, dropping one cache of equipment back at the inn and two more at storage lockers across the city. We didn't need it right now, but we might, and if one location went down like the houseboat, at least we had several backup sites. Clinging to Lance on the motorbike, we weaved around Oxford with the setting sun, a clear day fading to a starless evening so rapidly it was like we turned one corner and suddenly the world was in night mode. It mattered little what time it was because Oxford Castle and Prison was foreboding regardless, as was the intent of all such structures.

This place was over a thousand years old, having been remodeled from wood to stone and rebuilt from English Civil Wars to tourist attraction. It endured, century by century. Saxon St George's Tower was the easiest thing to spot as it soared higher above the stone perimeter than anything else as we wound up toward the site on the west of the city. *Why couldn't you have built your lab up there, Wilma?* I thought to myself. *Save us trudging into some probably freezing dungeon to save your butt.*

Slipping off the bike in the parking lot, I shook my hair free of the helmet and I hoped I'd get a chance to be mad at the old woman later. The opportunity to yell at someone was always much more appealing than the prospect of mourning them. There was a steady flow of people heading inside, the castle illuminated with dramatic lighting that did even more to enhance the very tangible impact it had on anyone approaching. It made you feel small, not just because of the size, because of the history. It was weighty.

"Are you here for the Spectre Ghost Tour?" a man in a bowler hat asked.

"My gosh, yes," I breathed. "What gave us away?"

"The shirt," he replied, pointing at Lance's chest.

"There is no Dana." Lance shrugged. "Only Zuul."

The guy gave him a cheery and very fake laugh, happy to take our tickets as I handed them over and probably thinking about all the money he was going to make off us when we hit the gift shop.

"Suppose you get a lot of the paranormally curious coming to these tours." I beamed.

"Oh yes," he replied, handing me a lantern. "And some who never come baccccck."

The "oooOoooo" that was added for dramatic effect was unnecessary, but from the giggles behind us an appreciated touch. I smiled when I saw it was a bachelorette party, the flash of amusement in Lance's glance telling me he felt the same. In terms of creating distractions for us to slip away and keep the guide's attention elsewhere, a tiddly bachelorette party was a gift from the heavens.

"Hear ye, hear ye!" our bowler hat wearer called after a few minutes of everyone mingling about.

"Hear ye?" Lance whispered.

"Ssssh, I would actually like to hear ye," I replied, elbowing him.

"Welcome to the Spectre Ghost Tour where I – your undead guide Professor D Ceased – will help you navigate the underworld at one of England's most haunted sites: Oxford Castle and Prison!"

There was a quick series of cheers and clapping as the group gathered leaned hard into his schtick. I counted heads quickly, coming up with fifty-four people which was good. The visual difference between fifty-two and fifty-four was barely noticeable.

"Now let's proceed into the bowels of the building and bring to light what you may not be able to see. Collect your lanterns and follow me!"

We did so, Lance and I immediately dropping to the back of the group where we needed to be. I had checked the route of this tour; it took us almost exactly to where we needed to go and I kept my eyes peeled for the landmark. When we hit the part of the castle that had been converted into a prison, I nudged Lance. He nodded and we scanned the bars and empty cells that we passed, each with keyholes of interest.

Yet there was only one section that corresponded with the position on the blueprints. It was elevated, unlike the others, with four stone steps leading up to a platform of four cells that were separated behind a railing.

"It's said that two of the most malicious ghosts still active on the premises today are women," the guide was saying.

"Ugh, of course," I scoffed as we slowly started dropping farther and farther back.

"Half Hanged Annie sprang back to life in 1650 after her execution for killing her own baby," he said, only his bowler visible now as we sank into the shadows. "She was so alluring after her revival that her sentence was entirely dismissed, and she went on to have three more children!"

The murmur of responses was inaudible now and Lance put our lantern out altogether, the light vanishing as we crouched behind a pillar and waited for the group to move on.

"Now as for the poisoner Mary Blandy…"

His voice faded away entirely as they left. We moved, heading straight for the quartet of cells, and soundlessly leaping the railing.

"Have you ever poisoned any–"

"Yes," I replied, examining each of the locks one after the other. Only one looked right for the key we had.

"Whoa."

"What? You wanted me to lie?"

He tilted his head. "Maybe? I dunno, you just replied *so* quickly. Yes. Definitive."

"If it makes you feel better, it was a war criminal and the dose was only to put them in a vegetative state."

"Pffft, vegetative state."

"Key," I said, extending my hand. He passed it over. I inserted it into the lock of the third cell, not quite understanding how this would work as the cell door was already open. Yet from the second I turned it clockwise, I heard the whirring mechanism as joints and bolts and pins unclicked against each other, causing a chain reaction. The seemingly solid stone wall behind us slid open barely an inch and looked like it was about to slide back to its starting position when Lance grabbed it. He positioned our lantern in the gap, propping it open and the sound of the stone against metal made me wince. Lance went first, drawing his weapon, and I followed, unsheathing my staves. My fingers stroked along the side of the shafts, activating the charge and affording us some light. Stone stairs stretched downward into seemingly impenetrable darkness as we hovered on the top two steps.

"Do you watch horror movies, Bobbi?"

"Just because I watch them doesn't mean I want to be in them," I whispered back, knowing exactly where he was going with that.

"I don't think we have much choice."

"Blondes tend to have a limited shelf life. You better go first."

He smirked, tossing me a look, before he took a step into the darkness. Then another. And another. I wasn't sure how long we were down there, it was impossible to gauge the time properly and I didn't want to risk a glance away from the steps to check my watch. Their texture was uneven, each one creating a different obstacle as it slanted this way or dipped that. One half crumbled under my weight and I tried not to take offense. There was a faint glow up ahead, the ceiling above us brushing against my skull and I stooped lower as we neared the end. Please let it be the end. Thankfully, it was. Unthankfully, we were in a crypt.

"See that arched stone looping from the column?" Lance whispered.

"Yeah."

"That's how I found this place. That kind of structure is unique and incredibly rare. It's one of the oldest parts of the castle, built way back in 1074."

"What are you, the bowler hat bro now?" I huffed.

"That's Professor D Ceased to you."

I stifled a laugh, the lack of steamed breath giving me pause. It had been freezing on the stone steps, the cold stinging my cheeks and making each exhale visible. Now, it was warm and growing warmer. In fact, the closer we moved towards the light, splitting up and using the columns as cover, the warmer it got until it felt like the heat being generated was borderline tropical. I was back in California with every additional step, the sound of an American voice doing even more to solidify the illusion. I recognized that voice.

Lance and I made eye contact from behind the stone structures we were leaning against, having crept as far as we could. I couldn't be sure what he saw when he looked at me, but the excitement in his gaze was tinged with wariness and a flash of something else. This was the "aha" moment we'd been desperately searching for. The space opened up after that, the sound of running water gently trickling nearby and mixing with the chatter of the radio as a BBC news program played at low volume. I stuck my head out just a touch, observing what I could, and the sight shocked me.

A state-of-the-art laboratory stretched out, the mix of tech and equipment a sharp juxtaposition to the ancient structure it was housed within. There was an enormous amount of space here compared to Pitt Rivers and even Chastleton House, with the square footage in this lab dwarfing where the others had been tucked and hidden and disguised amongst other pockets of life. The layout of this place was significant not just because of the size, but because of the way it mimicked the layout of S.H.I.E.L.D.'s Project Gladiator base almost exactly. There was a grid of cages, each one stacked two by two, but they were much too large for mice or rats. The yelp from inside one of them told me what they held: dogs. Puppies, actually. And right there at the center of it all was Dr Wilma Calvin. Her back was to me, but I would have recognized that silhouette anywhere. I'd spent years watching that woman work in that exact same position.

The emotional tug on my person was physical, my staves hanging limp at my side as I inched out from my cover. I heard Lance whisper my name, hiss it almost, but it felt like a tiny buzz at the base of my brain as I kept slowly stepping toward this woman I never thought I'd see alive again. His attempts to get my attention didn't work, but they clearly caught hers. She whipped around faster than you would have expected for an old bird and snatched up a piece of equipment to her left. Gripping it in her hands, she pointed it at me as I dropped my weapons and threw my hands up in surrender.

The shift in her expression from hardened stare to shock was a true metamorphosis as her eyes drank me in. Her hands shook, eyes welling up with tears as she digested who was before her.

"Bah… bah…"

"It's me, Wilma," I said, voice gentle.

"Bobbi?" she all but whimpered. "Bobbi Morse?"

"Yes." I smiled, relieved. "I've been looking for you for a long time. We both have."

"Oh, thank God, I'm so happy to see you."

Her glasses fogged up as she started to cry, shoulders shaking, and she dropped her weapon. I couldn't stand it and I rushed forward, arms extended. She folded into them naturally, the old scientist having seemingly shrunk over the years. Or maybe I'd grown more than I realized.

"You have no idea what it has been like," she said, voice muffled against my coat. "Working in these conditions…"

"Ssssh, it's OK. We're going to get you out of here."

I felt a familiar rage bubbling under my skin, mad at whoever had done this to her and all past transgressions on both sides forgotten. Rubbing her back to comfort her, the bench space behind her looked just as much like the organized chaos when I'd worked with her as I remembered. Notes and beakers and bubbling and… I frowned, eyes catching on the object she had spun around to defend herself with. It wasn't what I was expecting. It was a very specific and unique weapon that I had seen before. In fact, I'd laid my eyes on an entire crate of them at the Academy Museum what felt like a lifetime ago. At a glance, it looked like a water gun and my mind flashed back to the second lab, the trays of deconstructed weapons. As if someone had been trying to understand how they worked, how they could be made, how they could be improved. A prickle of unease started at the base of my spine.

"We?" Wilma asked. "You're not alone? Are S.H.I.E.L.D. here?"

"No," I replied, mind still catching up. "It's just me and Lance."

I turned around to look for him, but he was hovering farther back, as if reluctant to expose his position.

"Oh," she said, sighing with relief in a way that made me

lean back, examining her. She blinked away fat tears on her cheeks, sniffing. "Thank goodness for that."

I barely had a moment to register the change in her voice before she lifted up a canister pressed against her chest and sprayed me with it. I'd been clutching on to the woman, so I copped a full hit to the face as I lurched backward, gasping and spluttering at the brassy taste in my mouth. My eyes weren't stinging, so I knew it wasn't pepper spray, but I couldn't talk either as I tried to formulate words. My lips were moving, but no sound came out as I dropped to my knees, my legs giving out. It was a nerve agent, I realized, trying to fight my body's desire to shut down, to pass out, to give up. It was futile.

As I collapsed onto the hard, stone ground, all I could manage to do was roll to the side so I wouldn't choke on my own tongue. The swish of Dr Calvin's lab coat swept in front of me for a moment, my vision narrowing into a black tunnel like I was at the conclusion of a *Looney Tunes* episode. I could hear the tone of her voice, but not properly comprehend the words. The last thing I saw, the thing that made my heart slam against my chest in protest, was Lance's unconscious body being dragged away. Everything went dark.

CHAPTER NINETEEN

No big deal, but I knew a few people who'd been brought back from the dead. Not in a bribe the ferryman way, far as I knew, but with science. With cutting edge technology. And almost always, with excruciating pain.

My back arched as I came to, my body bucking against the restraints as I let out what was more of a strangled cry than an actual scream. The wave of agony faded almost as quickly as it had come on. I slumped, letting my body go limp and pretending to pass out again. The taste in my mouth made me want to throw up, but I swallowed the urge down – quite literally – as I tried to preserve my strength and listen to everything around me. It was coming back in chunks, the memory of creeping through this crypt with Lance and seeing Dr Calvin. Embracing Dr Calvin. Being attacked by Dr Calvin.

"Prepare two samples," the woman's voice said, sounding stiff and professional. "We can wait until Bobbi's awake then decide who goes first."

"I'll go."

Oh God, Lance! His voice was firm. He sounded strong, unhurt, and angry.

Dr Calvin snorted. "How chivalrous."

"Use me. I'll do it."

"Oh, you'll do it. That's not a question. It's whether you're first or whether you're second."

"First, then. I'll volunteer to be your tribute or whatever. Just let Bobbi go."

"You know I'm technically a genius, right?"

"I've heard," he said, spitting the words.

"Then treat me like one. I'd never be stupid enough to let her go when we're this close to perfection."

"She'sssss awake."

That voice. I didn't recognize that one. It sounded as if it slithered from the speaker's lips, dripping like ooze from their brain and into my ears. It chilled my core and I shivered to attention, feeling like an ice cube was slowly being run down my spine. Opening my eyes, everything was hazy at first. I could make out shapes, barely. Just foggy outlines of the same space I'd been in before. A figure moved, fading into the darkness, while the other sharpened to reveal Dr Calvin watching me with keen interest.

"No tears this time," I said, voice sounding as horrible as I felt.

She smiled slowly, yet the gesture didn't appear right. It looked dangerous. "I thought you'd be proud, Bobbi. Isn't that what they teach you at S.H.I.E.L.D.? Adapt to the situation."

She wandered over toward me and it was then that I was able to get a better sense of the predicament I was in. I was strapped onto an operating table that had been positioned upright, something I was initially optimistic about because vertically that meant I could utilize gravity to get free once I cut the restraints. With the weapon I didn't have. But still. A metallic clinking made me strain my neck upwards, where my hands were handcuffed above my head and linked around the table's steel bar. They'd used the handcuffs I'd had on me. I could work with that. My eyes met Lance's and I could tell he was on exactly the same page. He was in an almost identical position just a few feet away from me, yet his hands had been held in place with a combination of zip-ties. One you could snap out of easily, maybe even two, but they had seemingly used an entire supermarket's worth on him. It was clearly all they had, our appearance unexpected and unwanted.

"Adapt to what situation, exactly?" I asked, trying not to recoil as she checked my vitals. Her fingers were icy.

"I was under the impression you were dead," she said simply.

"*Linda*," Lance breathed, answering my question of why she would think we were dead. She'd sunk the houseboat.

"Who's Linda?" Dr Calvin asked. She remained a good scientist, albeit a mad one, right to the end. A good scientist asked questions.

"The houseboat," he replied.

"Oh. No. That wasn't me, but I should have been clearer in my instructions because when I said 'take care of it' that wouldn't have been my choice. *But* if it meant you were no longer a threat to the operation, then so be it."

"Your operation to resurrect Project Gladiator?" I scoffed. "Despite everything you lost last time? Despite what you promised me?"

"Everything I lost?" she said, a glint in her eye that gave me pause. I'd seen it before. In the Norman Osborns of the world. In the Doctor Dooms. Even Stark on the odd occasion. Men driven to mania by their quest for power. Wilma looked *just* like them. And I felt like an idiot for so wholeheartedly believing she was different.

"Think of everything I gained, Bobbi," she said, stroking my face gently. "We could never have succeeded under the constraints of S.H.I.E.L.D. and now, free, untethered, we're right there. I'm so, so grateful you'll get a chance to see it. It's what we worked so hard for all those years ago. Now you'll be the model system that brings our dream to life!"

Panic rose up in my stomach as I understood, properly understood.

"You're not ready for human trials," I replied. "What about those puppies? Whirl through a few more of them first."

Dr Calvin laughed like I'd made a cute joke about the weather rather than trying to negotiate for my life. "The corgis are much better than mice, I'll admit. But we were very close to human trials anyway when you two showed up, so this couldn't have come at a better time."

"I could think of a few," Lance grumbled.

"Hush," Dr Calvin snapped at him. "You'll be making a great sacrifice for science. We'll be able to learn so much from how your body responds."

"I will not be cooped up in some cage in a crypt!" Lance spat, drawing her focus in a way I appreciated. My eyes had been scanning and searching the whole time, looking for the source of the other voice I thought I'd heard. Yet it was just the three of us, meaning Dr Calvin had to ping-pong her attention back and forth between Lance and I. I'd been stripped of weapons, I could see them laid out on a far table, but they'd only searched me for the obvious ones. Using my toes to raise my height just a fraction, my fingertips could brush my hair and I released one of the snap clips there.

"Why is it the handsome ones are always the stupidest?" Dr Calvin asked, turning back, and I paused my movements for a moment thinking she'd sprung me. She hadn't. "Bobbi always had an appetite for good-looking morons."

"That's a himbo, thank you very much," Lance growled. As useful as his antagonizing of her was, I could tell he enjoyed it, too.

"Well, Mr Himbo, let me inform you that you will be no captor of mine. At least in the long term."

It was near impossible to do this without looking at the handcuffs and I wished that Lance's jokes about trying it blindfolded hadn't been so idle. Relying on touch and feel alone, with my hands at odd angles, was making this so much harder than I anticipated as I tried to pull the bar of the clip away from the teeth and into the groove I needed.

"I suspect your body will take poorly to the serum," Dr Calvin was telling him, checking his own vitals and extracting a blood sample. "So you won't be alive for long. We'll learn the most from you during the autopsy."

Lance had been wriggling, tugging against his restraints, trying to cause as much havoc as he could and draw her eye as she pivoted between the two of us. He fell still when she finished, hanging limp as the words sank in.

"It's the most comprehensive way to collect data, isn't it, Bobbi?" she pressed, not seeming to notice his reaction.

"More death," I spat. "That's your answer? I nearly died. And Ted is dead forever because of what you did! You said you learned, you promised, and I really believed you. What was it all for, Wilma? Nothing?"

"Sweetheart," she mused, patting my shoulder in a consoling fashion. "It was for science."

She turned her back to us, returning to her equipment as I watched her run the blood tests she'd taken from both of us. She'd be seeing whose sample responded the best, whose had the most likely path to success, and that's who would go first. When that subject eventually died, she'd learn what she could from the corpse, tweak the serum, and try again on the survivor. Dr Calvin had always been willing to push the limits, her personal and professional ones. The price she had paid for crossing that ethical line all those years ago had been so great, I really believed she'd learned her lesson. All this evidence had been slowly piling up in front of me and I'd been willing to think the best of her, believe her, when in reality what she'd learned was an internal hardening. Looking at this woman I thought I knew, who was as much a mother figure as she was a mentor, my blood ran cold. I couldn't see the soul behind her eyes, only the relentless ambition and desire to achieve her aim at any cost. Lance and I were just collateral.

"And you're wrong about Ted," Dr Calvin said, turning back to face me. "He isn't dead."

A chorus of sharp barks started immediately as the corgis in cages began to react, their high-pitched *yaps* echoing around the crypt like a pinball. It obviously didn't matter, with us being buried too deep for any noise to have a chance at alerting someone, anyone.

The darkness at the rear of the lab, the part that I couldn't see clearly, began to move. My throat went dry with fear as I tried to comprehend what I was looking at: a hulking, lumbering mass dragging itself forward. It towered over Dr Calvin, and

I felt my mouth hang open as I clocked the eyes, so human, staring back at me with intelligence. They were such a sharp contrast to everything else about this, this... monster. There was no other way to describe it.

"Hello... Barbara," it said. That voice was visceral, causing an immediate chemical reaction in my bloodstream as my instincts said *Run! Flee! Get away from this thing as fast as you can!* But the hair clip in my hand had paused midway into the handcuffs joint, my digits frozen with fear. And most horrifying of all, recognition.

"No," I whispered.

"Yesssss," it replied. But it wasn't just an it.

"What are you?" Lance balked.

It didn't turn to look at him, just kept staring at me as it addressed his question. "Professsor Theodore Ssallisss."

"Ted," I mumbled.

It gave what looked like a shrug. "Once, yesss."

Everything ran together, not sounding like a lisp per se but the letters feeling like they were disappearing into the ether along with his humanity.

"You... you're a man." Lance struggled. "But you're not! You're some kind of thing! You're something horrible."

Careful, Lance, I thought, watching as the creature that had once been Ted lumbered to the left to look at him.

"A Man-Thing," Ted said, a rumble of laughter bubbling up from what sounded like the bowels of hell.

"H-how?" I stammered. "How did this happen?"

"Who can really say?" Dr Calvin chirped, her tone telling me she had tried – and failed – many times to answer that question. "Best I can deduce is when Teddy injected himself with the Super Soldier Serum, it worked. His DNA permanently altered in all the ways we had intended it to, the stem cells stacking on each other rapidly, faster and faster, until his body couldn't keep up and he flatlined."

"Died," I said. "I was there. I saw the monitors, Wilma. I watched you try to bring him back. He was dead."

"Clinically, maybe," she shrugged, as if that was nothing. "Whatever the serum did to him, we couldn't perceive it. Besides, it was only half the metamorphosis. When your S.H.I.E.L.D. colleagues triggered the kill switch and the lab was destroyed, Ted was transformed."

"When?" I hissed. "Where? We never found his body!"

"Because there was no body to find!" she snapped. "Stop thinking so logically, Bobbi! The legacy of great science is going in with the best of intentions and not shying away when happy accidents occur!"

"He doesn't look too happy," Lance remarked. "In fact, I can't tell if he's looking at all."

"I'm right here, little boy," Ted said, words slow as he extended a limb towards Lance. I couldn't say arm, because it didn't exactly look like that as the texture seemed like moss and mulch shifting against each other. Outstretched, Lance turned his head away as something close to fingers stroked his face. My eyes were transfixed on Lance's cheek, however, as a translucent slime was left behind.

"His human form was destroyed at one location," Dr Calvin explained. "But the biological changes meant that it wasn't annihilated. He reformed nearby, at first with no memories of who he was or how he got there. Yet, over the years, he lived in the swamp, learned from it, and Ted started to come back."

"Of course," I murmured. "Nothing good ever happens in a Florida swamp."

"Not goooo-od," Ted told me. "Great. The next sssstep in human evolution."

"You don't look human to me," I noted.

"Ha!" Dr Calvin laughed. "Exactly! That's where we were going wrong. We were trying to manipulate human DNA, Bobbi. But it's so inferior."

"The data," I murmured. "I kept wondering why it didn't make sense, why it didn't correlate with any of the model systems, but your model system was–"

"Me," Ted interjected.

Dr Calvin was looking up at him lovingly and it didn't take an analysis of their astrology charts to understand their flame was rekindled. Even though they hadn't been a true couple when I'd known them, over time that had clearly changed.

"When Teddy found me, I couldn't believe it," she whispered, not shuddering away from his touch. "And if he could survive, then I knew I could find a way."

I felt the metallic *click* of the handcuffs against my skin and they nearly fell away. If they clattered to the floor, I would've been screwed. I managed to catch them with my fingers, gripped them, held them tight, and hoped they didn't realize that the biggest obstacle to my freedom was now gone.

"A way to what?" Lance pushed and I wondered if he'd seen the cuffs buck. "Sell yourself to Hydra?"

"Hydra?" Dr Calvin scoffed. "Those lunatics who wanted to slice and dice Teddy first chance they got? No, thank you, we took care of them back when I worked in other European countries."

But she did try them first, I noted. And when they didn't give her what she wanted, Ted handled it.

"Oxford was the next best thing," I said, catching up.

"You could get access to the best labs in the world and have the freedom to work on what you really wanted without S.H.I.E.L.D. prying into your business."

"Exactly," she said, handing a vial to Ted who moved away to prepare it. "It took some finagling, mind you. The dean was a little bit too nosy, ties to the Hellfire Club I learned. So I would move off-site to keep working freely and then when S.T.R.I.K.E. started sniffing around, too – you people sure do love an acronym – I had to disappear."

"You staged your disappearance." I frowned. "Just so you could Dr Frankenstein Project Gladiator again? I don't understand you, Wilma. I don't understand this."

"Your ratio of brains to brawn was always iffy." She smirked. "People were supposed to buy my family emergency. And it's called Project Romulus now."

Lance and I shared a look.

"That's foreboding," I noted. "Who's the Remus in this equation?"

"Captain America, of course." Dr Calvin gave me a look like I should know better. "That's the old, inferior product. Super Soldier Serum is just so… insular. This will be much, much more."

"You killed Agent Grist," Lance muttered. "You killed the dean. You tried to kill us on the houseboat–"

"He did those things," I cut in, jerking my head at Ted's hulking back. "He destroyed her lab the night we met, Lance. Look at the slime on your face. It's identical to what was in the dean's nostrils. Everywhere we've been has had some kind of water source nearby and I bet it's because he can be fluid when he wants to, transition in form. Sink a houseboat, for instance."

"That'ssss right," Ted said, returning and handing Dr Calvin a vial of a muddy green substance. "If you and all thosssse othersss had jussst stopped picking at a dead corpssse like vulturesss, then I wouldn't have had to take matters into my own–"

"Don't say hands," Lance scoffed. "You have mud mittens at best. And if you weren't working for Hydra, A.I.M., Hellfire, FiveFourThree then how the heck have you run this operation on a professor's sala–"

Lance didn't get a chance to finish. Ted backhanded him so hard, I screamed at the impact. When he pulled back, I was terrified Lance would be hanging there limp, neck broken and at an unnatural angle. Instead, he was hunched over in his restraints, blood dribbling from his mouth. He spat out a tooth and it bounced along the stone floor. His fingers were moving, and I realized he was tucking broken zip-ties into his fist, hiding the fact that Ted's hit had severed a few.

"Weapons," I growled, voice low and angry with the realization. "You've been funding this by selling biological weapons made from properties of Ted's DNA."

"It's a shameful affair," Dr Calvin admitted, flicking a syringe to remove any additional air bubbles as she approached me. "But it does pay. Now Bobbi, I want to make this very clear. It's better if you don't fight this."

Oh, I was going to fight it.

"I know resistance is in your nature, but our research has shown the formula grafts much better to the DNA of willing participants. That's why Ted's worked and so many others didn't. And if you were willing, this could be your chance," she continued.

"My chance for what?"

"Aren't you sick of watching men get praised for being

mediocre, when to get even just a morsel of the same acclaim you have to be exceptional, Bobbi? This could make you so much *more*."

She extended her arm with a grand wave, gesturing to where Ted was hovering near Lance. I understood then, finally. This wasn't Super Soldier Serum. She wasn't trying to recreate Captain America. Why would she, when she thought she already had the perfect success story right in front of her? This was Super Sallis Serum. She was going to turn me into another one of those *things*. If I survived. And that was a big if. I tried to slouch as much as I could, look like I had given up hope, and I felt a new mask slip into place.

"Fine," I whispered, voice full of despair. "Do it and get it over with."

"That's my brave girl."

She had to get up right close to me to insert the serum and I stayed still, waiting as she looked for the best place to inject it, given my full body tactical suit, to give the serum the best chance of success.

"Teddy, prepare the next vial," she called. I watched through the veil of hair that hung over my face as he turned and started doing as ordered. His back was to me. Wilma undid the restraint at my torso to cut a square in the fabric. Good luck with that. This was state of the art S.H.I.E.L.D. tech and lightweight body armor. And an additional obstacle? The woman in it was absolutely *furious*.

I swung my fist downward, fingers clutched around the handcuffs like a knuckle duster as I brought it down on her head. The contact was harsh, knocking Dr Calvin out in an instant and I lunged forward, grabbing her body so she didn't clatter to the ground and make a noise. I would feel bad about punching an old woman in the head later. Right now, I just needed her discreetly off the board. I pocketed the syringe of serum carefully, checking her pulse to confirm she was just unconscious. I used the cuffs to secure her to the bottom rail – both hands – and I used the jagged teeth on my clip to quickly cut through the final restraints at my feet. Keeping my eyes on Ted's back, who was dare I say it *humming* as he worked, I quickly rifled through Dr Calvin's pockets for anything of use. I grabbed Lance's butterfly knife and the bottle she'd used to spray me with, before quickly dashing over to where he was restrained. With a pad of my finger against the blade to minimize sound, I flicked the knife and quickly slashed upwards to sever all three of his restraints in one go.

Tucking the spray into his waistband, I had to awkwardly climb up his body to reach his hands at the top of the table. He bent his knees to offer me additional support, eyes wide and focused as they watched my six. I had to cut them all one by one, each plastic tie making a tiny *pop* noise that felt like a gunshot blast in my head but in reality was miniscule. Lance stayed dead silent, only moving his head to the side once to plant a kiss on my cheek. Just three more ties to go…

"It'sss ready," Ted said, and I didn't have to see him to know what happened. I could feel it in the tension of Lance's body as the monster turned around, eyes shifting from Dr Calvin's limp form to us breaking free.

"Bobbi, hurry!" Lance cried. Ted roared and I leapt away, leaving just one tie for Lance to snap himself as he pushed his wrists together and fell to the floor. We sprinted in opposite directions, the sound of the surgical table smashing as Ted collided with it. It told us precisely what our fate would have been. The noise was so magnified down here, it was disorientating and difficult to work out what was coming from where. I tried to use that to my advantage as I kept running. I plunged deeper into the lab then circled around, kicking over a table with equipment to create more of a ruckus and diving under another. This one I'd chosen specifically because it was loaded with weapons. *My* weapons. I felt immediately more secure as I gripped my battle staves against my side. Crouched and hidden, I tried to hide my panting as I waited to see where Ted was. What he was doing. I couldn't see him in the shadows of the lab and the confusing sound that had worked as cover for me was now working for him. Where was Lance? I couldn't spot him either and I hoped it was because he was being smart, tooling up like me, and not because he'd been turned into human horticulture. A hand slapped around my mouth and I went to fight it, but another quickly wrapped around my torso.

"Sssssh, it's me, it's me, not the Man-Thing."

Lance. I felt my whole being relax into him as I spun around, hugging him quickly.

"Are you–"

"Yeah. You?"

"Yeah. Where is he?"

Lance pointed and I followed the direction of his digit to Dr Calvin's body. I scanned her and missed this at first, my brain categorizing it as the woman having been covered in shadow. But that shadow moved. It breathed. He was cradling her.

"Did you kill her?" Lance whispered. "I mean, I'd understand if you–"

"She's alive," I said.

Lance held up a small remote in his hand and I nodded. It

was for the radio. He cranked the volume, and we watched as the figure shuddered against Dr Calvin, but didn't leave her. Yet. We observed the two of them for a moment longer, my eyes shifting to scan around us.

"How do we fight this thing?" Lance asked. "Cos sadly I don't think we can punch our way out of this."

"No." I smirked. "Definitely not. And whatever we do, we need to try and leave this lab as intact as possible."

"Why?"

I pointed to a map on the wall. It was of the US. Next to it were several other continents, locations and coordinates mapped out.

"That's their distribution network. I've seen what those weapons can do, Lance. I need to know everywhere they went, how many, and to whom."

"Let's use them, then?"

"I'm fairly certain it won't work," I said, shaking my head.

"How do you know?"

"The weapons are constructed from him. It would be like fighting fire with fire."

"There's an idea."

I tilted my head, watching Ted's form glisten as he started to slink back into the shadows, adjusting Dr Calvin as he made a move. To come for us.

"He's too moist," I replied.

"Yuck."

"You know what I mean. Wait, I know what I mean…"

"Mean it fast," he said. "Cos old mate looks like he's regrouping for the hunt."

I swiveled, looking for the sounds of the flowing water that I had heard since we got here. The castle had a moat once and this was a far cry from that, but the smallest sliver of water was running along a concrete gutter. It was little wider than rainwater racing along a drain, but this disappeared through an iron grate in the wall and went lord knows where.

"We work together, get him to the water," I said, pointing.

"Then what?"

"We throw in a toaster." My eyes darted to the tips of my staves. Lance's dimples twitched. He understood. "Now crank the radio, DJ."

He smashed the buttons, raising the volume as loud as it would go and setting it to automatic scan. I heard Ted's roar of annoyance, the sound clearly bothering him as the tuning landed on a station for two seconds then flicked to static, repeating over and over. I barely had time to celebrate before I was tugged away, a yank around my ankle dragging me from Lance at a rapid rate. The shock had my fingers slipping free and I scratched at the stone, my fingernails snapping as I fought against the momentum and tried to get back to my battle staves. I was hurled upwards, my head hitting the edge of a concrete pillar as I was dangled, the blood running through my hair. The once black orbs for eyes were glowing now, red, as I was held in front of the monster's face.

"Bobbi," he growled, rage thick. "I'm going to–"

His words cut out as something shattered at his feet. Then another, a beaker breaking against what should have been a shoulder. The fluid inside didn't do anything, just soaked into his form with a sickly wet sound. But they kept coming, Lance successfully correcting his aim and getting Ted's attention. He dropped me and I rolled off his body, bouncing down to the surface and landing with an ungraceful *oomph.*

"Come on, ya muddy sod!" Lance called, tossing objects

over his shoulder as he ran. He stole that move from me and I couldn't have been more pleased. He was weaving between the arched pillars of the crypt, making it as difficult for Ted as possible. I could see where he was heading. I looped around after him, wiping the blood from my forehead as I followed and turned just in time to watch Ted catch up with Lance. Yet unlike me, he was ready. He sprinted at one of the concrete pillars, running up it for a few steps before throwing himself backward into Ted. Lance spun through the air, his legs kicking outward in perfect form as they connected with the monster's head in two impressive blows. I could almost feel the power from where I was standing. That impact would have taken out a normal person under normal circumstances, but these weren't that.

Ted roared in annoyance yet seemed otherwise unaffected as he lashed out and destroyed an entire concrete pillar in one hit. It was right where Lance had been a second earlier, the stones and debris exploding apart in a brutal display of force. Lance had landed propped on one knee, and I saw the glint of two blades flash as he retracted them and tried a different approach. He slashed and stabbed, looking almost like a boxer as his quick steps brought him in and out of range while he tried to affect smaller but significant damage. It was seemingly impossible, Ted being too immense even if he wasn't swift. He was getting his own licks in and as I ran forward, I winced, watching a bloody laceration open up at Lance's torso when the hulking mass descended on him. Lance was smart enough to know when he was outmatched and he retreated, leaping over the small gap and stopping against the hard stone wall that created his dead end. Ted loomed in front, trapping him, but positioning himself perfectly over the water. Coming up behind him, I watched as his form naturally, seamlessly, flowed into the texture of the fluid.

"Bobbi!"

I leapt as Lance tossed my two staves over Ted's head, I caught them midair and dropped into a roll behind him. He'd swiveled with the movement, issuing a growl as he lurched toward me. A series of shots rang out, Ted grunting as the bullets connected with him but seemingly made no mortal wound. That didn't stop Lance though, who kept firing to make sure Ted's gaze was on him. He lashed out, his limb wrapping around Lance's arms like a tentacle and twisting. I heard the snap before I heard Lance cry out, screaming as his arm was broken. Planting my feet on either side of the water flow, I held my staves above the surface.

"Hey, Teddy!" I shouted. He spun, dropping Lance who slumped to the ground. "You should've stayed dead."

I activated the staves, plunging them into the water just as sparks began to fly out. Ted's enormous form lit up like fireworks, the electricity flowing through the water and into him as the fluid created the perfect conduit. He reacted like he was still human and I squinted, the light so bright. Yet I didn't want to look away, didn't want to pull out the staves too soon, and instead tried to maintain my firm grip as a smell like burning hair stung my nostrils. He exploded and I exploded with him, sent backward with the blast and into the same wall Lance had run to. The impact took me out for a moment and when I came to, I could tell it was only a few seconds later. Ted was gone, slime seemingly coating everything instead and I winced as I crawled forward. Lance was on his knees, face strained with pain as he gripped his arm.

My outstretched hand touched his back and he jumped,

spinning around like he was ready to go. The fight faded out of him just as quickly as he saw it was me, settling into the wall and bracing his back against it.

"Sorry about your staves," Lance choked out. My gaze could only look at them for a moment, both appearing like burnt Christmas crackers that had seen better days. They were destroyed completely, and their charred skeletons were still smoking.

"I'll get more," I muttered, resting my head on his outstretched thigh.

My whole world turned sideways as we lay there, covered in slime, panting through the pain and looking at the mass of goo that had once been Professor Ted Sallis.

CHAPTER TWENTY

The downside of being missing, presumed dead, was no one was officially coming for you. No backup. No help. No kicking in the door, guns drawn. All we had was each other. Unfortunately, neither of us was in great shape. Hobbling and holding ourselves up, we were able to get through the goo and back to the main section of the lab. Sitting Lance down on Dr Calvin's chair, it didn't take me long to find the first aid kit she'd have handy. Ironically, given where everything ended up, she took safety seriously and it was stocked. I also scanned her medical supplies, grabbing a syringe and quickly drawing a small amount of liquid painkiller. I turned back to Lance with the needle raised.

"If I'm about to be triple-crossed, just get it over with," he said, face strained with pain. "I haven't got any more fight left in me."

"It's liquidized OxyContin, you drama queen." I smiled. "Five mil will take the edge off so I can make a sling. It's a bad break, Lance."

"Oh, you don't say," he laughed, holding up his arm which was hanging limp like it had no bones remaining whatsoever. "At least we're not being lobotomized."

"That's the spirit," I said, cutting away his sleeve. I injected the good stuff, then quickly got to making a splint for his arm while I thought.

"Hold still."

I looked up, about to ask what for when he pushed an antiseptic-soaked bandage to the gash on my head. "Hey."

"Teamwork makes…"

I glowered at him, trying not to admit how much the cut was stinging right now.

"Makes the… come on, I know you know it."

I pulled the knot of the sling tight around his neck and he jumped with the pain.

"Ah!"

"The dream work," I winked. "Which, speaking of…"

What now? It was the question ringing loud in both our skulls, but I had an idea. I just wasn't sure how he would feel about it. His triple-crossed comment stuck with me, and I was conscious of the fact that although we weren't fighting for our lives anymore, our problems weren't exactly resolved. I bit my lip, trying not to frown and cause a fresh trickle of blood to streak down my face. Lance let out a sigh and I could tell the painkillers were doing their job as he leaned back against the chair.

"Do it," he said.

"Do what?"

"You know what," he countered.

"Lance," I began, pondering the stakes for him in the moment. "Just… think about it for a second."

"There's a leak at S.T.R.I.K.E. What's to think about?"

"You could plug it yourself."

"I'm a terrible plumber."

I rolled my eyes. "Take that information higher up. You know how these places are: if you go external, they could look down on you. Halt any upward progression. This could permanently impact your career."

He opened his mouth to reply, and I placed a finger on his lips to stop him.

"It's just you and me right now, no one else is involved. Whatever you decide, I'll support your choice."

To his credit, he did take a beat. He did think about it. He reached his good hand up, taking mine and toying with my fingers for a moment.

"I'm no help to you right now," Lance began. "I don't like the idea of you being solo and stave-less if we get one more curve ball thrown at us. I know you have a back-up plan. So do it. I trust you."

"You shouldn't," I sighed as I got the emergency beacon from my utility belt. "I was entirely and completely wrong about Wilma. This was her, all her. There was no one driving her ambition, just mad–"

"Love," Lance finished. "She loved him. Then and now, I'd guess."

"Yeah, and look what it did," I muttered, hitting the button and placing the beacon in front of us. With his good hand, Lance touched my chin, and I turned my head to face him.

"Not all love makes monsters of us."

His gaze was penetrating right through my skin, his stare intense and I tried to tell myself it was just the meds talking. Just the delirious relief from pain, even for a moment. I opened my mouth to reply, but a crackle from the beacon's speaker got my attention. An uneven hologram of Hill appeared at first, the image shaky before it solidified, and she was looking back at us.

"Good God," she began, face full of concern as her eyes ran over us and the absolute scene behind us. "Are you all right? What the hell happened? What do you need?"

"A micro team of about four agents," I replied, getting straight to the point. "At least one of them needs a science background, but any analyst you've got will do."

"Done." She nodded. "I had a holding team in the area just in case."

"You did?" I asked, genuinely surprised. I should've known, Hill was always thinking five steps ahead.

"They're on their way to your location," she added. "What about a med team? Neither of you look great."

"Oh, I like her," Lance mumbled. "She's direct."

"Big fan of your work, too, Agent Hunter."

Lance's eyes lit up like he'd just gotten an autograph from his favorite celebrity. He mouthed the words "oh my God" at me and I grinned, patting his knee.

"He has had some pain meds," I said, by way of explanation.

Lance ignored my comment as he spoke to Hill. "Listen, whoever you're sending, discretion is key. They need to not only remain unseen to any locals, but S.T.R.I.K.E. can't know they were here."

"You're S.T.R.I.K.E.," Hill countered.

"I'm Team Bobbi," Lance said, zipping his lips shut.

I smiled. "I left a chem trail to mark our route; if they switch to heat vision, they'll be able to follow it. I'll show them what they need when they're here, then they've gotta bounce."

Hill's gaze was still focused on Lance, and she addressed her next question at him. "Why?"

"Because there's a mole inside S.T.R.I.K.E. and we need a way to make them pop out of their hole," he replied.

"That could cost you," she answered.

"It nearly cost me my life. And Bob's. The price doesn't get much higher."

"Let's split the bill," I said, staring intensely at him before I pivoted back to my boss. "I'll volunteer to stay until this is all resolved. We don't know who he can trust in there *or* who they're really working for."

"That's generous of you." Hill smirked. "Fine. Now show me the scene."

I picked up the beacon, giving her a tour and explaining everything as quickly as I could, as best I could, as well as I understood it.

"Did you put that woman in a coma?" she asked when I examined Dr Calvin.

"Hey, she coma'd me first!"

"Fair call."

"Besides, I think she's just unconscious. Very, very unconscious."

Hill wanted to stay on the line as the agents arrived, so I set her on one of the tables and went to greet the four figures climbing down the staircase. I let out a cry of surprise when goggles lifted back to reveal the team leader, Tigra giving me her trademark toothy grin.

"Tig!"

I embraced my friend with a hug and she gripped me back, lowering her weapon so she could really get in there.

"Hey there, little bird, you look terrible."

"Honestly, it's just so nice to see you I'm gonna let that dig slide."

I nodded at the other three S.H.I.E.L.D. agents as they panned out, each looking around the space with interest. They were all from previous teams I'd led back home, because of course they were. Hill absolutely rocked.

"Where do you need us?" Tigra asked.

"Let me show you," I said, leading her over to the cache of weapons.

"Well, helloooooo there. Don't you look familiar."

"Right? Remove every weapon you can, we can't risk any getting into the wrong hands."

"And be careful," Tigra told them. "They're designed to be fatal and attack human biology, so pack 'em tight and pack 'em safe. What else?"

"The chemical properties, too," I continued. "That whole side of the lab was her weapons manufacturing wing, so anything you wouldn't want a potential enemy having–"

"Got it."

"We need samples of that huge pile of goo formerly known as Professor Ted Sallis." I pointed. "Who knows what we can get from it?"

"What about the doc?" Tigra asked, glancing at Dr Calvin.

"Leave her for now. she's only dangerous if she's in a lab and I feel confident saying that's never going to happen again. She's not worth exposing S.H.I.E.L.D.'s presence here, just yet. But this could be a problem."

I picked Hill's hologram up, carrying it over to the maps and chaotic cluster of paperwork.

"Was she doing *The Amazing Race*?" Tigra questioned, head tilting to the side.

"Tight version? Dr Calvin's Project Gladiator fails, Professor Sallis injects himself with Super Soldier Serum except it doesn't work, he dies, lab explodes, RIP or so we think. In reality, that dose combined with whatever else was blasted into him during the kaboom turns him into… something terrible."

"A Man-Thing!" Lance called from behind us, stumbling over to join in. Tigra looked around with interest, seemingly spotting him for the first time.

"Hey, dimples."

"Hey, Grizabella."

Tigra threw her head back with a laugh, elbowing me so hard I winced. "He's cute. What's the go there?"

"Focus," Hill snapped.

"Whatever part of him that can materialize, does in the swamps that were right next to the lab. He takes on physical properties of that setting, reunites with Dr Calvin, they weaponize parts of his biology to create these weapons and bankroll their real agenda, killing anyone who gets in the way."

"Super Soldier Serum, it's always Super Soldier Serum," Tigra tut-tutted.

"No, this wasn't. It was Super Sallis Serum. They were trying to fix him without losing any of the new abilities he'd gained."

"And the maps?"

"Their distribution network. It's where every weapon was sent."

Tigra let out a low whistle. "That's a lot of places. Bad places."

"Every war zone currently active," Hill noted. "And LA."

"Any of the survivors from the shipment we intercepted need to be checked," I said. "And monitored."

"You think they're gonna become Man-Thingies, too?" Tigra asked.

"Honestly, I don't know. I'll need time and help to analyze her data and experiments, but my concern is she wasn't hamstrung by ethics this time round. There was no overseeing body, so what happens when his altered DNA and her engineered chemicals all mix together on a subject that survives?"

"I'm mobilizing a team to get them into isolation now," Hill said. "Tigra, take all of that with you. Every map, every inch of paper, every hard drive. Bobbi, you're going to have to make it look like more of this lab was destroyed than it was."

"Done." I nodded, gathering two more key items. "Here's her laptop. It had been missing when I searched her office and home, but there'll be useful data on here and endless notes if I know Wilma. And you should take this, too."

I'd capped the syringe that had been destined for me and the one destined for Lance, handing them both over.

"Wait," Lance said. "If it's not a Super Soldier Smoothie, then shouldn't we leave it? If we want to lay a fitting trap..."

"I'll make something," I said, eyes scanning the materials I could use. There was more than enough. "Even though we know what it isn't, I don't like the idea of that concoction being freely available to those who know where to look."

"Agreed," Hill remarked. "How much longer do you need, Tigra?"

"Ten minutes," she said, getting to work as she began rolling up the maps and sliding them into cylinders.

"I'm gonna try and get those puppies out," Lance said, hobbling off in search of keys to release the corgis from their cages. I watched as he held his good hand up to the bars, the puppies licking his fingers as he scratched their heads.

"You ever gonna try dating outside of work or…?" Tigra mumbled, voice low enough so only I could hear.

"I have no idea what you're talking about," I replied, grabbing vials and mixing samples as quickly as I could.

"You're saying you haven't climbed that London Bridge?"

"Oh my god." I cringed. "Have you got any nano trackers with you?"

"Rode that double decker bus?" she continued, handing over what I asked for and entirely unbothered.

I emptied the nano trackers into the liquid and focused on the shaking of fluids while I glared at her.

"Buckinged that ham?"

"I thought you quit, huh? Remember that?"

She beamed, excited to get a rise out of me. "*Somebody* recommended me for a freelance lab tech role before dropping off the grid for a mysterious mission."

I rolled my eyes, filling six syringes with my Pseudo Soldier Serum.

"And then *somebody* had Hill worried, so I volunteered for the B team in case it all went sideways and oh, look! Here I am."

I laughed. "You were never the B team to me."

"I meant B for babe. Right, Team Babes?" she called out, the other three agents shouting an "aiyoooo" in response.

"I'm grateful," I said, voice warm because I really, really meant it. I could tell she knew.

"Ew, don't get emosh. Save it for when you're back and we've got frozen margs in front of us."

"Excuse me, Miss Morse?" Heck, that was a nice sound. I

turned to face a young agent whose entire demeanor screamed analyst. "I couldn't get that goo sample you mentioned, just some faint residue. Could you show me?"

I led her over to where the pile of Ted had once been, which was now little more than a few jelly chunks as the water streamed right through it again.

"It was here," I said, following the route of the drain. A weight dropped in my stomach as I glanced over the absence of a problem I thought I'd resolved. "Right here."

"There was a huge pile of him," Lance agreed, coming up behind me. "Like, imagine a jellyfish but at least… fifty times bigger."

"There's nothing left now," the analyst said as we came to a stop at the old, iron grate. I crouched down, glaring as the water trickled through it and on to the darkness beyond. "Looks like he got washed away."

"Looks like," Lance murmured. When I glanced up at him, he looked as concerned as I did except for the fact he was holding what I thought was a furry lump at first. It turned out to be a corgi puppy.

"Really?" I asked him.

"What? We saved him! He's adorable, look at him!"

"You have a broken arm, idiot. Now you're putting strain on your good one for that hairy bread loaf."

Lance covered the dog's ears. "How dare you!"

"All right, Team Babes!" Tigra called. "Let's wind it up."

The S.H.I.E.L.D. agents began to withdraw, and I thanked them as they left, Tigra in particular.

"Just sad I missed the fight, that's all." She winked.

"I'll see you back home. Frozen margs."

"Frozen margs?" Lance asked.

"Girls only." Tigra shrugged. "Sorry, dimples."

And with that, they were gone. The sound of them trudging up the stone stairs of doom echoed for a few moments longer, then we were alone again. A puppy licked my hand. Well, not quite alone.

"Have you got a way to call in S.T.R.I.K.E.?" Hill asked.

Lance shook his head. "No, all my tech went down on the boat."

"They don't know that," she replied. "I can patch you through, cloak the call from our end."

"Oh, you mean… like a shield?" Lance smirked. I pinched the bridge of my nose and closed my eyes. It was less than a minute before Lance was being connected, giving his access code and handing the puppy to me so he looked more serious. I stayed silent as he spoke, his version of the story coming easy and naturally because it was mostly true. When he hung up, I couldn't get rid of the dog fast enough as I settled down next to him, our butts in the dirt and backs against the wall while we waited.

"What should I call him?"

"Lance."

"What? Come on, I know you love dogs. You stop to pat every single one you see."

"Yes, because those are cute. And normally portioned."

"These guys are meant to be low riders, they used to herd cattle, nip at their heels."

I gave the dog with enormous eyeballs a sideways glance. "Aren't they supposed to be caramel? This one looks like a blue heeler."

"The others in there are, but this guy's a Cardigan Welsh Corgi as opposed to a Pembroke Welsh Corgi."

"I would have never given you the good pain meds if I knew it would turn you into Dr Dolittle," I groaned, leaning my head back. We were both quiet as we heard the S.T.R.I.K.E. agents approach the cells, all the way up at the ground level of the castle. I gently touched the vials next to me, waiting.

"You OK with me crashing?" I asked. "Until we…"

"As long as you and the Professor can find a way to get along, then it's A-OK with me."

I frowned, looking down at the wagging tongue of the puppy. Heck, either I was in too much pain and was turning delirious or that thing *was* kind of cute. Lance nudged my shoulder, him having no hands to spare.

"Of course, Bobbi," he murmured. "You're welcome as long as you want."

We watched as S.T.R.I.K.E. agents poured into the lab, guns drawn, and fanning out to cover as much space as possible. I sighed, resting my head on his shoulder.

In my dream, I could smell croissants. Specifically, almond croissants. My favorite. I smiled into a pillow made of almond croissants, promising myself that in a few moments I'd take a bite.

"Bobbi."

Just a few more moments.

"Bobbi, wake up."

My dream was rapidly trickling away and I squeezed my eyes tighter, trying to hold on to it in that impossible way. It was always futile.

"I've got almond croissants and coffee."

My eyes flew open, Lance's face hovering near mine and an enormous almond croissant held out on a plate.

"There she is." He smiled, backing up as I struggled into a sitting position in bed.

"You can't keep doing this," I said, rubbing my eyes and taking the plate in one swift movement. "I can't eat almond croissants for breakfast every day."

"Why not?" he said, plopping down next to me. "You love them."

"My blood sugar," I replied, my mouth full of almond paste and crispy pastry really undermining the point.

"Who cares?" He shrugged, sipping his coffee. "Look what I taught the Professor."

The sound of paws over wood came rushing toward us and I looked over the edge of the bed, watching as the little dog skidded to a stop at Lance's feet.

"Freeze!" he said, sticking up finger guns.

The dog froze, sitting up on its girthy hind legs.

"Bam bam!"

The dog barked dramatically, rolling over and playing dead. Lance beamed, glancing around to see my reaction.

"That's... that's really impressive."

"Ha! She loves it, mate. What did I tell ya?"

He flicked the dog a treat, the creature flipping over and chomping on it.

"Uh oh," Lance said, catching my expression. "Why the frown? Eat more croissant, that usually soothes your worries."

"No, it doesn't, it just distracts me."

"Tomato tahmartoe."

"Far as I can tell, all of the model systems Dr Calvin was using were around six weeks old," I mused. "They shouldn't have the cognitive function to learn, let alone master a complex trick like that."

"Maybe it's the teacher."

"Maybe it's enhanced brain activity from the experiments she was running."

"Ooooh, like *Deep Blue Sea*. Deep Blue Dog!"

I laughed. "I don't think the Professor is going to eat your face off in your sleep. But I swear, when we were playing chess the other day he was *really* watching."

"Yeah, watching me get my butt handed to me," Lance scoffed. "Everyone knows corgis love chess."

Licking the icing sugar off my fingers, I paused as I realized he was watching me intensely. I felt the heat rising in my cheeks and I climbed out of bed, shuffling toward him over the mound of blankets.

"Is that my New Order shirt?" he asked, said garment hanging off one shoulder.

"Maybe."

"Not complaining. You having bare clothes works out great for me."

His arm was in a cast, the previous pin in his wrist now having some additional company following a successful surgery. One more day and the limb would be free and healed enough to start physical therapy. It brushed against my waist as I climbed on to his lap, giving him a kiss that felt like the promise of a new morning. Caffeine and sugar and sweetness mixed into a very distinct cocktail I was steadily becoming drunk on.

It had been like this for a month after Oxford, us being treated overnight immediately after the incident. We'd both needed time to recoup and report on everything that had happened – at least that was the official story. The best lies always had a grain of truth to them and my relationship with Lance was what S.T.R.I.K.E. were really attributing to my extended stay as we tied up loose ends. Only he, I, the Professor, and Hill knew what we were actually waiting for, but I'd be lying if this wasn't a huge perk of the job. Lance was physically weaker as he recovered and, as far as the mole would think, largely alone. I was more than willing to be his backup and prove both things wrong if I needed to.

This apartment was starting to feel like home given all the time I spent in it. Croydon, too, felt familiar, the rolling flats of Lloyd Park now my regular jogging route and the Professor's favorite place to sniff the butts of much bigger dogs. I actually got to see the city, to *know* London properly through the eyes of someone who'd lived there their whole life. I bought a Polaroid camera. I took too many pictures. I went to museums. I made out with Lance on London Bridge. I bought the Professor a ramp so his dumb little legs could climb up onto the bed. I did silly touristy stuff. I sat on Lance's lap at a barbecue Tem invited us to. I got my stitches out, both lots. I drew on Lance's cast. I went to a soccer game and didn't make a single *Ted Lasso* reference. I read books I hadn't had a chance to. I let him keep me in bed a whole weekend. OK, maybe two. All the while, I waited and tried not to think about what came next.

When the alert went off on my phone that afternoon, I had almost forgotten what it was for. Lance and I had been working out, alternating between the boxing bag and a light circuit, drenched in sweat. I was swinging my leg for a roundhouse kick, holding the position on one foot as the noise cut through our playlist. I jogged over, analyzing the notification on my ops phone rather than my private one which was also active.

"They're moving," I said, watching the flashing notification on my screen. Lance jogged over to his tablet, which he'd used to piggyback off the S.T.R.I.K.E. security cameras.

"Where?" he asked.

"Coming up from the labs now," I said. "Tem's off today."

"I know," he replied, the relief thick in his voice. Neither of us wanted it to be him.

"Turning left toward the main exit."

"Got it." His fingers had been rapidly swiping between screens. They stopped now and he zoomed in, the two of us watching as the vials of Pseudo Soldier Serum were marched towards the parking lot. Daf waved merrily, getting only the stiffest of nods in return.

"You think he's going home?" I asked. "We can track him."

Lance tossed me his keys. "Let's meet him there then."

I drove, Lance only needing the one hand to grip my waist as we weaved in and out of traffic in London's peak hour. We made it to the destination half an hour early, making our way through the grand doors of a members' club in Mayfair. We didn't need to worry about the dress code, even though we were still in our leathers, or show ID. Some of Lance's old buddies from MI6 were at the counter, offering him a nod and handing over a briefcase. I already had Hill in my earpiece, listening as she told me her agents were in place on the street as well. We headed to the private room at the back, Lance opening the case to reveal several screens inside. It was split between the S.H.I.E.L.D. feed and MI6.

"Incoming, silver Land Rover," a voice buzzed.

I watched as someone pretended to skateboard in front of the car, causing it to stop. The driver wound down the window, waving angrily at the "kid" and while he was occupied, a businesswoman in a suit passed behind the bumper. She bent low at the rear, pretending to adjust her pantyhose as she planted a Disabler on the vehicle and kept moving.

"Success," the voice confirmed.

The car did a loop around the block, pulling into a spot vacated by a red Maserati. The window was still down, and the skateboarder zipped past just as it was winding up, a small object thrown into the vehicle right as the window sealed. The ride sat dormant for several moments and I could imagine what was happening inside. The interior was filling up with sleep gas that worked so rapidly, you'd never have a chance to get your gas mask on – if you were lucky enough to have one – before you took a big whiff and were out cold. All of the vehicle's functions were offline thanks to the Disabler doing precisely what it was supposed to.

"Appointment arriving."

I touched my earpiece, swiveling around in the chair so that its back was to the door and my identity hidden. Lance cocked his weapon and moved to the rear wall, slipping behind where the door would be opened. A waft of aftershave came in a wave as the doors were pushed open.

"Oh, you're here early," he said.

I spun around slowly as S.T.R.I.K.E. Director Tod Radcliffe was dropping into a chair. His butt had just made contact with the leather and his grin faltered as he realized it was me. He had been so keen, so desperate, to get this deal done that he already had the vials in their travel case and on the table.

"I'm nothing if not punctual." I smiled. He spun to find Lance shutting the door behind him, weapon visible.

"Uh-uh," he said. "Very well-manicured hands on the table please."

Lance gestured with his gun to really drive home the point.

"There's been some misunderstanding," Radcliffe started.

"Ha!" I beamed. "You owe me ten bucks."

"Fudge it," Lance sighed. "I had money on 'you're making a huge mistake.'"

"You are," Radcliffe said, trying to throw authority into his voice. "A *huge* one. Colossal."

"The only mistake I made," Lance began, "was not wising up sooner. Everywhere we turned there was some obstacle, someone on to us who shouldn't have been, and I just kept writing it off as the stakes of such a high priority target. It was Bobbi who called it, of course. She's the smart one."

I batted my eyelashes at Radcliffe. He looked *furious*.

"Any minute now, I'm going to have–"

"MI6 and S.H.I.E.L.D. agents pouring in here to arrest you?" I offered. "Cos you'd be right. See, this is the thing about having a hypothesis: you have to prove it correct or incorrect to be able to progress. So, although we knew someone at S.T.R.I.K.E. was – how do you say it? – chirpsin?"

Lance shook his head. "Please don't."

"We still had to prove it and you were patient. You waited a whole month before trying to sell the Super Soldier Serum to Hydra."

"How…" He looked baffled. "I'm not bugged, I check every day."

"No," Lance replied. "You're not. But they are."

Radcliffe's eyes looked down at the vials in front of him, mouth closing shut in a tight line. I glanced to the screen in the briefcase and watched as the Land Rover was opened from the outside, four slumped Hydra operatives were cuffed and carried away on gurneys. Someone offered a thumbs up. I closed the briefcase.

"You thought it was safe to make your move once the heat of the Oxford case had died down," I said. "Unfortunately for you, there'll be no sale today."

There was a knock on the door and Lance opened it, letting the agents inside. They cuffed S.T.R.I.K.E. Director Tod Radcliffe, informing him that he was under arrest for a huge list of crimes that started at conspiracy and rolled right through to treason, I think. I stopped listening somewhere in the middle.

"You're idiots!" he yelled as he was pulled to his feet. "You think MI6 are any better? S.H.I.E.L.D.? At least I would have made a fortune, all they're going to do is shoot themselves with this first chance they get."

I had been walking toward him slowly and paused in front of the vials, pulling one free. I stared at it with interest, shaking it.

"These li'l guys?" I asked. "Only thing they're good for is making icing on a cake."

He blanched.

"Food coloring, water, and a bit of embolic fluid to give it the right texture so… a gross cake, but still a cake."

"You switched the serums!"

"There never was any Super Soldier Serum," I whispered. "Just a mess."

He was hauled out of there by a sea of agents, Lance and I watching as he kicked and spat and fought them the entire way.

CHAPTER TWENTY-ONE

From the second the warm, Californian sun hit my face I couldn't help but grin. I was back in Los Angeles so I couldn't exactly inhale the fresh air, but even the morning smog and background noise of angry drivers honking at me felt like home. Because it was. The metallic rectangle of the lawyer's office usually filled me with dread, looking like something distinctly out of *The Matrix*. Today though, I was Neo. I was Trinity. I was freaking Morpheus. I was on a mission, and I could not be stopped as I took the elevator to the seventh floor and marched directly into the meeting room where Clint and his lawyer were waiting. Jen was pouring herself a glass of water from a drinks trolley and paused, catching the look on my face.

"Finally, she shows," Clint said by way of hello, throwing his hands up in the air. "Sorry this wasn't at a more convenient time for you, Bobbi."

"Apologies," I replied, meaning it. "Mr Vukojevic let me pilot and it has been a while since I flew trans-Atlantic."

"That's quite all right," Mr Murdock began. "We're happy to get right into it, unless you'd like to take a moment?"

Clint shot him an annoyed look and the blind lawyer smirked somehow, as if he'd seen it.

"Nope, let's go."

I flopped down into one of the big, fancy chairs that I knew cost more than my first car. Jen joined us, her own seat straining under her considerable muscles.

"I believe we were negotiating the vehicles," Jen said. "Mr Barton has expressed vehement disagreement to the ownership of the Scrambler Ducati 1100 Tribute Pro."

"I paid for it." He shrugged. "It was a gift, but it's still under my name."

"He can have it," I said with a bat of my hand.

Clint's head snapped in my direction. "What?"

"The Tribute Pro. He can have it."

"You loved that bike," he said, brow furrowing as if it was a trick.

"I loved you too once, now here we are. The Harleys were next?"

"That's right," Jen said, casting a sideways look at me like I was unwell.

"Mr Barton would be keen to–"

"Keep 'em," I interjected. "House?"

"Uh." Mr Murdock's fingers ran over his notes. "That's correct."

"You can have it," I told Clint. "You can keep the house, the dog, the Ducati you never liked and always crashed, but now want for some reason."

"We didn't have a dog."

"I know, what a relief." I beamed. "We never combined accounts, so all my savings are good, right, Jen?"

"Right." She nodded.

"Sweet, then... I think we're done here."

I got to my feet, Clint rushing to stand as well.

"You're giving me everything?" he scoffed in disbelief.

"No," I corrected. "I just don't want to sit here for months fighting over scraps. You said you wanted a divorce, remember? Out of the blue. No separation. No couples therapy. A clean break."

"I know what I said, Bobbi."

"Yet you've fought me every step of the way, keeping me here, keeping me tethered to you. And it makes sense! Our whole relationship started with us fighting side by side. You think it should end that way, too."

Clint stared at me, just stared, while Jen and Mr Murdock did a good job of pretending to be absorbed in their respective sets of notes.

"Here's exactly what you asked for," I said, gesturing to the table like it was all laid out. "You can have everything you want. And I get everything I want."

"Which is... what?"

"To leave you behind."

I watched the reply hit him like a slap to the face and I was sorry, genuinely sorry for the pain it caused. Yet his feelings were mercifully not my problem anymore. I turned to Jen.

"We good? I've got a briefing to make."

She winked at me. "See you there."

I gave the guys a mock salute and pivoted, strutting from that room like I was about to slo-mo fist pump in a John Hughes movie. It was done. *Oh my God, it was done!* I wanted to cartwheel my way to S.H.I.E.L.D. headquarters, but it would really undermine the composure I'd fought to maintain in that small interaction. In truth, the briefing wasn't until later that afternoon, but it was a cool exit line. I had enough time to go home, shower, and reacquaint myself with the Burbank bachelorette pad before heading back in. The plus side of barely surviving being drowned on a houseboat was I traveled home even lighter than before, with Mr Vukojevic dropping my one bag home for me which was a massive help. When I pulled up, my regular postie was placing a box next to it.

"Thanks, McGregor," I said, offering him a wave. My smile faltered as I got closer, recognizing the handwriting immediately. "Lance."

Keys in hand, it took two goes to get everything inside and I dawdled, opening the windows and back door to let the fresh air in before I tackled the package. It blended in amongst the half of my life that was already in boxes, and I sat down on the floor, legs crossed, mind clear. I removed one of the hair clips that was holding back my side part, using the sharp teeth to cut into the packaging.

It's not like either of us didn't know it was coming. The conversation loomed in the background of all our moments: the romantic ones, the normal ones, the sexy ones, the everyday ones. But after we busted Director Radcliffe, there was no more stalling. It had to be had. We didn't do much sleeping that evening, just a lot of celebrating. Afterward in bed, Lance was tracing the new scars on my back with his fingers, connecting them to a constellation only he could see.

"Stay," he said, voice quiet and clear. He knew I had heard him.

I lifted my head, turning to face him as I stayed laying on my stomach. It would have been so easy to say yes. Everything with him had been easy. The only relationship advice my mom had ever given me after my first big break up was "if it don't flow, it goes". This flowed all right. But...

"I can't," I replied, fingernails running through his stubble. He shivered against my touch.

"Why not?" His question was soft, like he'd expected this answer and wasn't antagonistic about it. He seemed genuinely curious. "You like it here, I know you do. Think of our chunky dog son."

I laughed, the sound punctuated by the Professor's snores as he slept soundly on the dog bed I'd bought that was supposed to look like a small castle. Yes, the hairy bread loaf had totally grown on me.

"S.T.R.I.K.E. would hire you in a heartbeat. Plus, I know someone who just got offered a very cushy promotion there..."

"I did that once," I told him. "Put a man first. Put our relationship first. I compromised on every little thing until I didn't recognize the pieces that were left. I won't do that again."

"I'm not asking you to compromise, to give up any part of yourself. We started as equals, and we'd stay equals. You know we have something special, personally and professionally."

"That's what worries me. We make a great team in more ways than one, but I need to concentrate on *the* one."

He pointed a finger at his chest.

"Me," I chuckled. "Myself, Lance. I don't need a therapist to tell me that leap frogging from a marriage to another serious relationship is a terrible idea."

He took my wrist, pulling me onto his chest. I lay there, inhaling his scent deeply and noting the way mine was now just as entangled with his. There was no distinction. No separation. He held me to him, his arms wrapped around my body like he could keep me there forever if he just cocooned me tightly enough.

"Running away to England doesn't fix my problems back home," I said, planting a kiss on his chest. "They just stay, growing, until I can't ignore them anymore."

"I don't want to lose you, Bobbi. We can't have gone through all this just to end up apart."

I lifted my head, making sure he could see my stare. "You're not losing me. If I stayed, you could lose me forever. If I go, you lose me for right now."

"Is there a third option?"

I smiled, climbing up his body and showing him exactly what that third option was. I'd left the next night. I'd had to. The longer I stayed, the harder it would get, and the pain would drag for both of us. Kissing him on the tarmac had felt very Kevin and Whitney, hair blowing around my face dramatically, yet the memory had kept me buoyed for the next several hours. The contents of this box would do so much longer, and I smiled, thinking about how he must have express posted this before I'd even left so it would be waiting for me when I got home. A postcard from Oxford sat on top, just a few words scrawled on the back.

"Great bants, Bobbi," it read, followed by "L" and an "x". It smelled like him, intensely, and I realized why when I saw a bottle of Armani Code in there.

"Just send a box of pheromones next time, Lance," I muttered. The following item was tea, several cartons of Twinings to be precise, and I laughed when I unwrapped the mugs he'd sent to accompany it. One was ceramic, the other was a travel mug, and both had images of the Professor on them looking *so* cute and *so* stupid. There were records and

I held each to my chest, all of them from key bands in our playlist. Lance's New Order shirt, the one I loved, was also folded up inside, along with his Adidas sweatpants he'd kept catching me stealing.

The best bit, though, were the Polaroids. I always took two of every shot, so he had one and I did. I'd left my camera behind for him to remember me. It seemed incredibly insufficient now given his thoughtfulness, but I was glad as I looked through the pictures he'd sent. The Professor wearing a crown, fast asleep in his castle. Tem and Lance holding up pints of Guinness in a pub. Then one of me I hadn't even realized he'd taken, sitting at his window seat with a book sprawled on my lap. The final shot was from our last day together. He'd told me it was bad, never let me see it. Yet there it was stashed in this care package. My arms were wrapped around him, and I was cheesing at the camera as he held it above us. I pressed the image to my lips, closing my eyes and letting myself miss him for just a beat.

The choice I'd made was hard. The right ones usually were. I grabbed my phone, hitting FaceTime on his number and laughing at the image that showed up with his contact details: Lance shirtless and sweaty, that block of chocolate abs very prominently on display following a workout. I'd left my phone unattended while taking a shower and only found his prank selfies later. I kept them all. His photograph was replaced with his actual face as he accepted the call.

"You got the box." He grinned.

"I got the box."

"Oh my god, Bobbi Morse, are you crying?"

"No!" I snapped, quickly wiping away the tears that said otherwise. "It's just raining here. On my face, specifically."

He smirked and diplomatically chose not to press it. "It's so you don't forget me."

"Please," I huffed. "Like I could."

"It's so you don't forget us."

I opened my mouth to reply, but he cut me off.

"Me and the Professor."

I laughed, nearly dropping the phone. "That bloody dog. Where are you?"

It was early evening there and I squinted, trying to make out what kind of tunnel he was marching through. He was dressed in mission fatigues, which made me even more curious.

"Sorry." I winced. "You don't have to tell me if it's–"

"It is," he replied. "But the new S.T.R.I.K.E. Deputy Director gave you level five clearance so I can tell you."

"Lance, you took the job!" I beamed. "That's so great, you're going to crush it!"

"Youngest double D ever," he said, wiggling his head, cocky.

"Don't call it that."

"And I'm heading to Thailand. That drain fed into the Thames, no surprise. The day after we were dragging our butts out of Oxford Castle there were some odd reports from a freight leaving Portsmouth."

"Portsmouth," I frowned, trying to invoke England's geography in my mind. "Could he have travelled that far in his condition?"

"It's over eighty miles so logic says no, but there's nothing logical about Man-Thing. We're planning to intercept the ship when it docks."

"Stay safe," I said. "Stay smart. Whatever he is physically, he's still Ted and Ted was a genius."

"*Teddy*," Lance teased. "How is the old bint?"

"Extradited and officially in a S.H.I.E.L.D. prison. Permanently. Hill saw to it herself."

"Good for her. Everyone needs a hobby."

I smiled, but the gesture didn't reach my core. The image of Dr Calvin in some cell was a painful one, but she'd backed S.H.I.E.LD. into a corner. She was ready to kill me, kill Lance, and had already tried unsuccessfully. It was blatantly clear that she couldn't be trusted and what she knew meant she couldn't be freed. What option was left? With a start, I realized that my initial goal had been to find Dr Calvin and bring her home alive. I couldn't have predicted the roundabout route it took to get there, but I'd achieved that aim. Someone called Lance's name out of frame and he turned his head, replying that he'd be there in a minute.

"I gotta–"

"Go," I told him. "I'll talk to you after."

"Deal."

He bumped his fist to the screen and I did the same. Hanging up, I lay on my back and stared at the ceiling. I had places to be. With a huff, I sprang to my feet. The roar and rumble of my Torana was like a hug from a long lost relative as I drove to S.H.I.E.L.D. headquarters, my beautiful, baby girl driving like a dream as I pulled into the parking lot. Tigra had started the engine once a week while I was gone to keep her ticking over, but I could just tell she was relishing a proper drive. There was still swagger in my steps as I headed into the building. If people's heads turned to look at me, I didn't notice. And I definitely didn't care as I made my way to Hill's office, which was exactly where the trouble was. The Deputy Director was there all right, hands crossed in front of her while she listened intently to a story Jen was telling her.

What concerned me was Tigra's excited expression, her eyes alight and her smile wide.

"And she goes," Jen said as I caught the tail end of the story. "*To leave you behind.*"

"Yoooooo!" Tigra whooped, Hill chuckling in a way that scared me the most. Hill. Chuckling. Jen's face blanched when she realized I was there.

"Don't be mad," she started. "It's the girls group chat. You know they're a vault."

I squeezed her shoulder, smiling, before turning to point at the other two. "Does not leave this room."

"Of course." Hill nodded, before adding another unnerving chuckle.

Tigra just yanked me into a hug. "Bobbi, does it feel good to be a gangster?"

"It feels good to be back." I beamed. "How's that?"

"Ugh, terrible."

"You know what's not terrible?"

"What?"

"Pursuing a militia equipped with very dangerous biological weapons halfway around the world."

Tigra whooped again. "I love my job!"

"Then let's bring everyone up to speed." Hill smiled, jerking her head. We followed her from the office to the briefing room nearby where a cluster of people were already assembled and waiting. For me. This was my new team. I was the leader of a very new and very important mission.

"Good afternoon and welcome to Project Gladiatrix," I said. A small smile twitched on my face with the realization that I had handpicked everyone here, from the analysts and tech support to Jen and Tigra standing at my back, ready to go in. In many cases, the people here were the best for the job. In others, they had real potential and just needed a guiding hand, a mentor, and an ally to help them get to that next level. They were also all women.

"I assume everyone has read the mission dossier," I began.

There was a chorus of confident affirmations as I tapped on a screen, a hologram of the compound we needed to infiltrate appearing in the center of the group.

"This is our target: what we believe to be the militarized arm of Beyond Corporation. Previously S.H.I.E.L.D. have considered them relatively small-time and that's a perception they're aware of, with Board Director Andrew Airs gaining some upward mobility thanks to the acquisition of extremely dangerous chemical weapons. Who hasn't seen the footage from the controlled tests?"

A few people raised their hands and I swiped across, bringing up the experiments Tigra had recorded in the lab with all of the weapons we had been able to access. The sound was off, but it wasn't essential as everyone made some impressed – or horrified, depending on how you looked at it – murmurs.

"Get familiar with it," I added. "There's two main weapons: a pseudo grenade containing spores that once breathed in have a detrimental effect to human biology in the short and long term."

"You'll die," Tigra simplified.

"Right." I smirked. "Slowly and badly. The operation masks are not optional, they're compulsory for this reason. The second weapon acts much like, well, imagine you're fighting an alien."

"Excuse me?" A junior agent blinked.

"The films. Acid for blood?"

"Oh."

"Except the acid blood is coming from a water gun, but there you go."

Tigra tapped at the keyboard, alternating between tests for an example.

"This is where one of what we've established now as eleven weapon caches developed by Dr Calvin and Man-Thing have ended up," I continued. "The only thing more dangerous than them being on the street is being in the hands of people like Beyond Corporation. Our mission is to infiltrate, immobilize, and confiscate. We cross this one off our list, then we keep going. Any questions?"

An analyst raised their hand. "Yes, uh, I've been part of several missions before that have tried to infiltrate this site and it's impossible."

Tigra snorted. "Ooooh, an impossible mission."

"The compound is on the north coast of the island of Borneo in Southeast Asia."

"You can just say Brunei," I offered.

They nodded. "OK, Brunei. Regardless, it's only accessible by roads, all three of them heavily monitored and even more heavily guarded."

"I know." I smiled. "That's why we're going in by air."

The motion of the Douglas C-47 Skytrain always put me to sleep. It was a much rougher ride than the Quinjet and all the creature comforts were absent, but it also lacked visibility on any form of modern flight radar. Very few people still flew these, let alone the kind of people Beyond Corporation expected to be coming for them. Least of all S.H.I.E.L.D.

"Wake her up, will you?"

Jen's voice was almost muted through the humdrum of the old plane, but it soon crackled through my earpiece.

"Bobbi, we're almost there," she pressed. "Bob?"

"Stop dreaming of dimples," Tigra added.

I smiled, eyes flying open as I glared at my friend with amusement. "This is not a closed line. Save it for the group chat."

"Fine." She smirked. "I've got all the juicy details anyway."

Jen's head jerked in her direction. "You do? She does?"

"No," I corrected. "Leave it, OK? You have the same amount of detail, chill."

"Dropping to four thousand feet, Miss Morse," the pilot chirped into my earpiece.

"Thank you, Hanelle," I replied, shaking my head slightly to brush off the jetlag.

Holding the railing above me, I got to my feet as I moved down the line of agents. I signaled using hand motions, everyone doing the checks of their packs accordingly. This was the exact same kind of aircraft that had been used to drop American paratroopers into France during Operation Overlord and my eyes flicked to the red light above my head. As if it could sense my gaze, it flicked to green, and I yanked the side door of the Skytrain open. My hair was tightly braided and clasped beneath the flight helmet. I slapped the hard plastic of the helmet's exterior and internal lights flicked on with the motion. The type of plane transporting us might have been old bordering on museum relic, but our suits were state of the art just like our training, our weapons, our team.

"Comms check," I said, calling to each member and receiving a report down the line. Everyone was online. Everyone was operational. Everyone was ready.

"At two thousand feet, Miss Morse," the pilot reported.

"We're green to go, Hanelle."

"Affirmative."

At this altitude, we couldn't risk dropping any lower without making the jump incredibly dangerous. Well, *more* incredibly dangerous, and this height still kept us out of range of the rather shoddy anti-aircraft missiles on site. Ideally, we'd be able to infiltrate the compound undetected. In the dark, sure, but as long as we followed our laser trajectories we'd be landing in the courtyard and hopefully right in the middle of a very unpleasant nightmare for the Beyond Corporation. I waved the first team member out, fist bumping as they went. Then the next and the next and the next. It was my turn, and I pulled the two battle staves free from the holster at my thigh. These were "new and expensively improved", as Hill had put it, and she'd had them waiting for me following our briefing like someone would present a lover with diamonds and pearls. Just whirling them around in my grip made me feel good. Powerful.

"You know," Jen said, her green complexion visible through the visor of her helmet. "Thailand is just a hop, skip, and a jump away."

"What are you saying?" I asked, pausing as I unclipped my security harness.

"Yeah," Tigra teased. "What *are* you saying?"

"Nothing." Jen shrugged, faux innocent. "Just that if we pull off a successful mission, Mai Tais on the beach wouldn't be so bad."

I sheathed my staves, looking between the two mischievous glances of my best friends, friends I was lucky to have in my life, and even luckier to have on my mission. Both of their eyes were crinkled in crescent moons, the only sign of their grins beneath the helmets.

"I'll think about it," I replied, trying to keep my voice neutral. Their excited whoops were the last thing I heard as I walked toward a black abyss, the smile on my own face feeling etched into my skin as I threw myself out of a plane and into the action.

ACKNOWLEDGMENTS

It seems fair and right to start by acknowledging the people who created Bobbi in the first place, Len Wein and Neal Adams. The late, great Len was so nice to me when I was a twenty-something idiot and I feel kind of baffled that all these years later I get to play with a character he worked to co-create. Life is truly the weirdest science of all.

My editors, Gwendolyn Nix, and her amazing ear for plot creaks, and Lottie, for her persistent guidance and hand holding as I navigated my way through this hedge maze of IP that means so, so bloody much to me. Frozen margs are on me! My agent, Ed Wilson, the GOAT (he won't know what that means). Amanda Bridgeman, the person who first told me I was five-foot-two and caused an existential crisis, but also a true super heroine who encouraged me to write this book.

My Oxford OG, Dr Jodi McAlister, whose time on those cobbled streets informed so much of this setting and story, as well as her invaluable insights into the world of academia. Michelle Wells, the first person who taught me how to write super heroes. Shari Sebbens, for always listening to yarns that span several voicemails and her undiluted (and questionable) belief in me. The Beyhive Group Chat, if I ain't got nothing, I got you. Taika Waititi, Toa Fraser, and Ra Vincent, the first Pasifika people I ever heard of working for Marvel, door kicker-innerers.

Nicola Scott for her guidance, wisdom and spells – always – Craig! Andrew! For being always a good ear and sounding board. Forrest Satchell, for letting me finish this book in his apartment of dead Hollywood stars. The Morely Bunch: Kezza, Adam, Jacinta, Emma, and my long-suffering teenage intern Jenna. Mackenzi Lee for Academy Museum dates we could write off on tax. Anna Jabour, my first fan and continuing biggest. Film Club! For keeping me mentally regular during this process: namely José Ortiz, Corey Te Wharau, Zak Hepburn, Laura Toista, Kubrick, Sose Fuamoli, KC and Tony, Chloe, Paige and Vanessa the Stresser.

The folks who kept me afloat: Dionne Gipson, Jeffrey Yohalem and Delano, Katie Walsh, Blake and Sam Howard, Michel "Bloody Sāmoan" Mulipola, Pocket's mum Kodie Bedford, Angela Slatter, Amy Remeikis, Ramona Sen Gupta, Rach Baker for allowing me to edit this in her chair, and so, so many friggen others.

Finally, I'm not a scientist. I did fine at science in high school, but that is a *long* way from the world of Bobbi: a bona fide baddie of STEM. So huge thanks to Professor Sebastian Alvarado who helped me bridge my background with Bobbi's via three simple words: "I don't know". Do I know how the Hadron Collider works? No! But his explanation of science being about not knowing stuff and asking questions is something I deeply relate to, having started my career as a journalist. Asking questions to the point of despair? That's something I do know, and it helped create an *in* for me when it came to the more technical aspects of Bobbi's life and hopefully an in for the reader, scientist and non-scientists alike.

ABOUT THE AUTHOR

MARIA LEWIS is a screenwriter, best-selling author, film curator and pop culture etymologist currently based in Australia. Over the past eighteen years of her career, she has built an international reputation as a storyteller across a diverse range of mediums including the award-winning *Supernatural Sisters* series of eight novels. In the film and television space, she has worked on projects for Netflix, AMC, BBC, Ubisoft, DC Comics, ABC, Marvel and many more. She is also the writer, researcher, presenter, and producer of audio documentaries *Josie and the Podcats* and *The Phantom Never Dies*, about the world's first super hero. In 2022, she made her directorial debut with *The House That Hungers*, based on her award-winning short story of the same name.

marialewis.com.au
twitter.com/moviemazz